A Death on Corfu

A Death on Corfu

EMILY SULLIVAN

KENSINGTON PUBLISHING CORP.
kensingtonbooks.com

This book is a work of fiction. Names, characters, businesses, organizations, places, events, and incidents either are the product of the author's imagination or are used fictitiously. Any resemblance to actual persons, living or dead, events, or locales is entirely coincidental.

To the extent that the image or images on the cover of this book depict a person or persons, such person or persons are merely models, and are not intended to portray any character or characters featured in the book.

KENSINGTON BOOKS are published by

Kensington Publishing Corp.
900 Third Ave.
New York, NY 10022

All Kensington titles, imprints, and distributed lines are available at special quantity discounts for bulk purchases for sales promotion, premiums, fund-raising, educational, or institutional use. Special book excerpts or customized printings can also be created to fit specific needs. For details, write or phone the office of the Kensington Special Sales Manager: Attn. Special Sales Department. Kensington Publishing Corp., 900 Third Ave., New York, NY 10022. Phone: 1-800-221-2647.

Library of Congress Control Number: 2024951044

ISBN: 978-1-4967-5141-6
First Kensington Hardcover Edition: May 2025

ISBN: 978-1-4967-5143-0 (ebook)

10 9 8 7 6 5 4 3 2 1

Printed in the United States of America

The authorized representative in the EU for product safety and compliance
is eucomply OU, Parnu mnt 139b-14, Apt 123
Tallinn, Berlin 11317, hello@eucompliancepartner.com

To Teresa and Marie and their love of Mystery!

A Death on Corfu

Chapter 1

I have been often asked how I first met the great Stephen Dorian, author of the beloved Inspector Dumond mysteries. And while many know that I was hired as his typist during his stay on Corfu in the spring of 1898—where I had been living with my children since the death of my husband—our story actually began with a newt.

More specifically, one I found on my pillow.

At the time, my son, Tommy, then eight, was obsessed with the local fauna on the island. I encouraged this interest of his, as any good mother would, but a woman must be allowed her limits. On the morning in question, I awoke as usual to the sounds of Mrs. Kouris, our housekeeper, yelling at the neighborhood cats, who liked to gather at the kitchen door meowing for scraps. I'd explained to her many times that they would stop coming if she stopped feeding them, but she would only shrug and grumble under her breath. Given that this was her response to most things, I decided that, despite her protests, she must have a soft spot for strays.

As I was mustering the energy to start the day, my gaze

caught on a rather large crack in the ceiling above my bed. I hadn't noticed it until that moment and immediately began to fixate.

The presence of a crack was, unfortunately, not unusual. A canny estate agent had christened the little seaside villa the Lemon Grove House, and my late husband, Oliver, and I had purchased it sight unseen, aware that it would need work. The exact *amount* of work remained a mystery until we were standing in the foyer, surrounded by stacks of trunks containing all our earthly possessions. My daughter, Cleo, then six, clutched my hand tightly, while little Tommy, still only a baby, dozed on Oliver's shoulder.

According to local rumor, the villa was originally built as a love nest for an English officer and his mistress, but hadn't been inhabited for many years—and it showed. I was aghast at the state of the place: weather-beaten walls, a floor covered in dust and debris, and a kitchen so primitive it took me nearly an hour to prepare a simple pot of tea. But I can still remember the grin on Oliver's face as he turned around and declared it "perfect." After over a decade spent in the Foreign Service, my husband had decided to retire early from his post with the British embassy in Athens. But rather than return to England, we moved our little family to Corfu. Thanks to a tremendous amount of grit and some very helpful locals, we got the house into general working order before poor Oliver died, but that was four years gone now. And lately it seemed like a new problem arose every week. While my husband had left us with a good bit of money, the sum grew steadily lower each year. I found work when I could, but it was never enough to fully recoup what was spent.

I turned on my side, trying to remember if Nico, our handyman, was visiting family on the mainland this week or the next when I came nose to nose with a small brown newt. Though it was hardly the first time I had seen a newt and knew very well that they are harmless creatures, one does not expect to find them in one's bed. The newt blinked its black, watery eyes at me, and I let out a very loud, very sharp shriek that woke the rest of the household, if not the neighborhood.

Tommy came rushing in, just as the terrified newt scrambled off the bed, while Cleo followed at the slower pace of someone who has suffered a great inconvenience. She was fourteen—a terrible age, really, both for her and myself.

"Tommy, darling," I began once I regained some composure, "are you missing a newt?"

His brown eyes lit up. "You found Newton!"

I pointed to the corner of the room, where Newton was currently climbing up the wall.

"Newton the newt," Cleo said with derision. "How original."

"Yes, I thought so," Tommy replied, missing his sister's sarcasm entirely, as he was too busy capturing the wily creature.

"Very clever, darling," I agreed as I threw on my dressing gown. "But I'm afraid Newton needs to live *outside*."

"It was only for the night," he admitted sheepishly, while gently stroking Newton, which seemed to put the creature at ease. "You weren't supposed to know."

I couldn't help smiling as I tilted his chin up. "And yet sometimes our best-laid plans go horribly awry. But my nerves won't survive finding another one of your animals in my bed."

Given that Tommy's interests lately had leaned towards snakes, lizards, and the occasional large, scary spider, I was lucky it had only been a newt that morning.

"May I still visit him?"

"As much as you'd like," I promised. "Let me dress, and we can find a nice spot for him in the garden."

That seemed to brighten Tommy's spirits considerably,

and he turned to his sister. "Would you like to come? I'll even let you hold him for a moment."

But Cleo looked appalled by the offer. "Absolutely not. I'm going back to bed," she said in a huff.

"Not for too long, my love," I called after her. "We're going to the market this morning."

She muttered something in reply that was punctuated by the slam of her bedroom door, and I cast a wary glance at the ceiling, praying the house would survive her.

After quickly performing my morning ablutions and throwing on one of the rumpled cotton caftans I wore around the house, I joined Tommy outside with my tiny cup of Mrs. Kouris's strong Greek coffee. Then I followed him around the yard as he scouted out the ideal place for Newton to live, occasionally offering my advice, which was politely ignored. The morning was still relatively cool, and the haze off the Ionian Sea was just beginning to lift. Though the house may have been slowly falling apart, our little patch of land remained as lush and vibrant as the day we arrived. Graceful cypress trees cocooned the property, while a large, twisting grapevine provided much-needed shade over the terrace, where we ate most of our meals. Bougainvillea, marigolds, roses, and more wildflowers than I could ever identify blossomed in every available spot, perfuming the air with a rich, heady scent, while clusters of pomegranate, fig, and, naturally, lemon trees were in various stages of fruiting.

I typically spent my free hours in the early morning and evening pottering around the garden, as I had better luck growing things than fixing them. Once I finished my coffee, I fetched a small watering pot and refreshed my little plot of herbs and spring onions. There was plenty more that needed watering, but Tommy called me over to the small olive grove at the back of the garden. It created a natural border with the neighboring property, a much larger and better-kept villa owned by Mr. Howard, a London-based businessman who usually visited the island during the summer months.

It was while we were wandering through the grove that I suddenly felt the sensation of being watched. I glanced towards the sprawling, Venetian-style villa perched on the hillside above and was surprised to find a man on the balcony staring down at us. Our eyes met, and even at that distance, I felt a shiver run through me. He wore a paisley dressing gown opened to reveal a white dress shirt underneath, and a lock of dark hair fell across his forehead in a rather rakish manner as he leaned against the ornate balustrade. Given that a glass with a fingerful of brown liquid rested by his elbow, I surmised that this man, rather than waking early like us, had not yet gone to bed.

I raised a hand in greeting, which he returned with a hesitant nod before retreating back into the house.

"Who was that?"

I looked at Tommy and shook my head, still staring at the now-empty terrace. "I don't know, darling."

"It wasn't Mr. Howard," he said. "Because he is *very* old."

"Yes," I agreed absently, though Mr. Howard would likely object as he couldn't be more than fifty. "We'll ask Mrs. Kouris if she knows."

A goat didn't bleat on the island without her hearing about it.

Tommy appeared satisfied with that answer and set about releasing Newton in a nice, shady spot.

"Another Englishman," Mrs. Kouris grumbled when we returned inside to ask after our mysterious new neighbor. "This island is already too full of them."

I had become well-versed on the intricacies of my housekeeper's dislike of the English over the years but did not take the slightest offense, as I had plenty of grievances of my own with my countrymen.

"Do you know anything else?" I asked. "Like how long he might be staying?"

But she shook her head with vigor, as if the question was repellent. I left her to finish making the spanakopita, a spinach-and-cheese pie we devoured by the trayful, and set about preparing the children's breakfast. Tommy and I were nearly done with our fruit and toast when Cleo deigned to join us on the terrace. She was in a much better mood by then, and I was relieved to see her ask after Newton with what appeared to be genuine interest. While Tommy filled her in, my gaze kept slipping past them towards the villa on the hill, even though from this angle it was mostly obscured by the tree line.

He certainly *looked* like an Englishman, or perhaps an American, though Mrs. Kouris wasn't interested in understanding the difference. I tried to remember all I could about Mr. Howard, but only a vague notion that he was somehow involved in book publishing came to mind. Now I regretted that I hadn't been more neighborly during his visits, as short and infrequent as they were. Oliver had always been much better at that sort of thing than I. He made friends everywhere he went.

"Mama?"

I blinked and turned to Cleo, who sounded impatient. "I asked if you're ready to go to town."

"Oh, yes. Absolutely."

She wrinkled her nose. "But you aren't wearing that."

I glanced down and realized I still wore the rumpled caftan. Given that I was an embarrassment to Cleo under the best circumstances, this would not do.

I excused myself to change into a pale yellow day dress she grudgingly found acceptable, and not long afterwards, we set out for town in our little donkey cart. Tommy stayed behind to visit with Mr. Papadopoulos, who lived down the road and was teaching him about the local flora and fauna. As we passed by the road that led up to Mr. Howard's villa, I told her about the mysterious man I had seen that morning.

She immediately began peppering me with questions, but I told her all I knew "Mrs. Kouris says he's English."

"I'll ask Juliet if she knows anything," she said with a decided nod. Juliet Taylor was the same age as Cleo, and her mother knew nearly as much about the British residents of Corfu as Mrs. Kouris knew about the Greeks.

"An excellent idea."

The rest of the drive passed amicably, and I enjoyed listening to Cleo's gossip about her little circle of friends. Like her, they were the children of people who had once worked for the Foreign Service or from families who had stayed on the island after the protectorate ended in the 1860s. She and Tommy attended a small English school in Corfu Town, and while it was admittedly not the most rigorous education one could receive, they supplemented it with lots of reading at home. Oliver and I had both believed the freedoms the children would experience living on Corfu would be invaluable. Indeed, Cleo and Tommy's childhood was nothing like the life Oliver and I had had. My younger sister and I had endured a series of mediocre governesses until I was old enough to attend Girton, though my parents had been quite against that idea at first. They wanted to send me to the ghastly finishing school my mother attended, where I would learn nothing more than how to catch a rich husband. It was only thanks to the intervention of my aunt Agatha, my father's eldest sister and the family battle-ax, that I was allowed to attend the school of my choice.

Meanwhile, Oliver had been sent to Harrow at age six. Then it was on to Cambridge. I knew it was the usual course for boys of our backgrounds, but I could not bear the thought of not seeing Tommy every day. Most of Oliver's colleagues in the embassy sent their children to school back in England as soon as they were of age, but our complete disinterest in continuing this tradition had been a large part of why we came to Corfu in the first place—and why I remained here after Oliver's death, despite the never-ending parade of inconveniences.

Soon we arrived in Corfu Town and found the narrow, cobblestoned streets bustling with activity. I greatly admired the Venetian-style buildings near the harbor and, on more than one occasion, had given serious thought to moving here, as it would be far more convenient for both the children and myself. But my last memories of Oliver were so entwined with the Lemon Grove House that, despite its many nuisances, I couldn't leave it, or him, behind. We tied up our donkey, Maurice, in a nice shady spot and set off to the market. I had only just reached my favorite stall, which sold the most delicious spice mixtures, when Cleo spotted Juliet with her mother and ran over to greet them.

"Mrs. Harper!" Virginia Taylor cried out as she waved her arm. She was an attractive woman with enviable blond hair and the kind of vivaciousness that made her an entertaining dining companion, though she was a bit exhausting in larger doses. Her husband had also worked at the British embassy in Athens, though not at the same time as Oliver, as he was quite a bit older than us. Now he did something in shipping, which, given the size and location of the Taylors' villa, appeared to be very lucrative.

Aside from Juliet and Cleo's friendship, I didn't frequent the same circles as the Taylors. They were very much a part of the British community that still populated the island, whereas I kept more to myself after Oliver's death. We chatted amiably for a few minutes about the weather and our favorite merchants until the girls ran off somewhere, giggling to one another.

"So then," Virginia said, leaning towards me conspiratorially, "have you seen him?"

I furrowed my brow. "Seen whom?"

"Mr. Dorian, of course! Don't tell me you haven't found a reason to knock on his door yet," she said with a laugh. "My goodness, if I lived next door, I'd be over there within the hour asking to borrow a cup of sugar."

"Do you mean Mr. Howard's guest?"

Her blue eyes widened at my confusion. "Minnie! You really don't know him? That's *Stephen Dorian*."

I gave her a bewildered shrug in return, and she laughed again. "He writes the Inspector Dumond series. He's nearly as famous as Arthur Conan Doyle!"

"Ah. I'm afraid I'm not much one for mysteries," I said apologetically.

That had been Oliver's preferred afternoon idle, and I had found him dozing in the hammock with a mystery splayed open on his chest more often than I could count. My tastes tended towards classic romances, history, or quiet little novels about everyday people. On more than one occasion, Oliver had playfully accused me of being a literary snob, and I suppose he wasn't entirely far off the mark.

"I know it isn't Shakespeare, but his books are so *good*," Virginia insisted. "And he's also terribly handsome."

I made a vague murmur in response, as I couldn't possibly comment on that, even as I instantly recalled his tousled hair and penetrating gaze. "Perhaps I'll pick one up. Do you know if he's here for long?"

"I've no idea. Oh! There's Florence," she said, waving to someone behind me. "She would know."

Florence Belvedere was a pleasingly plump woman in late middle age with sharp blue eyes and light brown hair streaked with silver. If Juliet was the young person's gossip, Florence was the oracle of the adults. Her family had been on the island since the days of the protectorate, but Florence had been educated back in England, where she'd met her husband, a barrister. They had returned to Corfu over a decade ago, once their children were grown, and settled in a charming white stucco villa not far from Mr. Howard's. Though Florence tended towards pretension, on account of her lineage, she and her husband had been particularly helpful to me in the wake of Oliver's death, for which I would always be grateful.

"Hello there!" she trilled, while a striking Greek girl with beautiful dark eyes and a mighty scowl followed a few steps behind her. "I'm so glad to see you both," Florence said, before turning to the girl and barking at her in Greek while she gestured to a nearby stall. The girl made no response, but dutifully trudged off. Florence let out a sigh and turned back to us. "That's our new maid, Daphne. I swear, it is impossible to find good help on this island. I'll never understand how my mother survived all those years."

Virginia hummed in sympathy while my smile tightened a little. Given that Florence had grown up not far from the site of the Achilleion, a literal palace that had once been a favored home of the late empress of Austria, I'd say her mother had done far more than "survived." But I learned long ago that no one liked having their privilege pointed out to them—least of all the wealthy.

"Anyway," she continued breezily, "we're having a little soiree tomorrow evening to welcome Mr. Dorian to the island, and I'd love for both of you to come."

Virginia shot me a knowing glance. "What a splendid idea, Flo. Mr. Taylor and I will be there."

I was just about to politely decline when Cleo was suddenly at my side and gripped my arm. "She'll be there too!"

"Cleo," I murmured in warning.

"But, Mama," she protested, "you never go anywhere."

"Because I have you and your brother to care for, my darling," I pointed out with a strained smile, which was true. But it was also true that attending a soiree was not how I wanted to spend my evening.

"I can watch Tommy. And Mr. Papadopoulos has been meaning to come round for supper. It will be fine."

I blinked in surprise. Cleo had not ever volunteered to watch her brother before. Her assistance usually involved heavy bribery that was seldom worth the cost of enduring the complaints that followed. I narrowed my gaze at her in suspicion, but she returned it with a sunny smile.

"Then it's settled," Florence said. "Come up to the house tomorrow around eight."

"*Eight*," I balked. I was usually asleep by nine, at the latest. But I felt Cleo's grip tighten, and I held back a sigh. "Sounds lovely."

We then made a little more meaningless small talk before parting ways, and I picked up a few spices at the stall before Cleo and I set off for home. She chattered away about the soiree and asked what I would wear and how I would do my hair, and I answered honestly. "I don't know. Why are you so excited about this? *I'm* the one going," I grumbled.

But Cleo was undeterred and let out a wistful sigh. "I wish I could go to a fancy party with a famous author. Do you think there will be dancing? Oh, what if he asks to dance with you? How exciting!"

I could only laugh. I hadn't danced with a man since Oliver and hadn't been very good at it, even in my youth. "I doubt any of that will happen, darling."

It was much more likely that I would spend the evening in a corner sipping a sherry and trying to think of clever things to say, only to then keep them to myself. I didn't like attending parties where I didn't know the other guests very well, but at least I used to have Oliver. Now, though, I would have to go it alone. The thought already filled me with a slick, nerve-wracking dread.

But Cleo didn't notice my lack of enthusiasm, which was just as well, and began discussing wardrobe options. I had never been much concerned with fashion, and after having my children, it was far easier to wear practical things that could be easily cleaned. These days, they managed to keep their sticky fingers to themselves, mostly anyhow, but I still kept the habit. Besides, I had no one to dress up for—though, frankly, Oliver had taken even less interest in my wardrobe than I did. But perhaps Cleo was on to something. By the time we reached our home, she had discussed nearly every article of clothing I owned and deemed them all unacceptable. She found this distressing and promised to put together something by tomorrow.

"Really, it's fine, Cleo," I said wearily. The afternoon sun had grown uncomfortably hot, and I was tired of listening to her malign my wardrobe, as sad as it was. "I'll wear the blue dress with the lace trim."

"*Mother*," she screeched in horror as if I had suggested wearing a dishtowel. She then made me swear not to wear the blue dress under any circumstances and hurried into the house, leaving me with the shopping.

"What is wrong with the blue dress?"

I turned to find Mr. Papadopoulos approaching with a quizzical expression. Our neighbor was a native of the island, but had left to attend university in Athens, where he taught botany before returning to Corfu to care for his aging sister. His wife had died tragically many years before in childbirth, and the loss of a beloved spouse was an unfortunate bond we shared. Now in his early sixties, Mr. Papadopoulos was still tall and lean, with just a dusting of silver in his black hair.

"I've no idea," I replied honestly.

As he helped me down from the cart, I explained the invitation to the Belvederes' and the apparently embarrassing state of my clothing. He chuckled. "It is hard to raise daughters, or so my mother always claimed. But then she had five of them, so perhaps you should count your blessings," he said with a wink. Like most of the local men, he had a mustache, though he kept it neatly trimmed and wore a pair of wire-rimmed spectacles that added to his scholarly air.

"Goodness," I replied, marveling at the thought of living with five versions of Cleo. "I will, though I suppose one must make allowances for her age."

He nodded his head sagely. "That is also true. People often wish to be young again, but you could not pay me. Once was more than enough."

"I agree."

He then helped me unhitch Maurice and led him to the pen, where Tommy was feeding our little passel of chickens. We chatted with Tommy about his afternoon, and I relayed my earlier encounter with Newton.

"You are a good mother, Mrs. Harper," he said with great warmth. "Most women would not have handled such an unwanted visitor that well."

"Most people," I corrected with a knowing smile. Lord knew, Oliver had been far more squeamish around bugs and other such creatures than I was. I often wondered what he would have made of his son's interests.

"Of course," Mr. Papadopoulos said, with a gracious nod. "But I stand by the first part."

I ducked my head at his praise. It was a trial most days not to feel that I was failing at some aspect of motherhood. "Thank you."

By then, we'd reached the little yard where we kept our ever-growing menagerie of animals. In addition to Maurice and the chickens, we also had a duck and a very grumpy, one-horned goat named Homer. For reasons that escaped me, the goat preferred that I feed him, and as if on cue, he came rushing over, bleating loudly.

"I've nothing for you, Homer," I pleaded and showed him my empty palms, but he was undeterred and stamped the ground with his hoof.

Just then, Tommy came up behind him, holding the bucket

of feed, and handed it to me, while chattering about the various plants he and Mr. Papadopoulos collected on their walk. Once Homer's voracious appetite was satisfied, I made sure Maurice had enough straw for supper, while Tommy fed the rest of the animals. Before I could even ask, Mr. Papadopoulos offered to visit the children tomorrow evening while I was out.

"Enjoy yourself with the Belvederes," he urged. "You spend too much time in the company of children and animals."

I gave Maurice a scratch in his favorite place, just behind his left ear, to avoid Mr. Papadopoulos's perceptive gaze, though I knew he was right. The years since Oliver's death had been overwhelming, between raising two children alone in a foreign land and keeping our home from falling into greater disrepair. But now that Cleo and Tommy were older and becoming more independent every day, I was left in a kind of fugue state, uncertain of what to do with myself at times. In truth, it was a tad disconcerting to feel de trop in my own home.

"You need to be with adults. To laugh and drink and celebrate the life you still have."

I bit back a sigh. That sounded exhausting.

"*You* are an adult."

He responded to my petulance with an indulgent smile. "I mean people your own age."

I let out a grumble. "Must I?"

"I'm afraid so, Mrs. Harper," he said definitively. "At least for an evening."

After he left, Tommy and I went inside and set about preparing the rest of our supper. In addition to Mrs. Kouris's delectable spanakopita, we had a hearty loaf of freshly baked bread from the market, some wild asparagus Tommy had collected on his walk, brined olives from the grove, and our favorite local hard cheese. We dined on the terrace to enjoy the soft breeze off the water, and afterwards, the children cleaned up while I sat with a small cup of red wine, watching the sun slowly set. When I finally rose to go inside, I glanced back at the villa on the hill and noticed a lone light flickering in the window of the upper floor, that was just visible through the trees. I stared at it for longer than I should like to admit, but there was no sign of movement from within.

I awoke at one point in the night, the edges of a dream slipping from my mind. I tried desperately to pull it back, certain it held some great importance, given the way my heart was racing, but all I could recall was the image of Mr. Dorian staring down at me from the balcony. I had not noticed it before, as I was too distracted by Tommy and Newton, but now I saw with perfect clarity the desolation behind his darkly forbidding gaze. My chest ached with sudden understanding, and I nearly got up from bed just to see if that light was still flickering in the window. I felt a strange compulsion to cross the back garden and traipse up the hill in the darkness to tell this man that I had seen his hidden grief. That it was a feeling I knew all too well. But, of course, I did nothing of the sort. Instead, I forced my eyes closed, and eventually Hypnos found me once again.

Chapter 2

"Honestly, Mother," Cleo huffed. "I would be done already if you'd stop fussing."

"But you won't let me *see.* Are you sure this looks good?" I asked for the tenth time, trying to crane my neck towards the mirror.

After one too many gasps, Cleo forbade me from watching her and turned me away from the dressing table.

"*Yes*. Now face forward and let me work."

I reluctantly obeyed and held my breath as Cleo pinned back yet another lock of hair. Whatever she was doing, it was taking an awfully long time, and now I was in danger of running late.

After a few more pins, she stepped back. "There," she finally declared with a satisfied smile. "Now, where do you keep your rouge?"

"Oh heavens, Cleo. I haven't worn cosmetics in years."

"I know," she said wryly. "But you must have a pot of rouge and a lipstick here somewhere."

I pursed my lips as we stared each other down for a moment before I relented. "In the bottom drawer of my dressing table," I grumbled and pointed over my shoulder. She retrieved a small cosmetics case, but as she moved to apply some rouge, I held up my hand. "Thank you, darling. But I can take it from here." Then I stood and turned around. "Now let's see what you've done to— " The rest of the words died on my lips while I stared at my reflection. I didn't recognize myself, which was rather unnerving at first, and for a moment, I was rendered speechless.

"I look . . ."

"So elegant," Cleo finished with a dreamy sigh. "Juliet and I practice on one another, and Mrs. Taylor always has the latest magazines in from Paris."

I continued to marvel at the woman before me. My mother, who had been considered the most beautiful debutant of her year, had told me long ago that I would never be a great beauty, especially when compared to my younger sister, who had been born with boatloads of charisma in addition to striking features. Though she did admit that my eyes were my best feature, while the rest would be "good enough to land you a husband." But given the witchcraft Cleo had performed on my hair, I was rather tempted to challenge that assertion. She had swept my light brown waves into a full knot near the crown of my head and teased the front before framing my face with a few loose tendrils. I had always thought my face too long, but the style drew attention to both my large eyes and my cheekbones. If we were back in London, I doubt I would have caused much of a stir in a ballroom full of beautiful, glamorous women, but I still felt a small surge of pride in my appearance. And I hadn't felt that in a very long time. Cleo then handed me my cosmetics bag with a look that would broker no argument.

"Very well. Just a touch of rouge."

"I also saw a kohl stick in there, Mother," she said, while arching a scandalized brow.

My cheeks turned so red the rouge wouldn't be necessary.

"That was for a fancy dress party!" I insisted, but Cleo didn't look convinced and pointed at the bag.

"Stop stalling."

A few minutes later, after I applied the rouge and, all right, a bit of kohl around my eyes, we admired our mutual handiwork.

"Oh, Mother," she breathed, "you look so lovely."

I patted Cleo's hand. "Thank you, darling."

From the neck up, I looked like one of those stylish Gibson girls the magazines were full of these days. Then I glanced down at the faded wrapper cinched at my waist.

"I need to dress."

Cleo's eyes lit up, and she raced over to my wardrobe, where she claimed to have found something appropriate. "I can't believe you've been hiding this back here," she said in a muffled voice as she rummaged through my clothes.

I frowned in the mirror and dabbed just a little more rouge on my cheeks. "I haven't the slightest idea what you're talking ab—Oh, God. Cleo, *no*."

I whirled around to see my daughter holding up a frothy lavender gown I had completely forgotten about. Why I had even bothered to bring it all the way to Corfu remained a mystery.

Because you are a sentimental idiot, a very unhelpful voice reminded me.

Oliver and I hadn't attended many formal events together. We married rather quickly, without much ceremony, and then left shortly afterwards for Athens, where our social calendar was usually dominated by afternoon gatherings with other British families or informal suppers at friends' houses, except for a dinner at the ambassador's residence not long before we left for Corfu. When, during a luncheon with the glamorous wife of one of Oliver's well-heeled colleagues, I had confessed to feeling unsure of what to wear, she gave the dress to me as a sort of good-bye present. She'd ordered the gown from Paris the previous season, but by the time it arrived, it was out of fashion—not that I knew or cared much about such things. To me, it was simply a beautiful piece of clothing that made me feel beautiful wearing it. That was also one of the best nights Oliver and I ever spent together, so much so that I was filled with regret over our decision to leave Athens altogether. But nothing I said would sway Oliver. He had made up his mind and was determined to live on Corfu, so away to Corfu we went.

I approached the gown slowly and fingered the delicate silk. It felt even softer than I remembered. Just as the image of Oliver in his black evening suit, giving me a fond smile as he leaned against the doorframe of my old dressing room, began to flash through my mind, I quickly pulled my hand away. "I can't wear this, Cleo. It's—it's much too formal."

She scoffed. "No, it isn't. Mrs. Taylor wears even nicer things to dinner."

I was both offended and incredulous, but then Cleo fixed me with a knowing look. Given the number of times she had attended dinner at the Taylors' house, I was forced to defer to her judgement on this point.

"I won't be able to make it up the hill," I protested.

"At least put it on first," she said, in a surprisingly gentle tone. "Before you decide."

Only then did I realize how nervous I was. Over a *dress.*

Now determined to squash such a ridiculous fear, I threw off my wrapper and took the dress from her hands. I wasn't even sure it would fit anymore. After all, it had been years—and they hadn't exactly been kind to my figure. But as I pulled the gauzy cotton and silk over my head and tugged it down around my corset, I knew instinctively that it would be fine.

Cleo set to work on the buttons, while I tugged the short, puffed sleeves into place. When she finished, I tightened the wide sash, which was a few shades darker than the dress, around my waist and shook out the full skirt before smoothing it in place. Whereas I had once needed to pad out my curves, now I had naturally fuller hips that did the job quite nicely on their own.

"*Please* don't change," Cleo said rather urgently.

I smiled at our reflections and swished the skirt a little. There was enough movement that I was confident I could make it up the path to the Belvederes' villa near the top of the hill. But a glance at Oliver's pocket watch resting on the dressing table said I would most definitely be late now, even if I hurried.

I managed a dab of rosewater, while Cleo grabbed my wrap and reticule. Together we rushed down the stairs to the sitting room, where Tommy and Mr. Papadopoulos were pouring over some old reference books our kind friend had brought. They both looked up at my entrance and made a great show of complimenting my attire. I promised not to stay out too late, but Mr. Papadopoulos and Cleo waved me off.

"And don't worry, Mother," Tommy said gravely. "I'll make sure there is nothing in your bed tonight."

"Thank you. That is very thoughtful." Then I kissed his chubby cheek and went out into the night.

Oliver and I had chosen our little villa in large part because of its close proximity to the water, which promised cooling breezes, convenient access for medicinal sea-bathing, and spectacular sunset views. And while all that is true, we hadn't given much consideration to its location at the bottom of the hillside. In our daily lives, this inconvenience far outweighed the benefits previously listed. However, on this particular evening, as I ascended the path in an evening gown and slippers, with my skirts hiked up nearly to my knees, I could only curse our decision. By the time I reached the Belvederes', my shoes were covered in dust, and I was fairly certain my hair was a wreck. As I approached the large villa, I did my best to straighten my gown and remove as much debris as possible, but I needed a mirror.

The young maid from the market opened the door, wearing the same insouciant expression from earlier.

"Kalispera," I cried out, hoping my cheery greeting would distract from my disheveled appearance. The girl either didn't notice or didn't care and silently ushered me inside.

She took my cape, then pointed towards the back terrace before leaving me alone in the entryway. Raucous laughter filtered through the villa's traditional whitewashed walls, and I took the chance to freshen up in the little alcove that Florence jokingly referred to as the powder room. I was relieved to find I did not look as disastrous as I feared. I reapplied my rouge, fixed a few pins that had loosened, and wiped down my shoes with a little cloth I always carried in my reticule.

Then I returned to the hall and was just about to head for the terrace when I heard two men in the middle of a conversation coming towards me.

"We're just waiting on Mrs. Harper. Have you met her yet?"

"I don't believe so, no," replied a smooth, deep voice.

I recognized the first speaker as Christopher Belvedere, whom I was very fond of. "She's your neighbor. Her husband passed away, oh, about three or four years ago. Terrible shame."

"She has a son?" the man asked after a moment, and I noted that his voice was distinctly clipped, especially in comparison to Christopher's plummy tones. Like Oliver, he had attended all the best schools.

"And a daughter."

"I know who you mean, then," he said. "I saw her yesterday morning from my balcony."

He must be this Mr. Dorian person. I couldn't help the thrum of anticipation that flooded my veins, and without thinking, I hung back in the doorway of the powder room. They hadn't moved any closer, and I surmised they had stopped at the drinks cart the Belvederes kept in the parlor. I really should have come out and made myself known then, but a foolish little part of me wanted to see what kind of impression I had made on Mr. Dorian.

"Ah, splendid," Christopher replied. "She's a Girton girl, though thankfully not one of the dreadfully mannish ones." I frowned at this description, though it was hardly the first time I had heard such a comment. "Still, she's very clever," he continued, blithely unaware of my presence. "Even worked for me for a time. Though my wife says she doesn't read detective fiction. Thinks them all a bit too lowbrow for her tastes," he added with a laugh.

I winced a little, as this sounded rather harsh and something I never would have admitted to Mr. Dorian, but just as I resolved to announce myself, he replied.

"If I cared what every frumpy middle-aged housewife thought," he began, sounding terribly bored and not the least bit offended, "I wouldn't have written ten novels."

This response must have stunned Christopher as much as it did me, for it was a long moment before he gave a startled chuckle. "Right, right," he said quickly before changing the subject. But I heard none of what they now said. I retreated back into the alcove, and their voices slowly faded as they returned to the terrace. I stood in the cool semi-darkness for a long while, battling the instinct to flee, when another pair of voices floated down the hall. This time, I recognized Florence and Mrs. Barthes, an older Frenchwoman with superb taste. I patted my cheeks and stepped out just as they approached.

"Minnie, there you are!" Florence cried out. "We were starting to worry. Oh, but don't you look lovely."

Mrs. Barthes also complimented my gown, and the genuine admiration in their eyes was a balm to my wounded pride.

A frumpy housewife indeed. What a ridiculous thing to say. Especially considering the state *he* was in that morning—though even I could admit that looking rakish was a far better description.

"Thank you. I'm so sorry I'm late."

Florence waved a hand. "Don't worry about that," she said as she took my arm in her own. "I know how hard it can be to leave the house with two little ones. Come outside. Everyone is here, and we're enjoying the delicious wine Mr. Dorian brought."

I frowned as I caught sight of the man's admittedly eye-catching profile. "Sounds delightful."

He turned as we stepped out onto the terrace, and our gazes locked together, much as they had that morning. His expression remained as stern and impenetrable as ever, but I noticed he quickly skimmed over my figure. I stood a little taller and tried not to let my satisfaction be too obvious as Florence led me over. Since Mr. Dorian was positioned at the far end of the terrace, there were a number of other people to greet first. I didn't look at him again, but all the while, I could feel his gaze upon me, and it spurred me to be more charming than usual. As I said hello to the other guests, I realized Cleo had been right. Virginia Taylor was dressed in a gown just as elegant as my own, as were the other ladies in attendance. If I had gone ahead and worn the blue dress I would have felt, indeed, rather frumpy.

Finally, we came to the guest of honor. I always imagined writers as pale, willowy creatures, given that they spent most of their time indoors typing away, too wrapped up in their own genius to bother with something as pedestrian as eating. But Mr. Dorian appeared to be in robust health, with his skin bronzed from the sun. He was taller than I expected too, about six feet or so, though not as tall as Oliver. But unlike my dear husband, Mr. Dorian possessed a surprisingly muscular frame.

With his strong jaw, straight nose, and thick, dark hair, I daresay I would have thought him one of the most attractive men I had ever met, if I hadn't overheard his callous description of me. Therefore, I was determined to think of him as nothing but a mean-spirited, vulgar fellow. He may have been beautiful outside, but I had every reason to suspect he was rotten to the core.

"A pleasure to meet you at last, Mr. Dorian," I said with far more graciousness than he deserved. "I confess I have not yet read your books, but I believe my late husband was a great admirer of your work." Indeed, when I had searched our bookshelves earlier, I had found quite the collection of his Inspector Dumond novels.

The author hesitated a moment before he took my hand. "Thank you," he said gruffly. "The pleasure is all mine, Mrs. Harper."

"And seeing as we are neighbors and you are new to our island," I continued with a beatific smile, "please feel free to stop by if you need anything."

There. Let's see what he would make of *that*.

His jaw tightened for a moment, but his dark eyes betrayed nothing. "You are too kind," he muttered with a short nod.

Then I didn't utter another word to him for the rest of the evening, both because I was still angry and refused to fawn over him like the rest of the guests—not that Mr. Dorian seemed to enjoy the attention. Every time I glanced over, his expression hovered somewhere between bored and saturnine. It turned out that Florence was also a fan, and she confessed to me that she and Oliver had spent hours dissecting the plots of certain novels.

"I had no idea," I admitted.

"Oh yes. Oliver was so clever, wasn't he?" she said, placing a comforting hand on my shoulder. "He always guessed the murderer correctly. I told him so many times he should write his own stories."

I will admit that this was not how I saw my husband. Oliver was intelligent, of course. One had to be in his line of work, but I had not realized his interest in mystery novels ran so deep. And I certainly had not thought him capable of writing one. In spite of my earlier dismissal of Mr. Dorian, I knew that writing a novel, even one I would not care to read, took a measure of skill and talent far beyond my own.

After about two hours and as many glasses of wine, I said my good-byes and retreated back down the hill, waving off Christopher's offer to escort me, as it was only a few minutes' walk. I was satisfied with my performance as anything but a frumpy housewife and determined never to be in the same room as Mr. Dorian again.

Little did I know that our association had only just begun.

Chapter 3

The next morning, I awoke much later than usual, feeling the full effects of both my delayed bedtime and the second glass of wine. I could hear Mrs. Kouris downstairs rattling around in the kitchen and Tommy and Cleo's muffled voices outside. As all sounded well, I didn't feel too guilty about lying abed for a few minutes more. But as soon as I settled my head back against the pillow, I heard another, deeper voice outside. Someone was with the children.

I was certain it was Nico, our erstwhile repairman, finally come to discuss fixing the roof. Given that he could be rather hard to pin down, I leapt out of bed and had nearly reached the window before I remembered to throw on my wrapper. But as I looked down onto the garden, Cleo, Tommy, and the visitor looked up. Only then did I realize that our guest was not Nico, but *Mr. Dorian.*

"Good morning, Mrs. Harper," he called out with a friendly wave, looking far more refreshed than I felt. This was most irritating, as no one had been close to leaving when I did last night.

I immediately clutched the gauzy curtain to my chest,

which must have looked very odd. "Oh. Hello there," I croaked, failing in my attempt to mimic his breezy tone. "I—I'll be right down." Then I moved away from the window before anyone could respond. I rushed over to the washstand to inspect my reflection in the mirror and let out a mournful little sigh.

I hadn't bothered to take my hair down last night, and now it resembled a bird's nest that had been tossed about in a windstorm. I did my best to smooth out the worst bits before I quickly washed up and threw on a white cotton day gown. Cleo met me at the bottom of the stairs and wordlessly handed me the straw hat I usually wore while gardening.

"Bless you, Cleo," I murmured as I put it on. "How do I look?" But just as Cleo opened her mouth, I shook my head. "Never mind. I don't want to know." Then I hurried outside to the garden, where I found Tommy enthusiastically showing Mr. Dorian something under a large rock and poking at the ground with a stick.

"Oh God," I muttered, praying that it wasn't anything too disgusting. "Tommy, darling," I called out as I hurried, "remember what we discussed."

"Not everyone likes bugs as much as I do," Tommy parroted as he reluctantly put the rock back in its place.

"It's all right," Mr. Dorian said. "I was once a curious boy myself."

As I drew closer, I could see that he wasn't as well-rested as I had first thought. The dark smudges under his eyes betrayed a night of sleep possibly worse than my own.

If he's even gone to bed yet.

But before I could ruminate on this, Mr. Dorian turned to Tommy. "Thank you for showing me those earwigs. Fascinating creatures. And do let me know when the eggs hatch."

I couldn't hide my horror while Tommy eagerly beamed up at him. "I will, sir."

"Now then," he began in a serious tone, "will you let me talk with your mother for a moment?"

"I suppose," Tommy said with a disinterested shrug, already eyeing the rock again.

Mr. Dorian gave him a short bow that I would have found charming if he had been any other man. "I'm much obliged." Then he gestured towards the back garden's gate and indicated for me to walk with him. "Mrs. Harper?"

"I don't suppose you'll be asking *me* if I want to speak with you," I said in a wry tone as I led the way.

"Tommy told me he is the man of the house," Mr. Dorian explained as we headed for the path, "so I thought it best to defer to his judgement."

"He said that?" I turned to him so quickly I nearly tripped over my own feet, and Mr. Dorian was forced to grab my forearm to steady me. The heat from his warm palm melted against my bare skin, and for one heady moment, I was very tempted to lean closer to him. Luckily, the urge passed.

"Thank you," I mumbled and stepped neatly out of his grip. "Only I . . . I've never heard him say anything like that before."

Mr. Dorian looked down the road with a thoughtful expression. "How old was he when your husband died?"

"Four. He barely remembers him." The words came out sharper than I meant them to, but Mr. Dorian didn't seem to notice. He simply gave a nod and hummed.

We continued down the road for a little way, with the chirping of birds, the rustle of the cypress trees, and the distant bleating of goats in the background. If it hadn't been for the company, I would have thoroughly enjoyed such an idyllic morning.

"This is a lovely place," he murmured at last and glanced back at the house. "You must be happy here."

"Very," I said, unable to keep the defensive note out of my voice.

He turned to me with a curious look on his face. "Belvedere said your husband worked in the Foreign Service."

"Yes, for over a decade. But he grew tired of the constant jockeying for position and influence," I explained, repeating Oliver's old explanation. "He thought it an utter waste of time and resources."

Mr. Dorian grunted in agreement. "I can imagine. Blasted bureaucratic nonsense."

I ignored his curse. "Oliver was much happier running his little export business."

Never mind that it had taken the better part of a year to get it started and had only just begun to turn a real profit when he died.

"But however did you end up on Corfu?"

"It is considered a nice place to live, and some of his former colleagues had settled here," I said. "So when he saw the listing for this house in a newspaper, he bought it."

Mr. Dorian raised his dark eyebrows in surprise. "You mean, you moved here sight unseen? And with your children?"

He was hardly the first person to question Oliver's decision, myself included, but between my lack of sleep and my growing headache, I didn't possess my usual patience. "He might have made a different decision if he knew he was going to die," I said dryly.

At least the man had the decency to look chagrined and cleared his throat. "I am sorry for your loss."

Though I hadn't cared for his judgement, I cared even less for his pity. I came to a halt and faced him. "Mr. Dorian, I suspect you didn't come here this morning to look at bugs with my son or—"

"Earwigs," he corrected.

I huffed. "Yes. Earwigs." Then I crossed my arms. "Well?"

He stared at me for a moment before letting out a breath. "Sorry. I don't mean to waste your time. Only I was remembering what you said last night about how I should feel free to stop by if . . . if I ever needed anything."

I had indeed said that, but hadn't expected him to take me up on the offer. And certainly not mere hours later.

At his silence, I narrowed my eyes and crossed my arms. "And?"

He glanced away and pulled a hand through his hair. For a moment, he appeared so shy—so vulnerable—that my heart began to thaw just a little. "This . . . this is a bit awkward for a man in my position, but I've found myself in need of a typist."

I dropped my arms. "Oh. Why is that awkward?"

He gave me an exasperated look. "I'm a professional writer, Mrs. Harper. I shouldn't need someone to type for me." Then he shook his head and looked away. "But the only way I've been able to make any progress on this book is if I write by hand. I'm already terribly behind on it, and my publisher, Mr. Howard, is expecting, nay, *demanding* a finished manuscript in a month's time. That's partly why he sent me here, but the change of scenery is not helping as much as I hoped." As he spoke, his shoulders hunched more and more until they were nearly touching his ears.

"That sounds difficult," I answered honestly. "But I'm not sure how I can be of help."

He raised an eyebrow. "Belvedere said you went to Girton."

"Well, yes. I did."

"And what did you study?"

I could sense where he was going with this and hesitated. "Literature. But—"

"I also understand that you perform secretarial work on occasion."

I had indeed provided such services for Christopher, as well as a few other of the island's more affluent inhabitants, when the opportunity arose, but that had only ever been simple things like correspondence. Not typing up an entire manuscript. "I did. I mean, I do—"

"Then surely you possess more than enough intelligence and skill to type up one of my terribly low-brow novels, Mrs. Harper," he said with a mocking smile.

My mouth dropped open, shocked that he would admit to hearing such a description. "I never—"

"And I'd pay you quite handsomely for your time," he cut in, before naming a figure that almost made my mouth drop open again, but I managed to keep it shut. Forget mending the ceiling. I could replace the whole *roof*.

"But you would need to start tomorrow," he added, "as I have a stack of notebooks waiting to be typed out."

Though I was in absolutely no position to refuse such an offer, what was left of my pride forbade me from accepting it outright. Well, that and the faintly smug look on his face.

I crossed my arms again and gave him an assessing look. "You aren't used to hearing 'no,' are you?"

He chuckled. "Not when it comes to business. But from ladies? More often than I'd like to admit."

I ignored this remark, given that this time he didn't even pretend to look chagrined, and pressed on. "But, Mr. Dorian, I really don't have any experience with this sort of project."

"That doesn't matter," he assured me. "I can help you with the formatting, and my publisher isn't expecting perfection."

"Just as long as it's finished," I guessed.

"Correct."

I let out a sigh and pretended to think about it for a moment while he indulged me. Then I threw up my hands. "All right. I accept. I can come tomorrow at eight for a couple of hours."

Mr. Dorian let out a laugh. "My dear lady, I am barely conscious by noon most days, let alone eight."

I cast a bewildering look at the sky. It couldn't be later than ten. "What about now?"

"I made an exception for you," he said, clearly expecting me to be flattered.

I suppressed the urge to roll my eyes. "Then you can either change your schedule to something less nocturnal or leave me a set of instructions. But I will not waste half my day waiting for you."

He stared at me for a moment, and I had the distinct sensation he was trying not to laugh. "I suspect you don't hear 'no' very often either, Mrs. Harper." I responded to this with a disapproving frown, but he was entirely right. "Let's compromise with, say, nine o'clock."

"Fine," I replied. "But I can't stay past eleven-thirty. The children will need their luncheon."

They were perfectly capable of eating without me, of course, but I felt the urge to retain the upper hand in this situation—or at least the illusion of it.

"Understood." Then he held his hand out to me. "So, do we have a deal?"

I stared at his outstretched arm for a moment, while a prickling sensation at the back of my neck gave me pause. But there was no turning back. As soon as he had offered me the job, I knew I would take it. I didn't have much of a choice.

"Yes," I said as I took his hand and gave it a firm shake, "it seems we do."

I silently prayed that the money would be enough to make up for my lost pride. If only I knew then how much more I stood to lose.

After Mr. Dorian and I parted ways, I returned to the house in desperate need of something to eat. Luckily, Mrs. Kouris had anticipated me and laid out, on the terrace, some toast, fruit, and more of the cheese we'd enjoyed the night before, along with a pot of strong tea. I had just sat down when Cleo appeared by my side, startling me. She seemed perfectly capable of being quiet when it suited her.

"What did Mr. Dorian want? Did you waltz with him last night? Has he come to court you?"

"Darling, please let me have my tea first," I said as I took off my gardening hat and ran a hand over my hair. Cleo's work from last night was entirely lost now. I took a long restorative sip before fixing her with a look. "No, we did not waltz, and he has not come to court me. I knew I shouldn't have given you that copy of *Evelina*," I added with far too much bitterness. Cleo seemed more consumed by romantic thoughts than most girls her age, or perhaps I had simply forgotten what it was like to desperately hope for love since my own experience had ended in heart-shattering grief.

"It was only a little gathering," I amended as her face fell. "Nothing so formal as a ball. There was no dancing. Just talking. And don't mind me. I'm tired and grumpy. You should read as many novels as you want."

She cast me a sly smile. "I intend to." Then her gaze turned thoughtful as she ran a finger over the well-worn surface of the heavy wooden table. "I was going to say you looked fresh-faced earlier."

My eyebrows rose. "Really?" Lord knew I hadn't felt that way.

Cleo shrugged and took the seat across from me before helping herself to my fruit plate. "You always have a sort of rosy glow about you."

I considered this as I took another sip. "But not as grand as last night."

"No, not like last night," Cleo said carefully. "But not bad, either. Just . . . different."

"Well, that's a relief," I said honestly and leaned back in my chair. Given that I currently felt like a wet sack of potatoes, I would have been happy to know I looked anywhere close to presentable. I closed my eyes and tilted my face towards the clear blue sky.

After a few blessed moments of peace, Cleo spoke again. "I wouldn't mind, you know," she began, her voice soft and hesitant, "if Mr. Dorian did want to court you. Or someone else, even."

I turned to her with a smile. "I appreciate that, darling, but he came here to offer me a job. Not because he wants to court me." The very idea was too ridiculous to even contemplate.

Cleo gave a thoughtful nod and went silent—until I closed my eyes once more.

"Is it because he's divorced?"

I sat up in my chair, fully alert now. "What? No! And how—how on earth do you know that?"

She shrugged. "Juliet."

Of course. "Juliet is a gossip," I said in my most disapproving tone. "And no one likes a gossip."

But Cleo appeared unmoved by my disapproval. "She said he wasn't married for very long, but his wife accused him of neglect, and he accused *her* of adultery. It was in all the London papers."

"Goodness," I breathed, unable to fathom having such intimate details printed for all the world to see and talk about. It made me uncomfortable just hearing about it. And yet . . .

"Who was he married to?" The question was out before I could stop myself.

"An heiress," Cleo said, as she waggled her brow. "And she's already married someone else. The same man she was accused of being unfaithful with."

"Goodness," I repeated, for what else could one say about such shocking behavior? "But you really should keep all this to yourself." Though if Juliet and her mother knew, it was only a matter of time before the rest of the island did too. Still, one must try to set a good example. "And you shouldn't believe everything you hear," I added, "even if it's printed in the papers."

There. That sounded like sensible advice.

When it became clear that I would no longer engage in gossip about Mr. Dorian, Cleo grew bored and loped off. I settled back in my chair once more, but after a few moments, I gave up. My mind was far too preoccupied for rest. I heaved a disgruntled sigh and stared out at the sea. *Divorced.* I had never met a divorced person before. Now it seemed perfectly clear why Mr. Dorian had dark smudges under his eyes and kept odd hours and was having trouble writing his book.

The poor man was suffering from heartbreak.

The rest of the day passed in the usual manner—Tommy was off observing whatever frightening creature he was currently fascinated by, Cleo disappeared somewhere with a novel, and I busied myself in the garden. By the time Mrs. Kouris had prepared our supper, I was covered up to my neck in a thin layer of dirt.

I quickly washed and dressed before going down to the kitchen, where she was putting the finishing touches on a tray of roasted chicken with lemon and potatoes.

"That smells delicious, Mrs. Kouris."

She grunted in reply. "Have you heard from Nico yet?"

I shook my head, and she let out a huff. "Useless man. I will go to his house tomorrow."

"He might not even be back on the island," I pointed out, but she only huffed again.

"Let us hope so, for his sake," she said ominously.

I was certain she was the only reason I had managed to get done half as much work on the house as I had. It seemed every man on the island was terrified of crossing her, and there were often whispers about the potency of her curses, but that was all nonsense. Besides, Mrs. Kouris didn't need any assistance from the dark arts. She was quite a force to be reckoned with all on her own.

"Thank you," I said, as I started slicing a loaf of bread. "Oh, and tomorrow morning, I'll be at the villa next door for a couple of hours."

She raised an eyebrow. "With the Englishman?"

"Yes, he's hired me to do some typing for him."

"Everyone says he is handsome, but I don't think so."

I laughed as she wrinkled her nose. "No?"

She made a dismissive noise. "Mr. Harper, *he* was handsome. Blond and so tall."

I smiled at this, as I was quite familiar with both Mrs. Kouris's preference for blond hair and her fierce affection for my late husband. Cleo had inherited her father's coloring, while Tommy favored my brown eyes and darker locks. "He was," I agreed, though it had not been his looks that had first caught my interest.

He had been at school with my brother Samuel, and for years I had heard about Oliver Harper, the impoverished second son of a viscount who was obsessed with all things Greek. His father steadfastly refused to support his endeavors, yet Oliver Harper still managed a number of impressive exploits: he worked on a boat one summer only because it had a stop in Piraeus and he wanted to visit Athens. Then, the next summer, he talked his way onto an archeological dig at Olympia. He even attempted his own translation of *The Iliad*.

By the time I actually met Oliver, he felt as familiar to me as a character out of a beloved adventure novel. I had just started at Girton, and he was back at Cambridge for some sort of symposium on Ancient Greece. Samuel came up from London for the day to see Oliver and invited me to lunch with them.

Oliver began working for the Foreign Office as soon as he graduated, but had finally achieved a coveted position at the

British embassy in Athens. He was brimming with an excitement that was contagious. I had never given much thought to traveling, and even less to Greece. It was enough of an ordeal to convince my parents to send me to Girton—and that had only happened because my father was more than a little afraid of Aunt Agatha. But listening to Oliver wax on about the beauty of a sunrise over the Aegean, the quiet majesty of the Parthenon, and the thrill of the Temple of Poseidon was contagious.

What he saw in me that afternoon, I still cannot begin to fathom. I was a girl of nineteen, the third of four children, who had lived a very sheltered life in Portman Square. Though my parents each came from families with distant but direct lines to the aristocracy, our lifestyle was largely the result of my father's lucrative banking career. I enjoyed literature, philosophy, and art, and indulged in writing a bit of terrible poetry, but I was hardly remarkable. Yet we began a correspondence that lasted all through Oliver's first year in Athens. When he came back to London for Christmas, he asked my father for my hand. I think my parents would have married me off right then, but I still had a term left at school, and Oliver supported my desire to finish. This shocked my father to no end, which only further convinced me that Oliver would be a good husband.

As soon as I finished my exams, we married in a private ceremony at the chapel in Cambridge, with only a few local people in attendance, and set off for Athens the day after that. I hadn't returned to England since. I blinked my eyes against the inconvenient moisture that began to gather at the memory of Oliver and hoped Mrs. Kouris didn't notice such an embarrassing display of melancholy. I had been widowed for four years now and should no longer be at the mercy of my emotions. Oliver was gone, and I had long since accepted my circumstances.

Luckily, Tommy came rushing into the kitchen at that

moment, babbling about some rare insect he'd found, and was even filthier than I had been. Before he could say another word, I took his hand and carted him off to the bath, grateful for the sudden distraction. The rest of my evening was consumed by the usual tasks of mothering, but Oliver was never very far from my mind. Here I was, living the life he had dreamed of, on an island in a country he claimed as his own. There were so many times, especially in the early years after his death, that I nearly packed up our home and fled back to England. But no matter how hard things became, somehow I always summoned the strength to stay, bound by the promise I had made to my husband to raise our children here.

Tomorrow, though, tomorrow I would start something entirely new. Something not connected to my role as a mother, or a widow, or my blasted promise, but rather those skills I had mastered long ago. When I belonged to no one but myself. I climbed into my bed that night exhausted to the bone, but with a steady thrum of excitement at what was to come.

Chapter 4

The next morning, Cleo once again insisted on helping me with my hair and clothes. Despite my protests that I simply needed to look professional, I was secretly grateful for her assistance. The excitement that followed me as I went off to sleep last night had turned into a bout of nerves by daybreak. After rejecting my first two outfits, we finally agreed on a white linen day gown with a blue sash that I hardly ever wore. She then arranged my hair in a simple but elegant chignon, but I drew the line at any more cosmetics.

"I'm only going there to type up some pages for him, Cleo. This isn't a social visit."

"That doesn't mean you can't look nice," she countered, but I would not be moved. It also seemed far too much effort for a man who had already seen the full range of my appearance.

As the children were about to go off to school in Corfu Town, I rode with them in the donkey cart until we reached the path that led to Mr. Dorian's villa.

"Have a good day at school, my darlings," I said as I climbed down. "I'll see you this afternoon." But as my foot caught on the hem of my gown and I fell onto the dusty road, I suddenly remembered why I hardly wore it.

"Mother!" the children cried out in unison as I was enveloped in a puff of dry dirt.

This was not an auspicious start.

"Are you all right?" Cleo asked.

"Yes, just a little rumpled," I said and picked myself up. Then I dusted off my gown as best I could. "How do I look?"

"Very pretty," Tommy replied, while Cleo narrowed her eyes.

"Like a woman who just fell off a donkey cart," she said dryly. "You need to fix your hat."

"Thank you," I said with all the dignity one could muster under the circumstances and straightened the brim. "Run along then, or you'll be late!"

The children both stared at me in mild horror until I shooed them away. I watched the cart disappear down the road, then headed towards the villa. I continued to brush my gown along the way, but a large streak still remained down the front. For a moment, I was sorely tempted to run back home to change, but then I would be late.

"He won't notice anyway," I told myself as I reached the front door.

Before I could knock, the door was opened by Mrs. Nasso, a very old, very small local woman who kept house for Mr. Howard when he was in residence.

"Kalimera, Mrs. Nasso," I said brightly. She was Mrs. Kouris's neighbor, but the two women were locked in a bitter, decades-old feud over ownership of a pomegranate tree on their property line. I had once asked Mrs. Kouris why they couldn't just share the tree, as surely neither of them could eat all of the fruit. But this question was met with a look so dark and forbidding that I hadn't dared broach the topic again. "Are you taking care of the house for Mr. Dorian's visit?"

She nodded and stepped back so I could enter. "Mr. Dorian here, yes."

I then recalled that her English was spotty and repeated the question in Greek. But she only stared at me for a moment, as if I had asked her to do a handstand. "Mr. Dorian here," she repeated in English and pointed to an open door down the hall.

"Thank you."

She gave a short nod and left, but not before casting a disapproving glance at my gown. I couldn't say for certain whether that was due to the sorry state of my clothing or the fact that I no longer wore black, as here widows were expected to dress in mourning until their own death, regardless of their feelings for the deceased. Mrs. Kouris, for example, had been dutifully wearing black for the last twenty years, yet the only time she ever mentioned her late husband was to curse his ineptitude. In any case, it all seemed rather excessive to me.

I had been inside the villa a few times before and vaguely remembered the layout. It was at least twice the size of my own home, with creamy stucco walls and large windows that faced the sea, and was decorated in an interesting combination of Grecian and English country style, while also offering the more modern comforts Mr. Howard no doubt enjoyed back in London.

As I drew closer to the room at the end of the hall, I could make out the sounds of Mr. Dorian muttering to himself. I paused before the doorway and peeked inside. He was hunched over a large desk piled with books and loose sheets of paper. A typewriter sat untouched by his elbow while he scribbled furiously, glowering as if the very paper had committed a grave offense against him, and entirely lost in his thoughts. I waited a breath before gently rapping on the door, and he startled before fixing that glower on me.

"I'm sorry," I blurted out, even though I hadn't done anything wrong. It was exactly nine o'clock, just as we had agreed upon.

It took him a moment to come back from wherever his mind had gone to, and I found myself wanting to know what he had been thinking of.

"Mrs. Harper. Welcome," he said curtly as his glower softened to mere indifference and motioned for me to enter while he attempted to straighten the papers on the desk. He was dressed in much the same manner as he had been that morning on the balcony, in a velvet dressing gown thrown over a crisp white shirt and dark trousers. His hair was still wet from a bath, but I was sorry to see that his features looked just as drawn as yesterday. He straightened, but then stopped short as his gaze fell on the front of my dress.

"Are—are you all right?"

"Oh yes," I said with a laugh. "I had a little accident climbing down from the donkey cart on the way here, but I'm perfectly well."

Mr. Dorian did not look entirely convinced, but gestured to a little seating area on the other side of the room that offered a view of the garden. "Have a seat, please. I've instructed Mrs. Nasso to bring us some tea, though I'm not sure she understood me," he admitted.

"You don't speak Greek?"

"Only a little, and not very well," he admitted with a wince. " I've had to resort to pantomimes more often than I'd care to admit."

"Mr. Howard should have warned you," I said with a smile.

"Oh, he did. But I told him I didn't care. At the time, it seemed preferrable to have a housekeeper who couldn't understand me anyway." There was a flash of bitterness in his gaze, and I recalled the salacious stories that had been printed about his marriage.

Was he implying that his own employees had been feeding information to the papers? It was a terribly distressing thought and the worst sort of invasion of privacy. But before I could respond, Mrs. Nasso appeared with the tea tray, and Mr. Dorian looked relieved. The pantomimes had done the job. She set down the loaded tray on the little table between us. In addition to a pot of fragrant mountain tea, she had included a few pieces of baklava, a Greek pastry made with honey and walnuts, and some braids of sweet bread.

"Efcharistó, Mrs. Nasso," I thanked her, before moving to pour the tea.

"Can you please tell her I don't want any more goat?" Mr. Dorian asked rather desperately. "I've tried and tried, but she doesn't seem to understand."

I passed on the message, but Mrs. Nasso only smiled and nodded before shuffling out of the room. I turned to Mr. Dorian with a meek look. "I believe she thought I was joking. The locals tend to think the English like to eat a great deal of meat."

He sighed heavily and sat back in his chair. "Well, I suppose I can't complain too much when the rest of her food is delicious."

"There are worse things to endure in a housekeeper," I said thoughtlessly and handed him a cup. An awkward moment passed as we both sipped our mountain tea in silence. Mr. Dorian seemed distracted by his own thoughts, as if he was too busy frowning at some spot on the floor to bother with conversation.

"So, then," I plowed on, "you seemed to be having a productive morning."

His gaze shot to my face, and he barked a laugh that sounded rusty, as if he was out of practice with the expression. "If only. No, I was composing a letter to my solicitor.

But I can type that out myself," he groused and set his cup down. "Must we engage in this meaningless small talk, or can I simply explain what I need from you and we can get on with it?"

"If you'd prefer," I said crisply. Goodness, if he had been this irritable when he offered me the job, I might have turned him down out of principle.

"Excellent." Mr. Dorian hauled himself to his feet and returned to his desk. "I have a devil of a headache and could use some rest." He pulled out the chair and moved the typewriter into a more accessible position. "I thought you could type up the first chapter or two today."

As I moved past him to sit down, I caught a whiff of his woodsy shaving soap. It must have contained a similar ingredient to the one Oliver used because my heart instinctively missed a beat. "That sounds manageable," I said before clearing my throat.

He opened a thick notebook and set it on the desk beside me. "I've labeled the chapters, but I am leaving it up to you to decide when a new paragraph is needed. Is that something they taught you at Girton?" he added in a droll tone.

I gave him a sharp look in response. He really was in an awful mood. Then I glanced at the first page and let out a gasp. "Mr. Dorian, your penmanship is appalling!"

He looked genuinely surprised and peered at the notebook. "Is it?"

"*Yes.*"

"Well, try your best." He shrugged, already moving towards the door. "I'm sure you will get the hang of it. If you need any more refreshments, call for Mrs. Nasso. I've told her she is at your disposal. Oh! And before I forget—" He pulled a thick envelope out of the pocket of his dressing gown and set it on the corner of the desk. "Your payment for the week, in good faith."

"Thank you," I said, bewildered.

"No, Mrs. Harper. Thank *you*," he said earnestly before he swept out of the room without another word.

I sat there for a long moment, collecting my thoughts while my gaze drifted over the study. I had never been in this room before and was pleased to see that it was rather cozy, especially as it seemed I would be spending a good deal of time here. The room was painted a calm blue color a few shades lighter than the slice of sea visible from the large picture window. A mixture of Greek and English artwork adorned the walls, including a rather majestic painting of the Parthenon above the small hearth.

Then I reached over and took the envelope. My eyes widened at the contents, and I quickly shoved it in my reticule, unused to having so much money on my person. I then let out a little huff and straightened my shoulders. It was time to get to work.

Two hours and several cups of mountain tea later, I had managed to finish typing the first two chapters of *A Murder in Middle Temple.* It had been slow going at first, and in a few places, I had to simply guess at the meaning behind Mr. Dorian's scratchings, but he was right, and it got easier as I went along. I was confident tomorrow's work would go much faster. Now, the contents of the book itself were another matter altogether, but I was not being paid to offer my opinion, and Mr. Dorian must have an editor back in England he trusted to tell him the truth.

I stood up and stretched before gathering my things and found Mrs. Nasso in the kitchen stirring what smelled like goat stew.

"Is Mr. Dorian still asleep?" I asked in Greek.

She nodded and clicked her tongue in disapproval. "Awake all night and asleep all day."

"Perhaps he's still adjusting to our time," I ventured, but Mrs. Nasso shook her head.

"He stays up drinking and thinking." Then she tapped her temple. "Too much thinking is not good for you."

"Well, he is a writer," I said weakly, but she fixed me with a look.

"He is not thinking about books, but about *her*," she nearly spat the word.

I raised my eyebrows. "You mean his former wife?"

"Oh yes." Mrs. Nasso nodded with an enthusiasm I had never seen her exhibit before. "When Mr. Howard wrote to me, he said that she is a bad, bad woman and that Mr. Dorian needed lots of rest."

I began to lean my elbows on the table, eager to ask her more, but that would make me no better than Juliet. "Well, then it is a good thing he is here," I said, straightening.

Mrs. Nasso seemed to approve of this response and nodded. "He needs to eat. He is much too thin."

"I'm not sure he cares for goat, though," I ventured, but she only shook her head in disbelief.

"No, Englishmen like goat. Mr. Howard always tells me so."

We then chatted idly for another minute before it was time for me to leave. Mrs. Nasso nodded good-bye before turning back to her stew.

As I tramped down the path towards the road, my mind reeled with all I had learned that morning.

A bad, bad woman.

Given that Mrs. Nasso wasn't exactly known for her loquaciousness, either Mr. Howard had disclosed the former Mrs. Dorian's adulterous behavior or she had done something even worse to earn such a title.

Despite my grudge, I couldn't help feeling a little sorry for Mr. Dorian. He was clearly in some kind of pain and wasn't dealing with it in a healthy manner. It was heartening to see that the old woman had taken a liking to him, though. A few more days rest, some hearty Grecian cooking, and the nourishing air enriched by the Ionian Sea could do wonders for a weary body and soul. But as I recalled the bleak look in Mr. Dorian's eyes, this observation was followed by a sinking suspicion that it would take far more to restore whatever had been taken from him. And, unfortunately, I knew all too well that some things once lost were gone forever.

I was so caught up in my own thoughts that I didn't notice someone coming up the path until they were nearly in front of me.

"Oh, kalimera!" I called out and stopped short.

It was Mrs. Belvedere's new maid, Daphne. I almost didn't recognize her without the scowl. "Hello," she replied in English with a pleasant smile. "I've come with some soaps I made for Mr. Dorian. Were you here visiting?"

"I am doing a little typing for him," I said, surprised she spoke so well and that this young girl had taken the time to present a stranger with such a gift. I also couldn't imagine Mr. Dorian being much interested in homemade soaps.

Daphne looked impressed. "Mrs. Belvedere says he is a very famous writer. She has all his books. Have you seen his newest work?"

Though we hadn't expressly discussed it, I didn't feel right talking about his work—and to my greater surprise, I felt almost protective. "Yes, but I was mostly just trying to make out his handwriting."

"How wonderful it must be to possess such a skill," she said on a dreamy sigh. "I wish I could write a book."

I made a noncommittal sound in response, as, given the state Mr. Dorian was in over his work, I couldn't exactly agree. "I must say, your English is very good," I said, attempting to steer the conversation in another direction.

"My mother and aunt worked on Corfu when they were young and made sure to teach me," Daphne explained, before giving me a sly smile. "Sometimes I pretend I can't understand Mrs. Belvedere in either language."

"Oh dear." I shouldn't have laughed at that, but I did, as Florence prided herself on her Greek.

Daphne joined me before turning serious. "You won't tell her, will you?"

"Absolutely not," I promised, having no desire to be the bearer of such news. "I know she can be difficult at times, but she does mean well."

"I suppose," Daphne said with a shrug. "And it is hard to find good work. That is partly why I came here to Corfu, like my mother did."

I nodded at the familiar lament. "Where are you from?"

"Paxos."

It was a smaller island nearby mostly populated by fishing villages, and I could see why a young woman such as herself had left. There was more excitement to be had on Corfu, and certainly more work, thanks to the number of visitors. Paxos, though just as beautiful, was not as popular with tourists.

"A lovely place," I said, and the girl beamed. "But your parents must miss you."

Her eyes dimmed, and she shook her head. "They are both gone."

I frowned in sympathy. "I'm very sorry for your loss."

But my words seemed to make her uncomfortable, and she shrugged. "It was long ago. I have only my aunt now, though she is very unhappy with me. She did not want me to come here," she added in response to my questioning look.

"Well, I'm sure it is hard having you so far away," I said. No doubt I would feel much the same way if Cleo left for another island, or farther.

She gave me a small smile, then gestured to her basket. "I should be going. Mrs. Belvedere will be missing me soon."

"Of course," I said. "But do try not to frustrate her too much, Daphne."

She let out a little sigh that didn't exactly inspire confidence. "I will."

"And Mr. Belvedere isn't so bad, is he?"

Her face lit up. "Oh no," she said. "He is the kindest of men."

I smiled at her description, as Mr. Belvedere was indeed very kind and had been a great help to me with some legal business after Oliver died. "I'm glad to hear that. Have a nice afternoon."

"Good bye, Mrs. Harper," she said with a nod and headed up the path.

I continued home, entirely unaware that was the last time I would see her alive.

Chapter 5

The next two weeks passed in a similar manner. After seeing the children off to school, I arrived at the villa each morning promptly at nine o'clock and immediately got to work typing out whatever Mr. Dorian had left for me the previous evening. Sometimes he had notes or corrections he wished me to make, but lately I had become quite adept at interpreting his terrible handwriting. Mrs. Nasso would bring me a pot of tea and something to nibble on while I worked, but other than that, I was left alone in his study.

I also made a point to rummage through Oliver's bookcase and found the first three Inspector Dumond novels. I flew through them in as many days, and though I still had grave concerns about Mr. Dorian's ability to craft dynamic female characters who had motivations beyond desiring the eponymous inspector, his talent for composing a gripping story was undeniable. I would have told him as much, but after my first day, I did not see Mr. Dorian again, save for an occasional brief encounter while I was on my way out.

I had gotten rather caught up in that day's pages, which

ended on a nail-biting cliffhanger, with the inspector suffering from a head wound alone at night in a disreputable corner of London, and left a bit later than usual. He came tramping down the hall as I was heading for the front door, but halted when he saw me. I was about to ask him what would happen next when a strange mixture of surprise and terror flashed across his face before he managed his usual look of boredom.

"Mrs. Harper," he said flatly. "I . . . I didn't realize you were still here."

"Just on my way out," I replied with a tight smile, unable to shake the feeling that he had been avoiding me this entire time. Then I scurried out the door before my suspicion could be confirmed.

When Florence Belvedere invited me to tea not long after this encounter, I readily accepted. I had been spending a little too much time alone as of late and was actually craving adult company. When I arrived on a balmy afternoon, I was shocked to see Florence herself open the door—and said as much.

"Yes, Christopher is at his office today, and Daphne has disappeared *again*," she groused as she led me onto the lush terrace, where tea awaited us. The comforting scent of lavender filled the air, thanks to two enormous pots that stood sentry by the doorway, and I inhaled deeply. Florence spent most of her free time out here, trying to create an English-style herb garden, and she was remarkably successful, despite the arid climate. "I swear, every time I look for that girl lately, she's gone off somewhere."

I hadn't seen Daphne again since my first morning at Mr. Dorian's, but every now and then, Mrs. Nasso would mention that she had stopped by. Whether she came simply to have a chat or give the man of the house more soap I couldn't be sure. If there really was something developing between Mr. Dorian and Daphne, at least they were being relatively discreet. I had never been a very good liar, and if Florence began to suspect them, she would sniff it out of me immediately.

"She'll turn up," I said blandly. Despite her lackluster work ethic, it didn't feel right to tattle on Daphne. She was allowed her privacy, the same as the rest of us, regardless of what she did with it.

"I must say, I'm rather surprised you agreed to work for Mr. Dorian," Florence said without preamble as we sat down under an arbor of grapevines. Florence was known for creating her own unique tea blends, and based on the heady scent of jasmine permeating the air as she poured, this one promised to be delectable.

"Why? You know I do that sort of thing now and then," I said, accepting the cup she handed to me. I had even worked for her husband for a few months, as I could never have afforded his legal help after Oliver's death. "Christopher was the one who recommended me in the first place."

"As well he should," she declared. "He says your work is excellent." Though I hadn't done anything more complicated than filing and general typing, I couldn't help blushing at this praise. "I was only surprised because I was under the impression you disliked Mr. Dorian, given that you barely said more than 'hello' to him at our party."

"Oh." Though I couldn't exactly deny it, I suddenly felt rather petty. Yes, the man had said some unkind things about me, but he had no idea I was eavesdropping. I glanced away and took a sip of the fragrant tea as I collected my thoughts.

At my continued silence, Florence leaned closer and lowered her voice. "Is it because he's divorced?"

I balked. "Florence, please tell me you don't think I'm so easily scandalized as that."

She sat back and shrugged. "No, but I would understand

if you were. Divorce is such a ghastly business. It shouldn't even be legal. It makes a mockery of the rest of us who have taken our vows seriously," she said with a nod towards me. "A woman swayed by a handsome face or a generous purse shouldn't require the state to save her from her own stupidity."

Her sudden venom on the subject shocked me. "But surely there are some circumstances when it is needed. After all, not everyone is lucky enough to marry noble men."

Predictably, Florence preened a little at that. "True, but I knew my husband was of excellent character as soon as I met him. And you must have known the same of dear Oliver."

Indeed, I had felt that way at the time, but I had also been very young and barely knew him. In truth, it was simply a matter of luck that Oliver turned out to be the man I thought he was. But I doubted Florence would credit the success of her marriage to something as capricious as chance rather than her own innate abilities. I could tell we weren't going to come to an agreement on this, so I just nodded. "Yes, I did."

"So then," she said conspiratorially, "if you aren't scandalized by his divorce, why don't you like him?"

I suspected Christopher must have told her about Mr. Dorian's initial impression of me, but I would rather attempt to swim to the mainland than admit to eavesdropping. "I hardly know him, Florence." There. That was at least honest. Then something else occurred to me, and I narrowed my eyes. "Does Mr. Dorian think I dislike him?"

Florence's mouth curved in victory. She had caught my interest. "I believe that was part of the appeal."

"That I *dislike* him?" I was incredulous.

She tilted her head with a thoughtful look. "I forget exactly how Christopher put it, but it was something about not wanting any distractions while he worked."

I scoffed, then thought of the way every other lady at the party had fretted and fawned over him. I certainly hadn't done anything like that. And yet, this reasoning still offended me. "And *I* am not a distraction?" I couldn't hide my indignation.

Florence raised an eyebrow. "Do you want to be?"

I sat back in my chair, dangerously close to slouching. "No," I grumbled.

Florence tactfully did not press me on this, though she very well could have. "Well, then do you at least like working for him?"

"Yes, actually, I do." I perked up a little. "I'm not really used to becoming so engrossed in my work—though don't tell Christopher."

Florence laughed. "I'm sure typing up a mystery novel is far more stimulating than legal correspondence."

"It reminds me of my time at university," I said fondly. "Though Mr. Dorian isn't paying me to analyze or interpret anything." But a growing part of me wished he would, as every time I sat down to work, I was swamped with ideas.

"I'm so glad." Then she waggled her eyebrows. "Though I don't suppose you'll tell me about the book?"

I smiled. "No, Florence. I'm duty bound to silence on that subject."

"Well, I had to try," she said with a grin. "But I'm happy for you. Perhaps this can be the start of something new. And heaven knows you'll need to fill your time once Cleo is gone."

I had just taken a sip of tea and choked a little. "What do you mean?" I asked once I recovered.

Florence looked puzzled. "You know. When she goes off to school. In England."

"Cleo isn't going to school in England," I said sharply and set down the teacup. My hand had begun to tremble, and I didn't want to risk spilling any more. "Wherever did you hear such a thing?"

"Why, from Virginia, who I assume heard it from Juliet," Florence explained, a bit bewildered by my response. Then she gave me a sympathetic look and patted my knee. "My dear, you can't really expect a girl like Cleo to be satisfied with that little school in town. She's so clever. Like you."

"We haven't discussed it," I murmured, but that wasn't strictly true.

A time or two, Cleo had vaguely mentioned wanting to follow in my footsteps to Girton, but she was only fourteen. That was years away.

"I'm so sorry. I didn't mean to upset you."

"I'm not upset," I insisted. "And don't apologize. I should speak about this to Cleo, though. Juliet must have misunderstood."

"Yes," Florence said with a diplomatic nod, "I'm sure that's it."

But despite this, the knot in my stomach stubbornly remained.

If anything ever happens to me, you must raise the children here. Don't take them back to England.

The unbidden memory surfaced, and I could still see the strange flash of desperation in Oliver's eyes when he demanded this of me. At the time, I hadn't a clue where such a morbid thought had come from. It was late in the afternoon, and we were relaxing out on the terrace together. I was planning our meals for the coming week, while Oliver was reading through the stack of mail he had picked up in town, as was his custom. In any case, I waved his concern away and readily agreed, as at the time it was unthinkable.

Of course, my darling. Whyever would we leave?

But he didn't answer and instead gripped my hand. I remember being surprised by how clammy it felt.

You must promise me, Min, he'd insisted. *Promise you won't go back there.*

He didn't let go until I'd said the words. Until I gave him my promise. But I hadn't pressed him on it. Hadn't asked why he felt the need to even say such a thing. Something had distracted me then, though now I couldn't remember what. One of the children had been crying for me or Mrs. Kouris had a demand or the supper was burning. And we never spoke of it again.

When Oliver died some months later, I began to think of that exchange as something like his last wish. By adhering to it, he would still have influence over our family, and it gave me something to base my decisions on. But now I felt a sudden flash of resentment towards him and my promise. For all that he would never experience as a parent, and all I had to contend with on my own. Even if Juliet had been mistaken, Cleo would likely wish to leave Corfu at some point, and it would be selfish of me to stop her. After all, I left home for my studies and then went on to travel halfway across the world. Yet despite this well-reasoned rationale, the very thought of Cleo leaving still sent a shudder through me. For what had once seemed like a far-off day in the distant future was now much too close. But time would continue marching swiftly, relentlessly on. And I was entirely at its mercy.

I left Florence's house that afternoon with a stack of Inspector Dumond novels, as she had all the books that had been published since Oliver's death. As for Cleo, I decided to wait for the right moment to broach her plans for school—preferably when she was in an excellent mood. Experience had taught me that the slightest hint of confrontation got her hackles up, and I very much needed this conversation to go as smoothly as possible.

A few days later, I arrived at Mr. Dorian's villa as usual, but it was a brilliant morning, and I had grown tired of being stuck inside at that massive desk. Behind it were a pair of French doors that led out onto a little sitting area. Mrs. Nasso usually opened them before I arrived to let in some air, but I had never ventured outside before. On a whim, I lugged the typewriter out onto the table, which was barely big enough for my purposes, and had just begun to work when the study's door was flung open.

Mr. Dorian tramped in, wearing his dressing gown and a mighty scowl. He swung towards the desk, obviously looking for me, and his scowl deepened considerably.

"Mrs. Harper!" he called out and put his hands on his hips.

"I'm out here, Mr. Dorian," I said in the same calm tone I used when the children were in a snit over something.

His gaze fell upon me, and he rolled his shoulders back as if preparing for a fight. "Well?" he growled as he charged outside. "What do you have to say for yourself?"

I tilted my head. "Excuse me?"

"This!" he cried out as he waved a piece of paper at me.

"Oh. Those were just a few ideas I had."

His cheeks reddened. "A few ideas?" he spat in outrage, then began to read from the paper: "'Miss Linley is rather poorly drawn and would benefit from deeper characterization.'"

"Yes."

"She is his secretary."

"I know that," I replied. "But other than being very good at her job and obviously having tender feelings for her employer, we know nothing about her."

"She has brown hair," he said with indignation.

I bit back a smile and nodded in concession. "All right, yes. She has brown hair."

He glared at me before reading from the paper again. "'The love triangle between Miss Linley, the duchess, and Inspector Dumond has also begun to stretch the limits of believability.'"

"It has lasted for nearly the entire series," I said, striving for delicacy. "Surely, by this point, the inspector has decided which woman he is in love with—though I will admit to a partiality for the duchess."

This seemed to catch him by surprise, and he raised an eyebrow. "Why?"

"Well, she suffered so terribly at the hands of her late husband. I suppose I wish to see her happy," I explained. "And, unlike Miss Linley, she is not dependent on the inspector for her livelihood."

He looked incredulous. "You think the inspector would dismiss her if their romance did not work out?"

"I'm not sure, as he doesn't ever seem to consider this himself. I think it would be much better for all of them if she marries that Peter Mayhew chap."

"You mean the cockney delivery boy?" he said, with surprising derision.

"He is far more than that, as you very well know," I said, fully prepared to defend poor Peter. "He has rescued the inspector from a number of tight situations over the years, thanks to his quick thinking, and he has aspirations to join the Metropolitan Police. All in all, a very industrious fellow. Besides, he must be about the same age as Miss Linley, which is more appropriate, given that the inspector is nearly old enough to be her father."

Mr. Dorian opened his mouth to respond, then appeared to think better of it. Instead, he sat down hard on the chair across from me and glanced at the paper again. "You also said the murderer was too obvious." Then he shot me a dark look. "Who do you think it is?"

"The bishop."

He stared at me blankly for a moment before muttering a curse. Then he stood up and walked over to the terrace's low wall. Mr. Dorian gazed out at the view for a spell before pinning me with another look. "How did you guess?"

I shrugged. "He seemed the least likely suspect—at first, anyway. I've noticed that you tend to introduce the true killer early on in your books. Then the inspector has to circle back to solve the crime. It isn't a bad formula," I added hastily, as his expression turned deadly. "And I'm not sure I would have noticed it if I hadn't spent the last few weeks reading them."

"Hmm," he replied and continued to stare at me, obviously thinking through something. But he was silent for so long that I began to shift, uncomfortable under his inspection. "So," he finally said, "you've read my books."

I paused, momentarily thrown by the subject change. "Yes. Though not all of them." The last three were still sitting on my nightstand.

He crossed his arms and leaned a hip against the wall, which came up to his waist. "And here I was under the impression that my work was beneath you."

Did . . . did he sound offended?

"I don't recall saying that," I began. "And I'm sorry. I truly didn't mean to upset you with my suggestions."

He scoffed. "Your suggestions didn't upset me, Mrs. Harper. It is your presumption. I am not paying you for your opinion. I am paying you for your ability to type. Therefore, kindly refrain from offering your thoughts about my work unless I ask for them. Which I *won't*," he added petulantly.

I'm not proud to admit it, but his complete dismissal got under my skin, and anger suddenly flared through me. I had had quite enough of men and their presumed infallibility.

"Right," I said as I came to my feet. "After all, what could I possibly know? I'm just a frumpy housewife."

I stormed past him then, propelled by both my indignation and my embarrassment. I had actually admitted to knowing about his unkind description of me. And there was no coming back from that. The terrace opened out onto the small back garden, which then gave way to the hillside where our properties met. But I didn't want to go home. I wanted to be alone. So instead, I headed towards the wooded area that ran alongside the villa. There was a well-worn footpath that connected his property and the Belvederes' with the main road, but halfway between lay a sloping meadow. One could step off the path and follow it all the way down to the sea, which sounded very appealing at the moment. I could faintly hear Mr. Dorian calling after me and moved faster.

Once I found the opening, I ducked down the path. It was pleasantly cool and a little dark, as it was shaded by a variety of old-growth olive trees and shrubs. I slowed my pace and had just let out a sigh of relief when I heard him.

"Mrs. Harper," Mr. Dorian shouted from the entrance to the path, "will you stop?"

"No," I called out over my shoulder. "I want to be alone."

It was childish, I knew, but I wasn't used to losing control over my emotions like that and needed to master this storm inside me. I heard him grumble something under his breath, but I didn't wait to see if he followed and moved swiftly down the path until the trees gave way to the open meadow. I paused to shield my eyes from the bright sun and cursed myself for forgetting my hat back at the villa. Perhaps I could send a message to Mrs. Nasso, as I really did hate to give it up. Then I looked down towards a cluster of spindly trees that bracketed the sea. Nothing but the faint rustle of the grass from the breeze off the water surrounded me. Mr. Dorian must have turned back.

Good, I told myself before I started to tramp down the gently sloping hill, forcefully swinging my arms as I walked. I would sit by the water for a bit, collect my thoughts, and then take the long way home, as I couldn't possibly pass by the villa. Though I would miss the rest of the money he promised, I had earned enough these last weeks to fix the house's most pressing issues. The rest would have to wait, as usual. I was nearly at the bottom when I spotted something crumpled by the edge of the trees. Or, as it turned out, someone.

Chapter 6

Once when I was a little girl, a swallow flew into my bedroom window. I had been playing alone with my dollhouse when there was a sudden, loud bang. My parents were out, and as usual my brothers were driving Nanny to distraction, so I ran downstairs to the kitchen. Mrs. Potter, our old cook, took my hand, and together we went outside. A gardener had already found the unfortunate creature, and he warned Mrs. Potter to keep me away, as the bird was in the last throes of life. I caught a glimpse as he picked it up and could see it twitching unnaturally. Somehow, I knew he was going to put the poor thing out of its misery, so I burrowed my face against Mrs. Potter's apron, comforted by her ever-present scent of flour and sugar. Once the deed was done, she took me back down to the kitchen and fed me tea and cookies until my parents returned. She must have told them what had happened, but they certainly didn't speak a word to me about it, and I was too afraid to ask.

I didn't have another encounter with death until I watched Oliver slip away in my arms. Aneurism of the brain, the doctor had said. It was fast, and he didn't suffer. For that, I would be forever grateful. But as I approached the still form by the trees that morning, a certainty came from the depths of my being that this person's passing had not been gentle, nor kind. I must have knelt beside the body and pulled back the cloak covering the face, but I don't actually remember doing this. For as soon as I recognized Daphne, I began to scream. I had been wrong about Mr. Dorian, for he arrived very quickly and pulled me back from the body. Then he pressed my face to his shoulder, and I shut my eyes, but the image was already hopelessly burned into my brain: Daphne's dark eyes frozen open, her lips slightly parted, as if death had taken her by surprise, and the mottled bruising at her throat.

He must have led me to the villa, but I don't remember that either. When I finally came back to myself, I was sitting on a chair by the hearth in the study with his dressing gown draped around my shoulders, clutching a mug of tea while Mrs. Nasso fussed over me.

"Where did Mr. Dorian go?" I eventually asked. I had no sense of time. He could have been gone an hour or mere minutes.

Mrs. Nasso raised an eyebrow in surprise. "To fetch the police, of course."

"Someone should tell the Belvederes," I said softly. "They'll be wondering where she is."

"It will be taken care of," Mrs. Nasso said, as she patted my shoulder. "And I will go tell Mrs. Kouris what has happened, so she doesn't worry about you."

I was still too dazed to fully appreciate the magnitude of this gesture and could only nod. "Thank you."

At some point, Mr. Dorian returned with a stone-faced policeman in tow who had one of the thickest, bushiest moustaches I had ever seen.

"I am Inspector Callas," he said in excellent English. "Please tell me what has happened."

I cast a glance at Mr. Dorian, who stood just behind him with his arms folded and an equally serious expression. Was I meant to tell him everything from that morning? Even our silly quarrel that had led me to flee in the first place? No, I decided.

"I was walking towards the sea not far from the footpath when I saw something up ahead. I didn't know what it was at first, and thought it was a forgotten piece of clothing. But as I grew closer, I realized it was a body . . ." My voice faded as Daphne's still form flashed through my mind yet again. I shook my head, desperate to rid my mind of the image, and fixed my eyes on the inspector. "I pulled back the cloak and realized it was Daphne Costas. The Belvederes' maid."

"Yes. Mr. Dorian has already told me all this," he replied, sounding a touch impatient. "Thank you, Mrs. Harper." He then tucked his notepad into his jacket pocket, but I noticed that he had stopped writing anything after I gave my address. "I will let you know if I need any more from you."

However, I had the distinct impression he wasn't terribly interested in anything I had to say.

"But do you know what's happened? I can't imagine why anyone would have a reason to kill Daphne." I suddenly felt very anxious. Everyone seemed to be acting quite normally, while a young woman was dead not far from where we sat. The man hadn't even asked what I'd seen when I found her.

Inspector Callas shook his head, though it seemed more of a chastisement than an admission of doubt. "I cannot say at this time."

I opened my mouth, but Mr. Dorian cut me off. "Come, Inspector. I will show you out."

I stared at them wide-eyed as they exited the room, neither one bothering to look back. Their deep voices slowly faded as they walked down the hall. When Mr. Dorian returned a few minutes later, I stood.

"That man doesn't seem the least bit concerned that someone has been murdered," I said, outraged. "He didn't even ask me about her body. About what I saw."

"Sit down, Mrs. Harper," he said calmly. "You are in shock." I was just about to deny this when I suddenly felt lightheaded. Mr. Dorian took my arm and gently guided me back to my seat. "I can't allow you to leave until you've eaten something."

"Fine," I muttered, though the mere idea of food made my stomach recoil.

He then left the room again, and I fully expected Mrs. Nasso to appear with a tray, but instead it was Mr. Dorian himself.

He set down the tray on the low table before me. "Here."

It was loaded with hearty brown bread, hard cheese, a dish of yogurt, and wedges of fragrant oranges rather artfully arranged—and far more than I could ever eat in one sitting.

"Did you do all this?"

"I am perfectly capable of slicing some bread and plating fruit, Mrs. Harper," he bristled.

"Of course."

I ate a few spoonfuls of yogurt and an orange wedge while he watched over me. After a few moments, I raised an eyebrow. "Do you plan to eat something as well, or will you continue to hover like that?"

He stiffened and sat down on a chair across from me, then helped himself to some bread and cheese. Nourishment did make me feel better, and as we ate in companionable silence, the fog that had surrounded me for the last hour slowly lifted. I caught a whiff of Mr. Dorian's woodsy scent and realized it was coming off of the dressing gown still draped around my shoulders. Then I noticed, really noticed, the scandalous state of Mr. Dorian's clothing. After making such a gallant gesture, he hadn't bothered to don another dressing gown or coat, and his shirt was open at the throat.

Despite my best efforts, I couldn't help noticing the exposed triangle of golden skin lightly dusted with dark hair. The inspector had seen him in such a state, and in my company alone. I shouldn't know such an intimate detail about his person, and my cheeks burned as I shifted my gaze to the floor. Then I noticed he wore a fine pair of leather slippers covered in dirt.

"What happened to your slippers? They're ruined."

Confusion flashed in his eyes as he glanced down. "Oh. I'm afraid I didn't bother to change before I . . . before I went after you," he said sheepishly.

Given what had unfolded, I was certainly grateful for his impulsiveness, but it seemed rather unnecessary. Before I could ask *why* he had gone after me, Mr. Dorian continued.

"It's fine," he added with a dismissive wave. "I'm sure they can be cleaned." He rose from the chair. "Stay as long as you'd like. I would also understand if you need a day or two to recover."

That caught me by surprise. "You . . . you wish me to continue working for you?"

He blinked. "Well, yes."

"Even after I stormed off?"

"Entirely understandable." I narrowed my eyes in suspicion, and he barked a laugh. "Mrs. Harper, admittedly I am not in a position to be selective with whom I employ at the moment, but I very much need, nay, *want* your assistance with this book. Though, again, please take some time for yourself."

I shook my head. "That won't be necessary. Working would be helpful." The last thing I needed was to be wandering around my house thinking about poor Daphne. "And please accept my apology. I didn't mean to overstep with my suggestions."

He raked a hand through his tousled hair and let out a sigh. "No, it's fine. I overreacted. Took me by surprise, is all.

But I think you're right. About some of it, at least," he added with a playful look.

Yet this didn't feel like any kind of triumph. Mr. Dorian was clearly in a state over this book, and I hadn't helped. "It's entirely at your discretion, of course," I murmured.

"I'm sorry as well," he began, "for my disparaging comment. It's no excuse, but I was . . . not at my best that night at the Belvederes'."

I could feel my cheeks heating again and nodded. "Understood. May we start anew?" I desperately did not want him to ruminate on that evening any further.

He smiled then. A real, genuine smile that I felt all the way down to my toes. "I would like that, very much." He then paused by the door and glanced back with a quizzical expression. "What did you mean before about the body?"

The body.

My mind clung to the words. Was that what Daphne, once so full of life, had been reduced to? A body? But Mr. Dorian was looking at me expectantly, and I hadn't the energy to needle him about his choice of words.

"What did you see?" he prompted.

"Oh . . ." I shook my head, feeling dazed. "There was some debris in her hair," I said, forcing myself to recall the ugly scene. "It was as if she had fallen down the hill." Or been pushed. But I did not share that with Mr. Dorian. It was disquieting enough to think the words, let alone speak them.

He turned fully to me then, but frowned in concentration. "I'm sure that will be discovered during the examination, but you may want to write it all down. Only if you feel able," he added quickly. "It might be helpful later, if the inspector does call on you."

"A good idea," I said with a nod, even though I highly doubted that would happen.

He then gestured to his desk. "Write it here, if you wish."

"Thank you. I will."

Mr. Dorian smiled again and left the room. The click of the door shutting seemed to echo in the small space, and I stared at the desk for a long while. Eventually, I found the strength to stand and got to work, driven by a certainty that once I put it all down in ink on paper, I would be rid of the images: Daphne's bruised neck, her lifeless brown eyes staring up at the sky, her dark hair, usually so neat, streaked with dirt and dried blades of grass. These details all came out in hurried strokes. I couldn't even manage proper sentences in places. It was as if I was making a confession. All of my thoughts and feelings poured out onto the page. Some were about Daphne, others about death in general. By the time I had finished, I had covered two pieces of paper front and back with my disjointed scribblings. But it would need a good rewrite before it could be of help to anyone. I let out a sigh and sank back into the chair, feeling depleted of energy. At that moment, I was sorely tempted to lay my head on top of the desk and take a rest right there, but instead I forced myself to my feet and folded the pages into my reticule. I had done my duty. Now, somehow, I needed to put the horror of the morning behind me before I left. For the children were expecting me, and I would not take this home to them.

Chapter 7

"I know I complained about Daphne, but I feel so awful for the poor girl," Florence said as she wrung her hands on her lap. "And to be *murdered*, my goodness. What a terrible shock it has been. Christopher is bereft as well."

Two days had passed since I'd discovered Daphne's body, and I was in Virginia Taylor's expansive parlor having tea with her and Florence. Cleo had begged me to take her there so she could visit with Juliet, since I had forbidden the children from going anywhere alone until the perpetrator was apprehended. Unsurprisingly, Cleo had been furious about this restriction, and even my sweet Tommy had kicked up a fuss, as he was used to wandering off alone for hours at a time. But I held firm, which was not an easy feat, especially when they teamed up together. I accepted the invitation to tea mostly to appease them, and so far it seemed to work.

The girls had shut themselves away in Juliet's room as soon as we arrived, and Tommy was playing with Joseph, the Taylors' younger son, in the large back garden, leaving us free to discuss the murder.

"And, Minnie," Florence said, as reached for my hand,

her eyes full of sympathy, "I'm so sorry. I can't imagine what it must have been like to find her."

I shook my head, even as the image of Daphne's lifeless body flooded my mind once again. I hadn't been able to sleep for more than a few hours at a time, but had no desire to speak about what I had seen.

I cleared my throat. "Have you been able to contact her family?"

"I sent a letter to her aunt," Florence explained. "She had no other relations to speak of."

She did not want me to come here.

I frowned as Daphne's haunting comment came back to me. It took on an entirely different meaning now, thanks to her death. Had her aunt been trying to warn Daphne away from Corfu? But then I shook my head at the ridiculous thought. I had been reading far too many mystery novels lately.

"It may be some time before we hear back, though," Florence continued. "And we can't wait much longer to bury her."

The Belvederes had generously offered to pay for Daphne's funeral expenses, but the days were growing steadily warmer, and bodies did not keep for very long here. We were silent for a moment at this sobering thought until Virginia broke the silence.

"Have the police uncovered anything?"

Florence sighed. "Not really. They claim someone saw that vagrant that is always about skulking around the hillside earlier in the week and want to question him."

I raised an eyebrow. "You mean Gregor? The man who sells wooden trinkets?"

"Yes, that's the one."

"I suppose he may have seen something," I mused.

"Oh, they think he did a good deal more than that," Florence pronounced.

I balked at her certainty. "But he's harmless. Truly." I had encountered him on at least half a dozen occasions and even purchased a small donkey from him. He was eccentric, certainly, but not violent.

"That is not for you or me to determine, my dear," Florence said loftily.

I suppressed the urge to roll my eyes. "Well, I certainly hope he isn't their only suspect. Shouldn't they be doing more?"

Thanks to Mr. Dorian's books, I learned that the longer a case went on, the harder it became to solve, as clues went missing and people forgot important details. And, unfortunately, we had no brilliant Inspector Dumond to rely upon here.

"Yes, they should," Florence agreed. "And presumably they are. Christopher was going to check with the inspector today, actually."

"Well, I'm glad to hear that," Virginia said. "I can hardly sleep at night, knowing there is a murderer in our midst." This seemed a touch dramatic, given that the Taylors lived in one of the island's most exclusive neighborhoods. Then she gripped my hand. "And poor Minnie. All alone in that little house of yours with no one to protect you. I don't know how you can bear it."

"I'm not alone," I said reflexively, though I knew what she meant. Tommy may consider himself the man of the house, but if we ever did have to contend with an intruder, it would all fall to me.

"Virginia does make a good point, though," Florence said. "Not to worry. Christopher and I will keep an extra eye out, especially where you and the children are concerned."

"I'm sure we will all be fine," I demurred. She only meant to be helpful, but the thought of being constantly watched was unsettling. I blamed my reading habits once more and changed the subject.

We then chatted a little about decidedly more banal topics until Florence declared she needed to leave. She wanted to be home when Christopher returned. We said our good-byes, and I promised to visit her soon. But she hadn't been gone for more than a few moments when Virginia leaned towards me with a familiar glint in her blue eyes.

"I wouldn't dare say this in front of Florence," she began, "but there have been whispers about Daphne."

I braced myself for whatever gossip she was about to share. "What do you mean?"

"That she was quite free with her favors, the discovery of which enraged one of her paramours."

That was far worse than I had expected. "And that is supposed to excuse her murder?"

"Of course not," Virginia said hastily, as she leaned back in her chair. "But you know how people can be here. She was an outsider and an unmarried woman. That alone would cause suspicion."

I reluctantly nodded, as it was true. "Do the police know this?" If so, I worried that it could affect their investigation.

Virginia lifted a shoulder. "I would assume so. If I heard it, I'm sure they have."

I stared past her towards the large open window. The Taylors' villa was situated in a prime spot on the hillside above Corfu Town and offered a breathtaking view of the tiled rooftops of the old town and the azure sea beyond. Something had been niggling at the back of my mind for the last two days, and this theory of a jealous paramour finally unlocked it.

Just beneath the bruising on Daphne's neck was a chain, though it was mostly hidden by her blouse. I hadn't gotten a good look at it, as I had been understandably distracted, but I closed my eyes now, trying to recall as many details as I could. I felt certain it was gold—and just the sort of thing a man might give to a lover.

My eyes shot open. Virginia had been calling my name, and I turned to her now.

"Are you all right?" She looked distressed.

"I've just thought of something. About Daphne," I said. "Would you mind terribly if I left to go speak about it to the police? I think it might be important."

I was much closer to the police station here and knew the children would be safe.

She blinked in surprise, as I was acting very strangely, but then shook her head. "Not at all. Take as long as you need."

I didn't wait another moment.

"I appreciate you coming down here, Mrs. Harper," Inspector Callas said in a tone that indicated the complete opposite. "But our investigation is nearly finished."

I had waited to speak with him for over an hour, but he was not as interested in my recollection as I expected. I hadn't seen any sign of Christopher either, so clearly he had not been occupying the inspector.

"Then you have a suspect?" I truly hoped it wasn't Gregor.

His frown deepened. "I cannot say at this time."

"But Daphne was wearing a gold necklace, wasn't she?"

He let out a sigh and gestured to the door. "Please, I must ask you to leave. I have other matters to attend to."

I very much wanted to ask what could possibly be more important than the murder, but no doubt that would only irritate the man further. So instead I left without another word, disappointed but not entirely surprised, especially if he really had learned of the rumors surrounding Daphne's private life. The world judged women harshly, and those who dared to fly in the face of convention were given no quarter if things went terribly awry. And it was always their reluctance to fall in line with the status quo that was blamed for their downfall, no matter the actions of others.

By the time I returned to the Taylors' villa to collect my children, I was filled with a bitter resentment that consumed my thoughts as we made the trek home in the donkey cart. Cleo and Tommy didn't seem to notice my silence, as they regaled me with tales of how they had spent the afternoon, which was just as well. I didn't feel like talking with anyone and escaped to Oliver's study as soon as I could.

After his death, I kept this room mostly untouched. His eclectic collection of books lined the walls, where one could find everything from old encyclopedias to the works of Sophocles and Shakespeare. And, of course, Mr. Dorian's novels, along with other mysteries, their covers battered and worn. I sat down hard on the old leather chair he had lugged from England to Athens, and then here. It had been his grandfather's, Oliver once explained to me, and he had many fond memories of sitting on the old man's knee while he regaled him with Greek myths, each more unbelievable than the next. He was the one who had inspired my husband's love of Greece, though the man had died when Oliver was still a boy.

I sat back in the well-worn chair, the leather as soft as butter from decades of use, and let my gaze wander over Oliver's desk filled with bric-a-brac: an old fountain pen, a few scraps of paper with his handwriting, a large, craggy rock a much younger Cleo had proudly given him to use as a paperweight, and a small piece of bottle-green sea glass I had plucked from the beach when we first came here. Oliver declared it his good luck charm and always kept it within reach. I picked it up and ran the pad of my thumb across the smooth surface, then turned it over in my palm. It was as if I was trying to channel him, to feel his gentle, reassuring hand on my shoulder, telling me not to give in to bitterness but instead find a way forward.

And it was then that I remembered.

One afternoon when we were newly married, Oliver and I

had been discussing our experiences at Cambridge and how different it could be for the female students. I had been complaining about how sequestered we were when he mentioned an incident that occurred while he was a student. A popular barmaid named Polly Henderson, who worked at one of the local pubs, had been found dead in the woods. Though the university tried to keep word from spreading, especially to the female students at Girton, it was too salacious to control, and soon rumors spread like wildfire. I was familiar with the story, but by the time I was a student, it was presented more as a warning to girls with loose morals rather than a heinous unsolved crime.

But Oliver knew the barmaid personally and said it was something of an open secret that she had been carrying on with the younger son of an earl who had a well-earned reputation as a libertine with a penchant for violence. Once the papers got hold of the story, though, it was Polly's reputation that suffered. The details surrounding her murder had become twisted into something that bore no resemblance to the truth until the writers could comfortably insinuate that she had brought on her death herself. There was never any mention of the earl's son, though Oliver was certain he had killed Polly and had even discussed his suspicions with a disinterested police officer. But it all came to nothing, for no one really cared that a promiscuous young woman had been murdered. Served her right was the general consensus.

Years later Oliver had been at a club in London with a group of classmates from Cambridge recalling their school days, when someone brought up Polly's murder. Another claimed that the earl had paid off the police to keep the investigation away from his son and arranged for the papers to demonize Polly to such a degree that the public was practically celebrating her murder. But it had all been for naught, as the young man had been stabbed in a brothel just a few years later. His classmates then moved on to other topics, shrugging off this terrible miscarriage of justice, but it left a heavy mark on my husband, as he felt guilty for not doing more. Our conversation had turned unexpectedly morose, but I will never forget what he said next. "If one has access to money and power, there is no limit to what they can get away with. But we must not stand idly by either. Justice should always be served."

I took those words to heart now and made a promise to both Daphne and my husband to see this case through. And make sure justice was served.

Chapter 8

"Are you going to the funeral?"

I glanced up from the typewriter to find Mr. Dorian hovering in the doorway. I hadn't seen him in person since our truce earlier in the week, as he still kept his odd hours, but I was pleased when he left a few pages for me to re-type in order to incorporate some changes to his manuscript. Though some were taken from my suggestions, most were of his own creation. And they were quite good.

"Oh, yes. I am."

I had arrived earlier than usual that morning since I needed to be at the church by eleven.

He stepped farther into the room, dressed in a sleek black suit. "Shall we go together, then?"

It hadn't occurred to me that he would be in attendance as well. "Certainly," I said. "I just need a few more minutes to finish this chapter."

He nodded and disappeared back down the hall. I rushed to finish my work and headed outside, then came to an abrupt stop. Mr. Dorian was cooing to Maurice with a rare smile of delight. As I approached, he gave Maurice a scratch just behind his ear, and the donkey made his pleasure known with an excited bray. Mr. Dorian threw back his head and laughed with such fondness that my heart thrummed with unexpected warmth.

"You've had a donkey, haven't you," I said.

He glanced back at me in surprise, too distracted by Maurice to notice my appearance. Then he shook his head as his hand fell away. "My grandparents did. When I was a boy. I used to spend my summers at their farm." Then he stepped back to help me into the cart. "Her name was Princess."

I smiled as I took his hand. "A wonderful name for a donkey."

"Yes. It suited her, too." He climbed up and sat down next to me. Then he let out a short laugh. "I hadn't thought of her in years. Funny, that."

I hummed in agreement as I took the reins. "It is amazing what the mind can recall when given the right inspiration."

We didn't speak much after that, but it was another one of those companionable kind of silences. I occasionally pointed out things of interest along the way, as Mr. Dorian admitted he hadn't left the villa much except to visit the Belvederes. He and Christopher had struck up a friendship, and I assumed that had compelled him to attend the funeral today.

"I hadn't even realized there was a church here," he said as we turned down the shady road.

"It's really just a chapel for the neighborhood," I explained. "There is a much grander church in Corfu Town, but I think the Belvederes wanted to discourage gawkers."

Mr. Dorian frowned in disapproval. "Yes, these kinds of things tend to bring out ghouls." Then he turned to me hesitantly. "Is . . . your husband buried here, then?"

I looked away, surprised by the question. "He is in the English cemetery in town."

Mr. Dorian muttered what sounded like a curse. "Right. Of course. I hadn't realized— "

"It's fine," I said quickly, filled with a strange need to make him feel comfortable about bringing up my dead husband. "It's a lovely place, actually. Though I suppose it would be nice to have him closer." But then I realized how ridiculous this sounded. Oliver and everything that made him him was lost to me the moment he died. What I had buried under a headstone was only remains. Nothing more. Which was why I hardly ever visited.

Yet Mr. Dorian simply responded to my babbling with a polite nod. "Quite."

Luckily, we had arrived at the chapel by then, so I was saved from further embarrassment. There were still a few minutes before the service began, and Mr. Dorian offered to tie up Maurice so I could go inside and pay my respects. The Belvederes might have chosen the smaller neighborhood church rather than the large one in Corfu Town in part to keep away gawkers, but I was still disappointed to see such a small turnout. Florence and Christopher were talking quietly with the priest at the back of the church, while a few other people I recognized from the neighborhood were seated, but it didn't look like Daphne's aunt was here.

In keeping with the Greek Orthodox tradition, her casket was open to allow one last viewing. As I made my way down the short aisle, my gaze traveled over the striking hand-painted iconography lining the walls. Dour-faced saints with enormous black eyes stared down at me, while the chapel air was a thick perfume of fresh-cut flowers mingled with smoky incense. I had always found frankincense comforting, and as I kneeled before the casket, Daphne looked peaceful, as if she were only sleeping. She had been dressed in a plain white gown with a wide collar, and her dark hair was plaited in a crown around her head. My heart ached for her once more, and I said a silent prayer, but just as I was about to rise, something glinted in the low light.

The necklace.

I leaned in for a closer look and saw that the dainty chain disappeared beneath the collar of her dress. I cast a quick glance around, but no one was looking my way. Then I took a deep breath, sent up a prayer of forgiveness, and gently tugged on the chain until I revealed a distinct teardrop pendant in hammered gold with an ornate pattern along the edges. If pressed, I would have called it rather hideous, but it looked to be made of real gold and thus must have been expensive. That alone narrowed the list of who could afford such a piece, and surely, if she had been killed by a vagrant in some botched robbery attempt, they wouldn't have left it behind. Before anyone took notice of my dawdling, I quickly tucked the necklace back in place and made the sign of the cross. Then I stood and took a seat near the front. Not long after, Mr. Dorian made his way down the aisle and paid his respects to Daphne, then slid into the pew and sat beside me.

"I found a shady spot for Maurice and gave him some water," he murmured.

I smiled and whispered my thanks. The Belvederes then took their seats, and the service began.

As anyone who has attended an Orthodox service knows, they can be quite lengthy, and funeral services are even longer. But I was grateful that Daphne was able to have the send-off she was owed. When it finally ended, we shuffled out into the bright sun to the little churchyard, where she was laid to rest. Florence let out a muffled cry as the casket was lowered into the ground, and I found myself overcome with emotion as well. She had been so young and, based on my brief encounter with her, very driven. That an entire life could be dismissed so easily because of rumors was sickening. Even if they were true, it certainly did not negate the need for justice. Someone had killed her, and they needed to be held accountable.

I felt a hand on my shoulder and turned to find Mr. Dorian handing me a handkerchief. I took it and dabbed my eyes. "Thank you."

He nodded, but kept his earnest gaze on the grave. By then, the gravediggers had started to fill in the ground, and the other attendees began to leave. We made our way over to the Belvederes. Florence had recovered, but Christopher still looked stricken.

"Thank you both for coming," she said as she grasped my hands.

"Of course," I replied. "It was a lovely service."

Florence nodded. "Yes, it was." She threaded her arm through mine and led me away, while Mr. Dorian spoke to Christopher. "The police found that vagrant and are holding him for questioning. Apparently he had one of Daphne's soaps in his bag."

"Goodness," I breathed. "Is that enough evidence to arrest him?"

"Probably not, but it is the best lead they have. We are going down there now."

"It's very good of you and Christopher to do all this," I said. "I'm sure her aunt will be grateful."

Florence gave me a weak smile. "I still haven't had a response to my letter. But hopefully when I do, I'll have some answers for her."

I hadn't told Florence about the necklace yet, or my suspicions, but it didn't seem like the right time. Besides, the police knew, and if Gregor really did have one of Daphne's soaps, then he should be questioned about it.

We parted ways shortly afterwards, as the Belvederes had

their appointment with the police and I wanted to get back to the children. Mr. Dorian led me to the shady spot where Maurice was happily munching on some dried grass.

"So then, do you also believe this rubbish about a vagrant murdering Miss Costas?" he said without preamble.

I turned to Mr. Dorian in surprise and found his sharp gaze already upon me. "I gather you don't?"

He let out a grunt and turned back to the road. "It's awfully convenient, especially since the police don't seem very motivated to conduct their own investigation."

"I didn't realize you had taken such an interest in this case."

Now it was his turn to look surprised. "The body of a young woman violently murdered was found not far from my home. Of course I'm interested." Nearly everyone else treated Daphne's death as nothing more than gossip, but it was wrong to make the same assumption of Mr. Dorian. I mumbled an apology, but he ignored it. "What were you looking at in the church?"

"Pardon?" I asked, blinking my eyes innocently.

But he wasn't fooled and let out an impatient huff. "I *saw* you, Mrs. Harper. There was something about the body that caught your interest."

I swallowed hard, reluctant to reveal my suspicions to him, as suddenly they seemed very silly. But Mr. Dorian stared at me expectantly, and I knew I had no choice.

"Her necklace. Did you see it?"

Mr. Dorian frowned in recollection and shook his head. "What about it?"

I looked away, certain I was making too much of it. No wonder the inspector had dismissed me. "The chain was made of gold with a matching pendant. It would have been expensive. Not the sort of thing a village girl would have. I noticed it on her body when I found her and wondered if it might have been a gift. But that doesn't— "

"From a man, you mean," he interrupted.

I nodded hesitantly. Then Mr. Dorian was silent for so long that I finally had to look at him. He appeared deep in thought. "Did you bring this up to the police?"

"Yes. The inspector didn't think it important."

He let out a dismissive snort.

"I'm worried they will pin everything on this vagrant, just to close the case because of Daphne's reputation."

Mr. Dorian raised an eyebrow in question. "What sort of reputation?"

I really didn't want to repeat such petty gossip, but I didn't know what else to do. "There have been rumors about her having a few different lovers. And that one of them killed her in a fit of jealousy."

Now he looked appalled. "Then why aren't the police arresting any of *them*."

I shrugged. "Because it would have served her right, if it's even true," I added.

"But this vagrant is already a nuisance," he inferred, "so arresting him will kill two birds with one stone, so to speak."

A heaviness settled over my shoulders. "I suppose."

"You do think she had a fellow, though."

"I think someone gave her that necklace," I said carefully. "And I would very much like to know who."

He stared at me for a long moment, then nodded sharply. "All right, Mrs. Harper. Then let us find out." With that, he climbed into the donkey cart, while I stood rooted in place staring dumbfoundedly up at him.

Us.

Finally someone was listening to me. And he wanted to look into this together. For the first time in days, I felt a faint glimmer of hope that this murder could be solved.

Mr. Dorian took the reins, then cast me a glance and frowned. "What are you still doing down there? Come. We've much to discuss."

"Yes," I said with a start. "Yes, of course." Then I hurried around to the other side of the cart and let Mr. Dorian help me onto the seat. In another moment, we were on our way back to the villa, while the most exciting chapter of my life thus far had just begun.

Chapter 9

"So then," Mr. Dorian began as the cart trundled down the road, "where shall we begin?"

I balked at his expectant look. "You're asking *me*?"

"Why not?"

"Because you're the mystery writer," I shot back. "I rather expected you to have an idea."

"And if I'm not mistaken," he said dryly, "you had quite a number of opinions about my methods."

I pursed my lips. The man was never going to forget my criticisms, was he?

"As I recall, they were mainly in reference to the inspector's treatment of the female characters, and the rather obvious villain," I pointed out, "not about his general approach to solving the murder."

Mr. Dorian tilted his head in acknowledgement. "Fair enough. But surely you must know that writing a mystery is nothing like actually solving one. I'm not a detective, Mrs. Harper."

"Perhaps not, but you seem to know how to think like

one. At least, far more than I do. What would Inspector Dumond do?"

Mr. Dorian rolled his eyes and let out a long-suffering sigh, then paused to think. "He usually begins by re-creating the victim's last day on earth. Sometimes that can be very fruitful—"

"Like in *A Fine Day for a Murder*!"

"Yes," he said with a faint smile. "But remember, he doesn't always get it right. You see, Inspector Dumond's biggest downfall is his steadfast belief in his own intelligence. That causes him to make assumptions that often lead him astray—"

"Which is why he needs his secretary, Miss Linley, to put him back on course!"

I couldn't contain my excitement. How had I overlooked such a basic element of his characterization?

"What most people don't realize about Inspector Dumond," Mr. Dorian began, as if he had heard my question and was warming to the topic, "is that in many ways he's remarkably average. Readers are used to brilliant characters like Sherlock Holmes. But I rather like writing about someone who is quite fallible and yet still manages to solve the case in the end."

My mouth curved in appreciation. "How did you begin writing?"

"I . . . I don't remember, actually," he said with a touch of surprise. Had no one ever asked him that before? "It was just something I always did, as soon as I learned my letters."

"But what about the first novel you ever wrote," I pressed. "You must remember that, surely."

"My first attempt was unfinished and largely unreadable." He chuckled. "The rest came out in dribs and drabs over years. I didn't go to university and had to work for a living until I sold my first book, a little adventure story for children. And that was only a middling success. So for many years, my writing time was limited to late in the evening or the odd day off."

"Oh," I said with a blush. I had just assumed Mr. Dorian had gone to Oxford, Cambridge, or the like and wrote his first novel during his studies. It was a common-enough occurrence among literary-minded men, and he was so prolific.

"And I didn't write my first mystery until about eight years ago," he explained.

"You mean . . . you've written all of your Inspector Dumond books in so short a time?"

Given he was currently finishing number eleven, this astounded me.

"Well, I will admit that the first two were already finished when I signed my contract," Mr. Dorian said with a smirk. "But once I started, I found I couldn't stop. And I was lucky that I—" He suddenly caught himself, and his shoulders tightened, along with his grip on the reins. After a moment, he cleared his throat. "I was lucky," he began again, "that Mr. Howard deemed them publishable."

It was patently obvious that was not what he was going to say, but while I was burning with curiosity, I wouldn't pry.

"Well," I said gently, "re-creating Daphne's last day on earth sounds like a good place to start."

Mr. Dorian's shoulders relaxed, and he nodded. "Then in order to do so, we must determine two things: what was the time of death and who was the last person to see her alive, or rather the last person who will admit to it? We'll need to speak to whoever performed her postmortem and hope they are willing to share that information."

I chewed on my lower lip. "Doctor Campbell usually sees to the dead."

"Do you know him?"

My breath caught. He had come to the house to declare

Oliver dead, then later told me it was an aneurysm that had taken my husband so swiftly and with such finality.

There was nothing you nor I or anyone excepting God could have done for him, Mrs. Harper, he'd said after the autopsy. *Take comfort in that.*

But I hadn't. Nothing short of a time machine could have given me peace at that point.

"Yes."

Mr. Dorian stared at me, no doubt curious about my awkward manner, but I pressed ahead. "He will speak to me, I think. We should also speak to the Belvederes to start recreating her last day," I said briskly, needing to move the conversation along. "One of them may have been the last person to see Daphne before her murder."

He tilted his head from side to side, ruminating on this. "It's certainly possible. You found her not far from the path that connects our properties."

"And Florence said she had been looking for Daphne all morning," I pointed out. "But we don't know if she was returning to the Belvederes' or leaving when she was killed."

"Or if the murderer simply left her body there," he murmured.

I turned sharply to him. "You think so?"

"We must be open to all possibilities, Mrs. Harper. And based on where you found her, I'd say that whoever left her there was hoping she wouldn't be found for a bit at least."

"The footpath isn't frequented very much," I acknowledged. "People don't usually have reason to use it unless—"

"They are coming to or from my house or the Belvederes'," he finished.

I pressed my lips together as my mind spun with each possibility. How would we ever determine which scenario was right?

"But if that isn't the case," he continued, "and Daphne was simply returning to the Belvederes' when she met her killer, then where was she coming from?"

If the rumors about her were to be believed, then she may have been coming back from visiting one of her lovers and was perhaps met by another raging with jealousy. But before I could speak, another thought wrestled its way into my mind.

"I—" Then I hesitated until he gave me an imploring look. "I've seen her on her way to your house before. To see Mrs. Nasso," I added, as the voice in my head suddenly whispered caution.

For that wasn't at all what Daphne had said the day I met her on the path. She had very clearly stated she was going to see Mr. Dorian. Had the man been unaware of her visit, or was he keeping their connection quiet in the wake of her murder? If so, that was an unsettling thought. I couldn't tell if I was being overly suspicious or if it was an avenue worth exploring.

But Mr. Dorian merely nodded, entirely unaware of the direction of my thoughts. "Well, we have a starting point at least. After speaking with Mrs. Nasso, the doctor, and the Belvederes, we should be able to establish a timeline."

I hummed my agreement while my mind continued to whirl.

We must be open to all possibilities, Mrs. Harper.

If Inspector Dumond's greatest downfall was his assumptions, then I would need to rid myself of the same habit. Beginning with my own assumptions about everyone I knew, including Mr. Dorian himself.

A short while later, we reached Mr. Dorian's villa and found Mrs. Nasso in the kitchen rolling out phyllo dough. I had endured enough chastisements from Mrs. Kouris to know that this was a delicate, time-consuming process and

was just about to suggest we come back when Mr. Dorian plowed ahead. "Mrs. Nasso, may we have a word?"

The older woman glanced up from her work. "You want food?"

"No, no," he said hastily, but she had already moved to pull a tray off the counter.

"It's about Daphne, Mrs. Nasso," I explained in Greek. "We have some questions."

She nodded. "Eat first. I made dolmades."

I turned to him with a helpless shrug. "She wants us to eat."

This wasn't exactly a hardship, given that she was an excellent cook, but Mr. Dorian still made a great show of sighing as he took a seat at the table.

"Well, if we must," he said, before enthusiastically tucking into the plate Mrs. Nasso placed before him.

I hadn't realized just how hungry I was and ate with equal enthusiasm, which seemed to please Mrs. Nasso very much. Once we filled our bellies, she insisted on making us coffee. And really, who were we to deny her?

Once we both had our tiny cups of the steaming concoction, I gave Mrs. Nasso a pleasant smile. But instead of directly asking when was the last time she'd seen Daphne, I chose a different approach. "What can you tell me about Miss Costas?"

The older woman took the seat beside me. "She came here with her soaps once," she began in Greek. "Said they were a gift for him." Mrs. Nasso gestured towards the man of the house. "And then a few times after that just to talk."

I forced myself to ask the question, even though I was swamped with guilt. "Did . . . did you ever see her and Mr. Dorian together?"

Mrs. Nasso shook her head. "No. He was always asleep when she came." I felt a strange mixture of relief and disappointment at her response. Then she turned thoughtful. "She was a lonely girl, I think."

"What did she say?" Mr. Dorian cut in before I could respond.

I shot him an irritated look. "Give me a moment, will you?" Then I addressed Mrs. Nasso once more. "What makes you say that?"

"Why else would she come talk to an old woman so often and ask me questions about the old days?" Mrs. Nasso chuckled before shaking her head. "She had no friends here. No family." Then she hesitated.

I raised my eyebrow at her silence. "No man?"

But Mrs. Nasso reared back at the question. "Daphne? No. She was a good girl," she said with a definitive nod.

"Make sure to ask when she saw her last," Mr. Dorian said.

"Yes, I'm getting to that," I snapped before posing the question to Mrs. Nasso.

She tilted her head in thought. "At the market with Mrs. Belvedere not long before she died. Maybe two days," she added.

I gave her a grateful smile, even as my heart sank. We were no closer to establishing Daphne's last moments.

"Thank you, Mrs. Nasso. Do let me know if you hear anything about Daphne. Anything at all."

She gave me an arch look. "You don't think Gregor killed her, do you?"

"We have our doubts," I admitted. "And the police don't seem to be taking her death very seriously."

"It wouldn't be the first time," she grumbled. "They only care about the foreigners or the nobility," she said, referencing the small group of local aristocrats largely descended from the Venetians who once ruled the island. "And Daphne was neither."

Mr. Dorian was now beside himself with curiosity. "What is she saying?"

"Mrs. Nasso has her doubts about the police as well," I

said. "And this isn't the first time they've prematurely closed a case."

The housekeeper then crossed her arms and shook her head in disapproval. "They are lazy," she replied in English.

Mr. Dorian leaned towards her. "Do you think that vagrant killed Daphne?"

Mrs. Nasso shrugged. "It is possible." Then she addressed me in Greek. "But he is also an easy target. They wanted to be rid of him anyway."

I nodded in agreement. "It does seem a bit convenient."

"I think so too," she replied with a firm nod. "She was strangled, yes?" Mrs. Nasso then held up her own hands, which bore the marks of a lifetime spent in the kitchen. "It takes much strength and determination to rob someone of their last breath. It is not a crime of convenience, but of pain. Of anger. I do not see why that man would have done that to her."

I blinked in surprise. "You have given this a lot of thought."

She shrugged again. "I have much time to think while I am working. And when Mr. Howard is here, he talks about his new books with me," she added. "So I have learned to think like a detective."

I let out a surprised laugh. "I see."

"Mr. Howard likes those kinds of stories. Mysteries," Mrs. Nasso continued. "Especially when there is a twist." She nodded towards Mr. Dorian. "He is very good at them, or so I was told."

"Yes," I replied softly. "He is."

We exchanged smiles, but then she quickly sobered and shook her head. "But this is not a story. And I don't think murders are so easily solved in real life."

"No, I doubt they are," I admitted.

Mrs. Nasso grabbed my arm then. "But you will find who

really did this. You and Mr. Dorian." Her dark eyes faintly glistened. "For Daphne."

My throat went dry. "We will," I rasped.

After we finished our coffee, we left Mrs. Nasso to her phyllo dough. As Mr. Dorian escorted me outside, I repeated what she had said—well, most of it anyway. I felt it best to omit my question about him and Daphne.

"A dead end," he admitted with a sigh, looking as disappointed as I felt. "Though I suppose that is to be expected."

I nodded in agreement. "It was only our first interview. It can't be as easy as that. And no self-respecting mystery novelist would write it that way," I added with a smirk.

"Yes," he agreed, returning my smile. "The critics would be merciless."

As we stepped into the bright sunshine, I shielded my eyes with my hand. It was just after noon, but the day had already grown uncomfortably hot.

"You look tired, Mrs. Harper," Mr. Dorian said. "We can save the rest for tomorrow."

Indeed, the weight of the morning's events had taken a toll, and I was in great need of a nap. Still, I would have preferred he kept that comment to himself.

I stood a little straighter in response. "All right. It's best if we give the Belvederes their privacy now anyway."

"You will be here at nine tomorrow, though?" Mr. Dorian's mouth tightened, betraying a hint of nerves. "I'm afraid I've grown rather accustomed to our work schedule," he admitted sheepishly.

Right. The book. I had nearly forgotten. "Yes, of course. Typing first, then sleuthing."

He smiled a little at that. "Until then," he replied and gave Maurice a pat.

The donkey snorted his pleasure, and I felt a twinge of envy over how easily they had taken a liking to each other. If

I hadn't already known I was in desperate need of rest, this ridiculous thought would have sufficed. I said good-bye and accepted his assistance up onto the seat of the cart. Then Maurice and I plodded off down the road. I looked back just once when were nearly at the bend, and he was still standing there, watching us.

Chapter 10

As soon as I entered the house, Cleo practically leapt upon me. She must have been awaiting my return for some time.

"A letter from Aunt Agatha came. I set it on the table for you," she said in a great rush before I had even removed my hat.

Given that my aunt wrote every month, this was hardly usual. But Cleo's interest certainly was. I arched a brow and finished untying the ribbon that held my straw hat in place. "Thank you, my dear. I'll get to it. Let me change first."

But Cleo's eyes grew as round as saucers, and she grabbed my arm. "No! You must read it now. Please," she added in a syrupy tone I rarely heard from her unless she truly wanted something.

"Very well," I said suspiciously and headed for the kitchen where Mrs. Kouris was kneading bread.

I greeted her, and she shot me a veiled look in response. Something was most definitely afoot. I placed my straw hat on the table and picked up the letter. From the outside, it looked just like every other one Aunt Agatha sent, with my name and address written in her perfect script. Aunt Agatha was very proud of her penmanship.

I tore open the envelope and began to read.

My Beloved Minnie,

I hope spring has come to Corfu as the weather has been absolutely dreadful here . . .

So far nothing out of the ordinary. She always began her letters complaining about the weather in London. Or Paris. Or Berlin. Wherever she found herself. As a shy young woman, my aunt had been married off to a much older business acquaintance of her father's. Her husband was, according to her, kind but disinterested, which was the best she could hope for. They had no children, and when he died only a few years later, she came in possession of a large fortune and her own independence. Aunt Agatha had never married again and instead spent a good portion of her time traveling abroad. But she always made sure to return to London quite regularly—and never failed to send my stodgy father into a snit over something or other. She was, without a doubt, one of my very favorite people.

I cast a glance at Cleo, who was watching me like a hawk and clenching her hands. I pursed my lips and resumed reading a few more lines about the weather, a sentence stating that my parents and siblings were all in good health, two paragraphs about Colette, her prized French bulldog gifted from a friend who was rumored to be a famous Parisian courtesan, and then—

I've spoken to Lady Artemis D'Arcy and she would be delighted to have Cleo as a student next term . . .

I looked up from the letter and cleared my throat. "Cleo, who is Lady Artemis D'Arcy?"

Mrs. Kouris chose that moment to head outside and feed the chickens, leaving us alone.

Cleo shifted on her feet. "She runs a girls' school in Hampstead. It's very well-regarded."

"And *why* did Aunt Agatha talk to her about you attending this school?"

"I—I asked her to."

I did not respond to this and resumed reading:

If Cleo hasn't told you about any of this yet, then I am sorry you heard it from me first.

I let out a heavy sigh and closed my eyes for a moment before I could continue:

But may I remind you that nearly two decades ago, I received a similar request from you.

My chest contorted with a strange kind of pain, born of both guilt and embarrassment.

Now, I don't mean to suggest that you are purposely dismissing her educational needs the same way your parents did. Your father didn't believe in educating his daughters beyond what was needed to run a household, and your mother, well, the less said the better.

I snorted a laugh. My aunt had never hidden her disapproval of my mother. She thought her a shallow, vapid woman more concerned with the latest fashion than her own children. Meanwhile, my mother claimed my aunt was a self-important busybody with too much time on her hands. In public, however, the two women nearly fell over themselves complimenting the other while also trading barely veiled insults. It was a performance I had always found both fascinating and highly entertaining. During family gatherings, my brother Samuel and I used to keep track of their insults and then tally them up afterwards to crown a winner. But more often than not, it was a draw. My aunt may have been right about my mother's vanity, but she also possessed a great deal of wit, and they were well-matched competitors.

No, this situation is far more complicated because of the very real loss you have suffered. And it is because of this loss that I believe you may have inadvertently given Cleo the impression that you do not want her to leave you. Perhaps ever.

Your daughter has a deep love and concern for you, so much so that she might very well do just that. But I can't imagine you would want her to give up her dreams. You are too good a mother to ask that of her.

My eyes began to prickle, and I bit my lip. Of course, I didn't want that. My parents' initial refusal to support my education had driven a wedge between us, one that remained firmly in place even after they had relented. I promised myself that once I became a parent, I would never be like them. And yet I had skated dangerously close without realizing it. That my children might ever feel that way about me was equal parts distressing and horrifying.

That being said, my aunt continued, *Cleo is determined to go to Girton, and in order to do that, she must be prepared for the rigors of a university education, as you very well know. And based on what you have shared about her current school, I am doubtful it is up to the task. Please write to me at your earliest convenience so that I may begin the arrangements. And don't worry about the cost. I am happy to—*

I set the letter down on the table. The rest of it could wait. Cleo was still looking at me anxiously, and I realized I was frowning.

I relaxed my expression and let out a weary sigh. "Cleo—"

"I'm sorry I didn't tell you first," she burst out. "It's only that, every time I tried to talk to you about going to school in England, you changed the subject."

"I don't think it was *every* time," I huffed, but that wasn't really the point. Aunt Agatha was right. I had given Cleo the impression that I didn't want her to leave because, well, I didn't. And that was purely selfish at this point.

I shook my head and began again: "I'm sorry I didn't listen to you, so much so that you thought this was your only recourse," I said, gesturing to the letter.

She perked up for the first time since I arrived home. "Then I can go?"

"I still need to think about that. Next term is quite soon."

"In September," she said with an easy shrug.

I let out an exasperated sigh. "Cleo, you've never even been to England!"

"I've read about it enough," she pointed out. "And I like the rain."

I narrowed my eyes. "It's more than Jane Austen and galoshes."

Much more.

But Cleo ignored this. "I can finally meet Grandmama and Grandpapa."

Somehow I managed to hold back my grimace. When we still lived in Athens, Oliver was far too busy with work to even consider a trip back to London. But Samuel often came to visit, as he was working at the embassy in Istanbul at the time. He moved to Bombay not long after we left for Corfu, though. And Aunt Agatha had stayed with us a few times over the years, but the rest of my family had never met Cleo and Tommy.

It was terribly far, I knew, and my father got violently seasick. There was no chance that my mother would travel without him either, seeing as she groused over the very thought of leaving Mayfair. Meanwhile, my eldest brother, Jack, was an MP with a family of his own and my younger sister, Delia, was busy galivanting around London—at least according to my mother.

We all kept in touch with fairly frequent letters, though Jack was the worst correspondent by far, and my parents always sent the children wonderful presents for their birthdays, but I had been away from home for nearly half my life now. My family had become little more than words on a page and faded memories—many of which I would have preferred to forget altogether. I had lived an entire lifetime in the years since I had left England, and in so many ways, I had become an entirely different person. As, I'm sure, they had too.

In the wake of Oliver's death, my family constantly asked when we were coming to visit, but I always begged off. First, the children were too young for such a long journey. Then I didn't want to take them away from school. Then their friends. It was never the right time for them. But those were all just poor excuses for the truth: it was never the right time for *me*. Eventually, they stopped asking.

The very idea of seeing them all again, and without Oliver by my side, twisted me in so many knots I couldn't begin to untie them. But Cleo's eyes sparkled in a way I hadn't seen since . . . well, I couldn't remember.

You won't be able to say no to her forever.

My stomach sank with a newfound certainty. But I wasn't ready to say yes yet either.

"We'll see," I replied, but it sounded horribly weak to my ears. Cleo must have sensed she had won this fight too, for she didn't press me on this and was uncharacteristically agreeable for the rest of the evening. She even listened with what appeared to be genuine interest while Tommy spent most of dinner giving us an extremely thorough update on Newton's resettlement in the garden. I wondered how he could even tell Newton apart from the dozen or so other newts inhabiting the area, but I kept that to myself, as he seemed quite certain.

Later, after the children had gone up to bed, Mrs. Kouris and I were cleaning the kitchen together. I had just finished wiping the table when I suddenly blurted out the question that had been nagging me for hours. "How long have you known about Cleo and this school in London?"

The older woman didn't miss a beat. "Since last year, at least."

I sat down heavily in a chair. "I've been deluding myself for that long?"

"It is a part of being a mother," she said with a sage nod. Mrs. Kouris had four children herself, all grown up with families of their own. "One day you are wiping their bottoms, and the next, they are sneaking off to meet boys. It takes time to catch up."

I groaned and pressed my forehead against the table. I hadn't even thought of boys yet.

Mrs. Kouris patted my shoulder, which was a huge show of affection from her. "You will grow used to it."

The thought was hardly comforting, but I gathered that wasn't the point. I had buried my head in the sand long enough, and now I must face the truth—and all that involved. For if Cleo really was determined to go to school back in England, I could not imagine staying here, no matter what I had promised Oliver.

Chapter 11

I awoke the next morning much later than usual, as I had been up half the night tossing and turning over thoughts of the future. Luckily, Cleo was still in a helpful mood and had gotten herself and Tommy ready for the day. They were just leaving for school when I rushed downstairs, having barely managed to run a comb through my hair, and dutifully submitted to my longer than usual good-bye embraces.

Mrs. Kouris then insisted I eat something and made a disparaging comment about Mrs. Nasso's cooking under her breath. I should have admonished her for the unkind remark, but I was far too grateful for this small return to normalcy. After downing a hot cup of bitter coffee and a piece of flaky phyllo stuffed with tender cheese, she pushed another into my hand as I was leaving. I raced up the hill at twice my usual pace and was huffing from the exertion when I knocked on the door. But instead of Mrs. Nasso opening it as usual, it was Mr. Dorian himself.

"Why Mrs. Harper, you're late," he teased. Technically it was true, but by no more than five minutes.

Only when I saw that he was already dressed for the day did I recall our plan.

The Belvederes.

He kept any comments about my state of disarray to himself and ushered me inside while chattering on about all the work he had gotten done since yesterday.

"My goodness," I said once we reached the study, "are you sure you still need me?"

I was only joking, but there was a distinct energy about him. Whatever had been blocking him before seemed gone, and if he'd dismissed me on the spot, I wouldn't have been entirely surprised.

But Mr. Dorian looked properly shocked by the question. "Of course, Mrs. Harper. I won't make my deadline without you. Besides," he continued as he pulled out my chair, "we had an agreement, and I always keep my promises."

I couldn't help but think of his marriage vows, which was something I never would have voiced. And given the immediate relief that swelled in my chest, I needed this man far more than I wished to acknowledge.

"Thank you," I said and took my seat. "Now, where would you like me to begin?"

He proudly handed me two notebooks' worth of scribblings. "I came up with a new culprit last night. One that might just surprise even *you*," he added with a wink.

"We'll see about that," I said archly.

Mr. Dorian laughed as he headed for the door. "I'll return in time for luncheon. Then afterwards we can visit the Belvederes."

I nodded my approval, and he disappeared down the hallway, whistling as he went. For a moment, I could see a glimmer of the man he must have been back in London. The kind that appeared in gossip columns and won the hand of a beautiful young heiress before he drove her into the arms of another man.

If that is even the truth.

But it did not matter either way, I reminded myself as I got to work. The source of Mr. Dorian's marital discord was one mystery I had no interest in solving. Not in the least.

At twelve o'clock sharp, Mr. Dorian rapped on the doorframe before he entered, followed by Mrs. Nasso with a tray.

"Good afternoon," he said. "I've come bearing food."

I pushed back in my chair with a grateful smile. "And not a moment too soon."

The morning had passed faster than usual, as I had become quite immersed in his revised story, but now my wrists were stiff, and my stomach was rumbling. He helped Mrs. Nasso set down the tray in the room's little seating area as I made my way around the desk. She had outdone herself once again, with dolmades, steaming rice, cold chicken, bread, and a simple salad of tomatoes and cheese.

"This looks delicious," I said. "Thank you, Mrs. Nasso."

She waved her hand as if it were nothing and hurried out of the room, saying she had to get back to the kitchen.

Mr. Dorian gestured for me to start. "I think she's making more goat for supper," he said with a sigh.

I chuckled and began to make myself a plate of food. "Do the Belvederes know we're coming?"

Mr. Dorian shook his head. "The element of surprise is essential in an investigation."

I balked. "But surely you don't suspect them."

He shrugged and reached for a piece of bread. "Everyone is a suspect, Mrs. Harper, until proven otherwise."

"And I suppose that includes me," I said dryly. "Even though I'm the one who found the body."

"Well, it wouldn't be the first time the perpetrator pretended to find the body. But once the time of death is better established, I'm sure you'll have an alibi. Several, in fact."

Something about his utterly blasé tone rankled. This man was completely confident he had me figured out. "You don't think *I* could kill anyone?"

He shot me a look. "You? No. Women in general? Absolutely."

I huffed and fixed my attention on my plate, where I began to stab the dolmades with my fork using far more force than necessary.

"I can see I've upset you," he began, but I could hear the smile in his voice. "And for that I am sorry. I'm sure under the right circumstances, you would be perfectly able to murder someone."

"Of course I could," I said primly, though I very well knew how ridiculous this sounded. But I refused to give him any satisfaction. "You are the one who said we shouldn't be making assumptions, and yet you seem to have no trouble making them about me."

I regretted it as soon as the words came out of my mouth. The last thing I wanted was for this man to know just how deeply his careless words had wounded me. I peered at him through my lashes and found him looking at me thoughtfully.

"And yet you continue to surprise me, Mrs. Harper. You should know I have always been something of a slow learner," he added with a chuckle.

"I'm sorry," I said with a sheepish smile. "I didn't sleep well last night, and it has put me in a bit of a mood today."

He tilted his head in concern and gave me a searching look. "Is that all?"

"Well, no," I admitted before letting out a short sigh. "My daughter wants to go to school in England next term and has enlisted the help of my domineering aunt to convince me."

"Ah." He sat back in his chair and folded his hands. "Because you don't approve."

"No, I don't. At least, not this soon," I explained. "But it's more than that."

He raised an eyebrow at my silence. "Do tell," he prompted.

I shook my head. "You can't want to hear about my domestic quibbles."

"Why not? Most of life is made up of domestic quibbles. And . . . I'd like to think we're friends. Or, at least, friendly," he added. The uncertainty in his gaze took me by surprise. "It can be good to talk about such things."

Was my loneliness so obvious? But then, I had no trouble noticing it in him. I placed my napkin on the table and cleared my throat. "You see, I did something similar when my parents forbade me from attending university," I began. "I even wrote to the very same aunt for help. So I always promised myself that I would never do the same thing to my own children. That I would encourage them in all their endeavors. It's just that . . . it's been harder than I thought."

The corner of Mr. Dorian's mouth curved. "It sounds like she's more like you than you realized."

"I was *never* that stubborn." But even as I said the words, my own mother's exasperated cries rang in my ears. I buried my face in my hands. "Oh God. I really am no better than they were."

"There now, Mrs. Harper. Obviously, I have no personal experience with child-rearing. But it seems to me that your regret over your own behavior indicates that you are doing better," he said. "Perhaps, in the end, that is the best one can hope for: to make mistakes different from those of their own parents."

"That isn't exactly comforting," I said with a frown.

"Well, I was trying to be practical, not comforting," he insisted, adjusting the lapels of his jacket as he straightened in his chair. Before I could respond, he glanced at the clock on the mantel. "Now, if you're finished, we should be going."

I bristled as the feeling of comradery all but vanished under his business-like tone.

"Yes. Let's."

We decided to take a short detour to look over the place where I had found Daphne, on the off chance any clues the police had missed still remained. Mr. Dorian marched ahead along the footpath, while my feet dragged against the packed dirt. The closer I came, the slower I moved, until he nearly disappeared from sight. Once I stepped off the footpath and reached the hillside, the sun moved behind a stray cloud. As a shadow fell over the area, I shivered. My mind flooded with images of Daphne, both alive and dead, until I could take no more and raced to the bottom of the hill to catch up to Mr. Dorian. He had already passed the cursed spot where I found Daphne and was examining the surrounding wooded area. I hurried over to him while carefully averting my eyes.

Then he abruptly stopped as something caught his attention. "What do you make of that?" He pointed at the ground a few feet away from where I had found her.

Grateful for the distraction from my macabre thoughts, I followed the direction of his finger and saw a hint of pale purple among the mix of rocks, sticks, and grasses.

"It looks like a flower." I gingerly brushed aside some debris. It was a single flower petal, dried and half brown. How Mr. Dorian even spotted the thing was beyond me. I held it to my nose and caught the faintest whiff of scent. It smelt vaguely familiar, though I couldn't place it. "I think it's from a potpourri," I said, though I wasn't at all sure what, if anything, that could mean.

For his part, Mr. Dorian didn't seem terribly interested, but he held out his gloved hand, and I dutifully dropped the petal into his palm. Then he pocketed it and started back up the hill to rejoin the footpath.

I stood there for a moment, blankly staring at his back, before I shook my head and hurried after him. "You think it's a clue?"

"Possibly. Though anything can be a clue when you aren't quite sure what you are looking for."

"It might not have come from Daphne," I said rather unnecessarily. "Other people do come here on occasion. It could have fallen from someone's skirt or gotten stuck to the bottom of their shoe."

Mr. Dorian's jaw twitched. "I know. But that is the point. It shouldn't be here, regardless of who brought it. It hasn't rained since Miss Costas's body was found, and I've been keeping a close watch on the path, which one must use to come here."

"You have?"

He raised a lofty brow at the shock in my voice. "It is not uncommon for the perpetrator to return to the scene of the crime."

It was on the tip of my tongue to ask if that was actually true or simply something mystery novelists wrote about, but decided against it.

"Has anyone used it, then?" I asked instead.

He hesitated then shook his head. "No. And from what I understand, the locals are avoiding the area altogether now because of . . . of what happened."

We had reached the top of the hill by then, and I looked around us. The shadow had passed, and the midday sun now shown as usual, but my discomfort lingered. *Persisted.* Death had marked this place, and it could never be the same. I had always felt perfectly safe here on Corfu, and I bitterly regretted the loss of such a presumption in that moment.

"People can be very superstitious in these parts," I said.

Mr. Dorian barked a laugh. "People are superstitious everywhere, Mrs. Harper. My God, even Arthur Conan Doyle has gone ghost-hunting. And he's a doctor."

I was very curious to ask if he knew the man personally. But I didn't think Mr. Dorian would appreciate the question, especially given the snide way he had said the famous author's name, so I filed this bit of information away for another time.

Mr. Dorian had come to a stop and was staring at the bottom of the hill. "You mentioned before that, when you found Daphne, her hair was filled with debris. As if she had tumbled down the hill."

I cleared my throat. "It appeared that way, yes."

He hummed and took a few steps down the hill, scanning the grass as he walked, while I stayed firmly rooted in my spot. After a few moments, Mr. Dorian spotted something.

"See how the grass is tamped down here? It runs all the way," he said while pointing towards the spot where I had found Daphne. Reluctantly, I moved to his side. Indeed, this section of grass did look more trampled on than the rest. And wide enough for a body.

"Do you know what this possibly means?"

I shook my head, distracted by that cursed spot. Mr. Dorian let out an impatient huff, and I finally turned to him. "What?"

"That she wasn't killed here," he said, with far too much excitement. "The murderer must have brought her body to this spot."

"I fail to see why that would excite you."

Mr. Dorian tilted his head. "Because not everyone has the strength or means to move a body. Especially at night."

"If that was when she was killed."

He smiled at my petulance. "Yes. *If.* Which is all the more reason for us to speak with the Belvederes and Doctor Campbell to establish the time of death."

I turned away and headed back up the hill. I had no desire to spend another moment here. "Then let's get on with it."

We returned to the path and made our way to the Belvederes' home, which was a little higher up the hill than Mr. Dorian's villa. Within a few minutes, Florence's lush terrace garden was in sight just above us. The footpath wound around to the front entrance, but when we were nearly there, Mr. Dorian suddenly stopped short and turned to me. "Are you very good friends with Mrs. Belvedere? I want to make sure you can be objective," he added in response to my look of surprise.

"I wouldn't call her a very good friend," I said carefully—I wouldn't call anyone that, as a matter of fact. "But we are friends, certainly. Though she was closer to my husband," I added. "They had quite a lot in common."

Mr. Dorian scoffed. "Ah yes, a paragon of men."

I balked at both the descriptor and the distinct edge in his voice. Oliver had a great many wonderful qualities, but it was hard to think of someone as a paragon when they had to be reminded to pick their dirty socks off the floor. "Who on earth called him that?"

"Mrs. Belvedere," Mr. Dorian said, as if it was perfectly obvious. "From the way she goes on about him, I rather think she was a little bit in love with him."

Now that was ridiculous. "She is old enough to be his mother," I snapped.

But Mr. Dorian only shrugged. "A little thing like age doesn't usually stop people."

"I would hardly call a twenty-five-year age difference *a little thing*," I said before realizing my faux pas. Hadn't his own wife been much younger?

But Mr. Dorian didn't look offended. Rather the opposite. "My good lady, that is usually part of the appeal," he said, with a wicked smile that set my teeth on edge.

"Well, even if that was true, the feeling was not mutual," I gritted out and fixed my gaze firmly ahead.

"No," he murmured. "I'm sure it wasn't."

I glanced back at him, surprised by this sudden sincerity, but then the Belvederes' front door swung open, and the lady of the house appeared in the doorway.

"Hello, there!" Florence called out, while furiously waving her arm as if she was on a deserted island and we were a passing ship.

Mr. Dorian and I exchanged a look before he stepped ahead, greeting her with a charming smile. "Hello, Mrs. Belvedere. Have we come at a convenient time?"

She nodded with similar enthusiasm. "Yes, yes. Do come in, please," she urged and extended her arm.

In truth, Florence looked more out of sorts than I had ever seen her before. Her face was flushed from exertion, while locks of hair spilled out from her chignon. But the most surprising thing, by far, was that she wore an *apron*. Given that she was one of the most talented gardeners I knew, Florence no doubt wore aprons daily, but never in front of company. She usually dressed with a care and precision I hadn't the patience for even before I had children, so this was truly unprecedented.

As I followed Mr. Dorian into the house, she gave me the same tight smile I used in my most harried moments. "How are the children, Minnie?"

"Very well. And Christopher?"

"At his office, as usual," she said blithely before shutting the door behind me. "Always working, that one. Even when he doesn't have to."

I nodded in response. Christopher did seem quite dedicated to his profession for a man who was supposed to be at least semi-retired.

"Let us go out onto the terrace," Florence said as she charged ahead.

As usual, her terrace was a lush mixture of English and Grecian flora. Large pots of blushing pink roses, which Florence had brought over from her former home in Surrey, were just beginning to bloom, and the air was wonderfully fragrant. I inhaled deeply and marveled, not for the first time, at Florence's commitment to keeping so many native English plants alive and flourishing in this arid climate. I had become a fairly competent gardener over the years, mostly out of necessity, but my tally of the plants I had inadvertently killed in my lifetime was still higher than the ones I'd managed to keep alive.

She led us over to a table shaded by a large grapevine, and we all sat down. "I do apologize. The house is at sixes and sevens, and I just don't have it in me to find new help at the moment," she said with a sniffle.

This was surprising, given how freely she had criticized Daphne when she was alive. Privately, I wondered if this was more a case of being unable to find help, given Florence's reputation as a difficult employer.

"Not to worry," Mr. Dorian replied smoothly. "My goodness, you have quite the collection of plants, Mrs. Belvedere. I confess, I did not notice when I was last here."

"Well, it was nighttime, so I will allow you that one discrepancy," she said with a trilling laugh.

Mr. Dorian smiled politely and scanned the assortment of pots. I had the distinct sensation that he was looking for something. I tried to catch his eye, but he pointedly ignored me.

"Shall I fetch us some tea?" Florence asked brightly.

"Please don't trouble yourself," I said. "We can't stay long anyway. We've just come to ask a few questions about Miss Costas."

Florence's eyebrows rose in surprise. "Whatever for?"

"We believe the police have the wrong culprit."

She stared at us in shocked silence for a moment. "Nonsense," she then blustered. "That vagrant has long been a nuisance, and he was roaming about the area only days before. I saw him myself. And they found a bar of her soap on him. Of course he killed her."

"Florence," I began gently, "being a nuisance doesn't make someone a murderer. As far as we can tell, his only plausible motive for such a crime would be to rob her, and aside from a bar of soap, which could have been a gift, none of Daphne's personal possessions were missing. Including her necklace."

Florence stiffened. "What necklace?"

"I saw it on her when I—" My throat suddenly went dry as the image of the poor dead girl flashed in my mind once again. It was a long moment before I could continue. "When I found her."

"Oh." Florence's eyes softened, and for the first time, she looked truly grieved. "Do the police know about this?"

"I told them myself. But they weren't terribly interested."

"Which is why we are looking into it ourselves," Mr. Dorian put in.

"Hmm." Florence sat back and gave us both an assessing look. Then she nodded. "All right. What would you like to know?"

Mr. Dorian wasted no time: "When did you last see Miss Costas alive?"

"The evening before she was found. I had a meeting with the Ladies Guild that afternoon, but I left early with a headache. You can ask Mrs. Barthes if you need confirmation of my attendance," she added dryly and arched a brow in challenge.

Mr. Dorian pursed his lips. "I'm sure that won't be necessary. Please, continue."

"Then I came home, had a light supper, and went straight to bed."

"Do you remember the time?"

"I didn't feel well," she said peevishly. "I wasn't exactly watching the clock." But Mr. Dorian looked at her expectantly, and Florence heaved a sigh. "Sometime between six and seven, I suppose. The next morning I couldn't find her. But that wasn't unusual. That girl was always going off somewhere," Florence groused.

I recalled Daphne's words when I met her outside Mr. Dorian's villa. *I've come with some soaps I made for Mr. Dorian.*

Did Florence know about Daphne's visits to the villa? It seemed unlikely that she would have approved, given the girl's habit of disappearing. I couldn't help casting Mr. Dorian another look, but his focus remained firmly fixed on Florence.

"And what of Christopher?"

Florence sighed heavily once more. "He dined out in town that evening, as he went to the office that day. I don't believe he saw her when he returned home, but you'll have to ask him."

"I will," Mr. Dorian said with a firm nod. "Was there anyone else at home with you that evening?"

"No," she said stoutly. "Wednesday is Mrs. Georgiou's half day."

My shoulders sank. This was starting to look like another dead end.

"Is she here now?" Mr. Dorian asked, undaunted. "May we speak with her?"

"She didn't see Daphne the next morning, either," Florence snapped before turning to me. "I've already told the police all of this."

Mr. Dorian looked about ready to snap back when I cut in.

"I understand," I said in my most soothing tone. "We simply want to make sure the police didn't overlook something. But only if you would allow it, of course," I added, hoping this show of supplication would appeal to her.

Florence's mouth tightened. "Fine. Just you, though," she said to me. "Mrs. Georgiou wouldn't think it proper for the two of you to be traipsing around the island together."

Though I would hardly call looking into a murder traipsing around, I held my tongue.

"That's just as well," Mr. Dorian replied. "As I can go speak to Christopher in the meantime."

Florence narrowed her eyes at him before addressing me once again. "Don't keep her for very long. She's doing the work of two people now."

"Of course," I said, as graciously as I could manage.

We all rose, and Mr. Dorian made a swift bow.

"Thank you for all your help, Mrs. Belvedere," he said in a tone that indicated the exact opposite before turning to me. "We will speak later," he murmured.

I nodded in reply, and Mr. Dorian strode off the terrace.

Florence frowned at his retreating back. "That man is becoming a nuisance himself," she said when he was barely out of earshot.

"He only wants to help, Florence."

"We don't need his help," she sniffed. "And you would do well to stay away from him."

I sucked in a startled breath at her chastisement. "I'm working for him. On your husband's recommendation, I might add."

"The typing is one thing. But larking about in full view of the neighborhood is quite another."

My jaw tightened, as I knew very well what she was implying. "That is hardly the case here, I assure you," I said coolly, trying to keep hold of my temper.

But, maddeningly, Florence didn't look convinced. "I'm only looking out for you, Minnie. The man has a reputation, and a well-earned one at that. Who knows what he's been getting up to at the villa since he arrived—and with whom."

"Florence!"

"Think of your children," she insisted. "Of what people will say."

This coming from the woman who only weeks ago had been quite publicly fawning over him. It was disturbing how quickly her opinion of him changed. Or perhaps it was her opinion of me that was shifting now that I wasn't just Oliver's lonely widow.

I rather think she was a little bit in love with him.

Though I still didn't agree with Mr. Dorian's assessment, it felt as though I was walking a fine line with Florence—and if I put a foot wrong, she might quickly turn on me. But I would not be shamed simply for being seen in Mr. Dorian's company. Despite our rather combative relationship, I confess I felt a bit protective over him.

"Then I suppose you had better keep this to yourself," I said.

Florence had the decency to look chastened. "Of course I will. I didn't mean to suggest that I would spread—"

"Is Mrs. Georgiou in the kitchen?" I had no desire to listen to her any further. At times the careless things Florence said annoyed me. But that was never anything close to the absolute disgust I felt now.

Florence bit her lip and nodded. At least she looked properly mortified. That was somewhat heartening.

"Thank you," I said and turned on my heel.

Chapter 12

Once I entered the house, I followed the aroma of simmering spices down the hall. Though Florence may have trouble finding a maid, most of the island was green with envy over her cook. Mrs. Georgiou was a local legend, and even my impossible-to-impress housekeeper was a little in awe of her. Rumor had it that as a young woman Mrs. Georgiou had worked in the household of a countess, under the tutelage of a Parisian chef, before Florence's mother snapped her up. She then served the family faithfully for many decades, and theirs became one of the island's most sought-after dinner invitations, in large part because of her culinary prowess, which seamlessly combined French methods with traditional Greek cooking.

When the Belvederes returned to Corfu over a decade ago, she immediately came out of a well-earned retirement to work for them. In short, one couldn't find a more loyal servant than Mrs. Georgiou. I found her at the worktable, kneading dough with the vigor of a much younger person. Though her wrinkled brow was furrowed in concentration, as soon as I greeted her, she immediately looked up.

"Hello, Mrs. Harper."

The woman might have been swiftly on her way to eighty, but she had lost none of her sharpness.

"I wanted to ask you a few questions about Miss Costas," I said.

She paused in her work and raised an eyebrow. "What did Dia say?"

I smiled at her use of Florence's childhood nickname, a diminutive of the Greek name Florentia. "That I could, but not to keep you long since you are doing the work of two people now."

Mrs. Georgiou let out a grunt. "That girl wasn't much help anyway. Give me a moment to finish this," she said, gesturing to her dough.

"Take your time," I replied and sat down.

Mrs. Georgiou worked the dough a few more times before she transferred it to a wooden bowl and covered it with a cloth to let it rise. Then she cleaned her floury hands before fixing her full attention on me.

"What do you want to know?"

I had the sense that Mrs. Georgiou would appreciate brevity rather than wasting time on formalities, so I got right to the point. "When did you last see her alive?"

The woman didn't even blink. "The morning before she was found. It was my half day, so I prepared luncheon and a cold supper, then left around noon. When I returned on Thursday morning, she was nowhere to be found. Dia was very upset."

I tilted my head. "Florence said it wasn't unusual for Miss Costas to go missing."

"No, it wasn't. But Dia needed her, and where was the girl?" She threw up her hands in agitation, as if this was a grave offense on Daphne's behalf.

Dead not half a mile away.

I kept this to myself, but Mrs. Georgiou didn't seem at all

concerned that someone she worked with had been murdered.

"Do you know where she went off to when she couldn't be found?"

"I know she liked talking to Mrs. Nasso on occasion. And she never missed a chance to sell those soaps of hers," Mrs. Georgiou added, with a disapproving eye roll. "She should have been more focused on doing her job rather than making extra money."

A tightness in my chest loosened, and I let out a sigh. Then her visit to Mr. Dorian's villa really had been about the soap. I felt dreadfully ashamed for ever having entertained the thought that something more untoward could have been going on. Thank God, I hadn't voiced my suspicions to anyone.

Mrs. Georgiou gave me a shrewd look. "You don't think that vagrant killed her, then?"

"I am reserving judgement until I have more information," I said carefully.

She gave a thoughtful nod and seemed to mull this over. "There is something else." Mrs. Georgiou hesitated. "She was sick."

"With what?" Florence hadn't mentioned this.

"With something that makes you ill only in the mornings," she said with a knowing look.

My mouth dropped open. "How long was this going on?"

"A week maybe?"

Then it could have just as easily been a stomach ailment. "Did you ask her if she was with child?"

Mrs. Georgiou looked appalled. "I would never! But if she was, she should have gone back home to be with her husband."

"Daphne was married?"

Florence hadn't mentioned *that* either.

"I don't know for sure," Mrs. Georgiou said hastily. "And

I hope that, for the sake of the child, she was. Otherwise, it is a grave sin for them both. But she did have someone back on Paxos. A fisherman. She mentioned him when she first came here. He sent her some letters."

But if Daphne really was newly pregnant, it seemed unlikely that this fisherman was the father—unless he'd paid her a very clandestine visit. However, an unplanned pregnancy could certainly give someone a reason to kill her. Someone who was either already married or uninterested in supporting her. My stomach turned at the thought of such an utterly cruel and callous act.

"Don't tell Dia about this, please," Mrs. Georgiou suddenly said, her eyes full of worry. "I know the things people have been saying about the girl, and if Dia knew she might have been with child as well, it would upset her greatly. She . . . she does not always understand the ways of the world."

Given that Florence had three grown children of her own, I didn't see how that was possible, but Mrs. Georgiou still seemed to see her as the girl she had once been.

"I won't," I promised, but not because I wished to preserve Florence's nerves. Daphne was already the subject of enough salacious rumors. It could simply be that Mrs. Georgiou's recollections were being influenced by what she had heard. The fisherman, though, that was an avenue worth exploring.

The older woman sighed with relief. "Good."

"Did you tell the police about any of this?"

She nodded reluctantly. "The inspector, but he didn't seem interested. Only wanted to know where I was when she was found."

I bit back a curse. Then they really had done nothing. This was an important piece of information that should have been explored, like the necklace. And yet still they focused all their attention on Gregor.

"Thank you, Mrs. Georgiou," I said as I stood. "If you think of anything else, you will tell me?"

"I will. But wait here." She plucked a few biscuits off a plate and wrapped them in a napkin, then handed it to me. "For the children. And you," she added with a wink.

I returned her smile and thanked her again, then left.

As I walked back through the house, there was no sign of Florence in the sitting room or on the terrace. She must have gone to town or was having a lie down. Either way, it was just as well. I didn't wish to speak to her, or anyone, for that matter. It seemed very important that I write down everything I had learned here before I could forget. Next time, I would need to bring something with me.

As I hurried back home, I went over my conversation with both Florence and Mrs. Georgiou again and again. Tommy and Mr. Papadopoulos were outside feeding the chickens and waved hello, but I didn't stop, just returned their wave and continued on. Inside, Mrs. Kouris was rattling around in the kitchen, and there was no sign of Cleo, so I raced up the stairs and shut myself up in Oliver's study. I grabbed one of his old leather-bound notebooks and quickly turned the pages until I found a blank one and began to write.

I inscribed every single word, every minute detail I could recall. After a while, my hand began to cramp, but I refused to stop—not until my entire exchange with Mrs. Georgiou was put to paper. And when I was done with that, I worked on Mrs. Nasso's interview next, including her insights into the murder.

It is not a crime of convenience, but of pain. Of anger.

The full weight of Mrs. Nasso's words struck me anew, especially in light of Daphne's potential pregnancy and this mysterious suitor. It seemed utterly ridiculous now to think that a stranger had murdered her at random. No. Whoever had done this must have had a motive. They knew Daphne.

Knew her movements. And knew when she would be most vulnerable to attack.

When the work was finally done, I let out a sigh and leaned back in Oliver's chair. I flexed my hand, but that did little to relieve the tension that had gathered there. Then I glanced towards the window and was surprised to see that it was late afternoon. I must have been up here for well over an hour. I stretched my back, which was nearly as bad as my hand, and stood. Then I caught a glimpse of Tommy running around the yard waving a stick and smiled.

I made my way back downstairs and stopped in the doorway of the kitchen, where Mrs. Kouris was chopping vegetables for our supper. "Do you need any help?"

She shook her head without looking up. "That man is here. Outside."

I frowned in confusion. "Mr. Papadopoulos?"

"No," she practically spat. Then shot me an arch look. "The writer."

Oh.

Mr. Dorian must have come to see what I had learned from Mrs. Georgiou. Without thinking, I wiped my hands on my dress, which had the unfortunate effect of smearing ink on the skirt.

"Blast!"

Mrs. Kouris clicked her tongue. "I will fix it later. You go. He's not been here long."

I muttered another curse under my breath and headed for the door.

As I stepped outside, I caught sight of Tommy, still with his stick in hand, and Mr. Dorian with one of his own. They were fencing on the lawn, I realized, with Mr. Dorian showing Tommy how to assume the proper stance, while Mr. Papadopoulos appeared to be their audience.

"Good form," Mr. Dorian said as he stepped back and assumed his own position. "Then when you're ready you say 'en garde'!"

I wasn't sure that was technically correct, but Tommy looked absolutely thrilled.

"En garde!" he shouted, while proudly waggling his stick.

Mr. Dorian threw back his arm and similarly extended his own stick, parrying a little with Tommy.

I stood next to Mr. Papadopoulos, who gave me a smile. "You've come just in time for the match."

"Mama! Look at me!" Tommy shouted before he lunged towards Mr. Dorian's chest.

I let out a surprised gasp, but my employer easily blocked Tommy's thrust. "Goodness," I murmured to Mr. Papadopoulos. "They're taking this rather seriously."

"Yes, Tommy was adamant that Mr. Dorian not let him win."

"I see."

Based on the competitive glint in Mr. Dorian's eye, he seemed perfectly happy to accommodate my son's wishes.

I then asked Mr. Papadopoulos about his day, and he related a funny anecdote about Tommy and his ongoing obsession with Newton. I laughed, and Mr. Dorian looked over at us sharply. This provided Tommy with the perfect opportunity to attack, and he wasted no time thrusting his stick against Mr. Dorian's arm.

"I did it!" He threw up his hands and let out a cheer. "I got a hit!"

For a moment, Mr. Dorian was stunned, but then he gave Tommy a wry smile. "So you did," he said and rubbed his arm. Tommy must have hit him a bit too enthusiastically. "But remember, a gentleman never gloats."

My son immediately sobered. "Sorry. You're right."

"That is enough for today, I think. Besides, I need to speak to your mother for a bit," Mr. Dorian said as he caught my eye. "But we will have a rematch very soon."

"May we use proper foils next time?"

"I neglected to bring mine with me when I left England," Mr. Dorian said drolly. "But we certainly can if you manage to find some."

"I will," Tommy promised.

They then bowed very neatly to each other and Tommy scampered off, likely already on the hunt for some fencing foils. I bit my lip and hoped Mr. Dorian wouldn't regret his words. My son had a knack for finding the most peculiar items on this island.

"I admit, I'm a little embarrassed to have an audience for my defeat," Mr. Dorian said with a smile. As he walked towards us, he rolled down his shirtsleeves, and I confess, I was distracted by the movement. When I glanced up, Mr. Dorian's dark eyes were fixed upon me. A fierce blush heated my cheeks as I immediately turned away, but it was useless to pretend. The man had caught me full on staring at him.

"You put on an admirable defense," Mr. Papadopoulos said as he rose. "But it is well past time I take my leave."

"Actually," Mr. Dorian began, assuming a casual air before fixing that dark gaze on Mr. Papadopoulos. "Would you mind staying? This concerns you."

My neighbor stilled for a moment before replying. "Certainly."

"I was in town earlier, speaking with Mr. Belvedere, and learned that the suspect in the murder of Miss Costas was released today," Mr. Dorian said. "After *you* provided an alibi."

I inhaled sharply and leaned forward.

Mr. Papadopoulos replied with a grave nod. "I wish I could have done so sooner, but I only learned of his imprisonment a short while ago."

Mr. Dorian raised an eyebrow in disbelief, but I cut in.

"Mr. Papadopoulos does not go into town very much," I explained, "and has far better things to concern himself with than the latest gossip."

"I'd hardly call the murder of a local woman gossip," Mr. Dorian said, keeping his skeptical gaze on my neighbor.

Mr. Papadopoulos smiled at me. "Yes, you make me sound rather sanctimonious, Mrs. Harper. It is more that I simply prefer a quieter life," he explained to Mr. Dorian.

But he did not look convinced. "Then how was it you came to invite this vagrant into your home?"

"His name is Gregor, and on the day in question, I happened upon him as I was returning from my weekly trip to the market," Mr. Papadopoulos began. "He wanted to sell me some trinkets, which I have no use for, so I offered him a home-cooked meal instead. I live with my older sister, you see, and she always makes far too much. We all dined together that evening and stayed up later than usual, as he had a number of entertaining stories." Mr. Papadopoulos then shook his head. "My sister tried very hard to convince him to sleep inside, but he said he preferred our barn, as he had grown used to sleeping rough. Then we breakfasted with him early the next morning, and he offered to fix a patch of our roof that was leaking. I suppose he could have snuck out then and murdered the girl, but as I understand it, she died while we were all eating our dinner. A terrible tragedy, to be sure, but not one Gregor is responsible for." Then he turned to me. "I was actually going to suggest him to help with your roof if Nico is still off island. He does good work."

Before I could answer, Mr. Dorian scoffed in outrage. "You would bring that man to the home of a helpless widow and her children?"

I rather objected to being called helpless, but Mr. Papadopoulos remained as calm as ever. "Well, he isn't a murderer, Mr. Dorian. I am quite certain of that."

Mr. Dorian opened his mouth to respond to this, but then took a different approach. "And do you make entertaining strangers in your home a habit?"

"No, but I wouldn't call Gregor a stranger. He may not have a home of his own, but he has lived around here for a good while now. And it is not the first time he has stayed with us, either."

Mr. Dorian looked properly shocked, but the generosity of Mr. Papadopoulos and his sister was well known. It was not surprising the police had released Gregor on his word.

"Now that I have satisfied your curiosity, it is time I take my leave," Mr. Papadopoulos said. "My sister will be waiting for me."

I gave him an apologetic smile. "Thank you for spending time with Tommy today."

"It is always my pleasure, Mrs. Harper. And it was good to meet you, Mr. Dorian," he added with a swift nod.

"Yes, you as well," Mr. Dorian replied flatly.

I shot him a frown before walking with Mr. Papadopoulos towards the road. "I'm sorry Mr. Dorian was so short with you," I began once we were out of earshot. "I have had my doubts about the police's investigation into Miss Costas's death and asked him to help."

"Not to worry. I gathered as much. And I can understand how my actions look to a man such as him." Then his expression turned wary. "I do hope you are being careful, though."

I reared back a little. "Whoever killed Miss Costas seems to have had a personal vendetta against her, but I will keep the children close at hand until someone else is arrested."

He glanced over my shoulder back towards the house. "I wasn't speaking of that." Then he met my undoubtedly surprised gaze and looked rather sheepish. "But I think I have said too much. You are a grown woman, after all. Good night."

I managed to wave my good-bye before he walked in the direction of his home. When I turned around, Mr. Dorian stood not far off, with his hands shoved in his trouser pockets and a disapproving look on his face.

"I didn't realize you two were so close," he said when I joined him.

The comment took me by surprise. "Mr. Papadopoulos?"

He cut his eyes to me. "Who else would I mean?"

"Not that I need to explain myself to you," I said as I lifted my chin, "but he's very good with the children. Especially Tommy."

Mr. Dorian's gaze softened slightly. "Sorry. I didn't realize— " But then he seemed to catch himself and shook his head. "Never mind." Now I was thoroughly confused by his behavior, but I didn't have the chance to respond before Mr. Dorian pressed on. "There's something I need to show you," he said abruptly and pulled something out of his pocket. It was a letter. "I found it in Miss Costas's bedroom."

For a moment, I was entirely speechless. "How did you manage that?" I sputtered.

"Before I left the house," he said with a touch of pride.

"And Florence didn't see you?"

He shrugged. "She was still out on the terrace with you. And I was quick about it."

Then I sincerely hoped he hadn't heard any of the disparaging remarks she'd made about him. But Mr. Dorian seemed only interested in the letter. "Go on, then," he urged. "It's in Greek. I can't read a word."

I let out a sigh. "Well, I might not be much help." I was ashamed to admit that even after all this time, I had never managed to master written Greek.

"But you can speak it," he insisted, as if that would change things.

"Yes, but I'm hardly fluent. And it's an entirely different alphabet," I said, feeling defensive.

Still, I opened the envelope and pulled out the letter. It wasn't very long, which was a comfort.

"It's from her aunt," I said. That much I could gather, given that it was addressed to "my dear niece" or something similar.

"That's a start," he said dryly.

I shot him an irritated look and read on, but I only understood every few words, and it was hard to make sense of them together. Once I came to the end, I shook my head.

"We need to find someone else. I can ask Mr. Papadopoulos."

Mr. Dorian grimaced. "I'd rather not."

"But I can go right after him. He can't have gotten very far."

"It needs to be someone we know won't go running off to the police," he insisted.

I really didn't think Mr. Papadopoulos would do that, but Mr. Dorian seemed set against the man for some reason. "All right."

"Do either of your children—"

"*No.*" The word seemed to erupt from me, taking us both by surprise. "They are not to be involved in this in any way," I said more calmly.

Mr. Dorian bowed his head in acknowledgement. "Understood. What about your housekeeper," he suggested after a moment. "Is she literate?"

"Yes," I said tartly—though the truth was I didn't know to what extent.

Mr. Dorian held up his hands. "Well, I couldn't assume."

I didn't like the thought of involving her either, but couldn't think of an alternative.

"Fine," I said reluctantly. "But we can't tell her where this came from."

Mr. Dorian raised an eyebrow. "You don't trust her?"

"She certainly won't go to the police. However," I paused and glanced over towards the door that led to the kitchen before lowering my voice, "Mrs. Kouris is a bit of a gossip, which can be quite helpful at times. But . . ." I tilted my head to the side, and Mr. Dorian nodded in understanding.

"All right. I'll think of something." Then he extended his arm in the direction of the house.

"After you."

I entered the kitchen just as my housekeeper set down a hot tray of roasted chicken.

"Mrs. Kouris, may we trouble you for a moment?"

She glanced up from her work and frowned. "I was just going to leave."

"It won't take a minute. Mr. Dorian has a letter he'd like you to translate."

Her frown deepened. "Why?"

I resisted the urge to roll my eyes. I had forgotten to tell him that in addition to being a gossip, the woman was also wildly suspicious.

"I found it," Mr. Dorian interjected. "And I'd like to return it to its rightful owner."

She turned her sharp eyes on him. "Then why not ask Mrs. Nasso?"

Mr. Dorian blinked. "It is her night off."

I silently prayed that he was telling the truth, as I was quite certain Mrs. Kouris knew the answer. The two women may have been sworn enemies, but that didn't stop them from being in each other's pockets.

After a moment, her mouth curved in a slight smile. "So it is." Then she cleared her throat and held out her hand for the letter.

"Thank you," I said graciously as I gave it to her.

Mrs. Kouris let out a grunt and began to read. After a few moments, she started to shake her head. Then she began to click her tongue in disapproval. I exchanged a bewildered look with Mr. Dorian.

"This person is asking for money. Well, not asking," she amended. "More like expecting. It sounds like it could be a payment of sorts for their silence."

"You mean, it's a *blackmail* letter?" Mr. Dorian said before addressing me. "I thought you said it was from her aunt?"

"It is," Mrs. Kouris said and pointed to the salutation. "*Anipsia* means niece." Then she clucked her tongue again. "But this is not something one should write to their family."

I grimaced. This was very damning indeed. "Is there anything else?"

Mrs. Kouris was quiet for a moment as she scanned the letter again. "The writer says that she does not approve of something the niece is doing."

"And yet they are willing to keep their silence in exchange for money," I posited.

Mrs. Kouris shrugged and handed the letter back to me. "It appears that way."

"Is it signed?" Mr. Dorian asked as he craned his neck over my shoulder to look at the letter himself.

"It only says 'your loving aunt,'" she replied.

I let out a very undignified snort, while Mr. Dorian muttered something in disgust.

"Do you really think you will be able to find the rightful owner?" she asked Mr. Dorian.

He was deep in thought and gave her a blank look until I gently nudged him with my elbow.

"Ah, well," he blustered, buying himself some time. "I certainly mean to try," he added with a charming smile that no doubt had gotten him out of more than a few awkward situations.

Predictably, this did not work on my housekeeper, who only frowned. "Then I wish you luck," she said. "Good night."

Mrs. Kouris shot me a speaking glance as she headed for the door, and I knew I would have much to answer for in the morning.

I let out a sigh. "Well, that could have gone better."

But Mr. Dorian seemed unconcerned. "What cause would an aunt—a supposed loving one at that—have to blackmail her own niece?"

"I haven't a clue," I replied and moved towards the tray of chicken and rice that Mrs. Kouris had left for supper. Investigation or not, I still had an evening full of mothering to attend to.

Mr. Dorian clasped his hands behind his back and began to pace around the table. "What did Daphne's aunt disapprove of? And how much money was she meant to send her? Was Daphne selling these soaps because she needed to make a payment?"

I tied my apron around my waist and began slicing up a loaf of bread. "Are you actually asking me or simply talking aloud?" The question came out sharper than I intended, but that seemed to get his attention.

Mr. Dorian stopped his pacing and glanced over at me. "Sorry. It helps me think." Then he began patting his pockets and looking around. "Where is my jacket?"

I took a deep breath. One of my biggest irritations was being asked the location of some random item. Despite the fact that I rarely knew the answer, the children and, at times, even Oliver himself seemed to think I possessed some kind of mental map of our house along with a current inventory of all our possessions.

But instead of scolding Mr. Dorian as I did my children, I decided that once again he must be thinking aloud because, really, how on earth would I know? But after a few moments, he cast me the same pleading look I had seen on the faces of my family members nearly every day.

My jaw tightened. "Outside, perhaps?"

His face lit up at my suggestion, and he raced out the door. I resumed slicing the bread with more enthusiasm than usual and made quick work of it.

He hurried back in with the jacket in question slung over his arm while he scribbled in a small leather notebook. "There. I've written down everything regarding the letter." Mr. Dorian then gave me an expectant look. "Now, what did the cook tell you?"

I should have gone upstairs to retrieve my own detailed record then, but Mrs. Georgiou's concerned expression flashed in my mind. She hadn't wanted me to tell Florence about Daphne's possible pregnancy, but now it felt wrong to share her suspicions.

After all, it really was just hearsay. And Daphne had already been branded a harlot. Would Mr. Dorian be quick to judge her, like most other people, or was he able to remain neutral?

You are stalling. And hardly remaining neutral yourself, an accusatory little voice in my head pointed out. *You certainly wouldn't want him to withhold anything from* you.

That was true, but I needed more time to think about this. To ascertain Mr. Dorian's true character. And there was still plenty for us to look into in the meantime. So I ignored the little voice and told him everything else we discussed, which he then dutifully recorded in his notebook. Only the mention of the fisherman momentarily broke his concentration and he glanced at me in surprise. But then, I had the same reaction to this bit of information.

"I don't suppose you found any other letters?" I asked once I finished. "Mrs. Georgiou seemed to think this fisherman had sent some to Daphne."

Mr. Dorian shook his head, distracted. "I didn't see any,

but I was trying to be quick. Even still, this is something, Mrs. Harper," he said. "Truly something." His boyish enthusiasm was rather endearing, even if it was in response to a murder. "And we still need to speak to that doctor."

"We can go in the afternoon," I said. "He usually closes the surgery then."

"All right." But then Mr. Dorian grimaced. "Although perhaps it is better if you go by yourself. If we are seen too much in each other's company, people might talk."

I opened my mouth to reassure him, but then I thought of Florence and her remonstrations. Perhaps Mr. Dorian had heard her after all. "That is . . . sensible," I said with a nod.

He hummed in agreement before his head shot up. "And Paxos. We have to go to Paxos to talk to the aunt and the fisherman," he added.

I was just about to point out that traveling to another island together would draw far more suspicion than visiting the local doctor when Cleo entered the room. "Is supper ready yet? I'm so hungry I could gnaw off my own arm."

"Really, Cleo," I chastised. "Don't be so disgusting. And in front of company!"

But rather than look at all embarrassed, Cleo simply smiled. "Are you staying for supper, Mr. Dorian?"

"I wouldn't want to impose," he said a bit sheepishly.

"But there's plenty," she replied. "Mrs. Kouris always makes far too much, and Tommy doesn't eat chicken anymore."

"What?" I set down my knife. "Since when?"

"Since this afternoon when he was feeding the hens and realized the chickens we eat are the same animal as the chickens we keep," Cleo said with a prideful grin.

I closed my eyes and took a breath. When I opened them, Mr. Dorian was giving me an amused look. "I am sure Tommy has made that connection before, dear," I said to Cleo, though I wasn't entirely sure. One never knew what went on in Tommy's head, and I had learned long ago not to ask too many questions.

But Cleo merely shrugged, already bored with the conversation, and wandered towards the terrace. "I'll go set the table. You'll stay then, Mr. Dorian?"

He looked to me and raised an eyebrow. "If you'll have me."

"Yes, of course," I replied and then sent up a silent prayer that the children would refrain from their usual suppertime conversation.

"Good. Then I'll have time to make my case for Paxos," he said with a roguish smile and followed Cleo outside to fetch Tommy before I could object.

Chapter 13

I should have known my prayer would go unanswered. Tommy talked of nothing but bugs, reptiles, and arachnids, while Cleo only wanted to hear about the London social scene. But Mr. Dorian patiently listened to each of Tommy's anecdotes with genuine interest and answered all of Cleo's barely veiled attempts to fish for gossip with far more grace and consideration than she deserved. That didn't stop me from cringing every time she opened her mouth, though, as I was worried she might be bold enough to actually ask the man about his former wife.

By the time supper was finished and the dishes cleared, it was later than usual, so I shooed the children upstairs to wash and get ready for bed. Thankfully, they didn't protest too much.

Once Mr. Dorian and I were alone in the kitchen, I let out a long sigh of relief.

"I'm sorry about them. I'd say they're usually better behaved than that, but I'm not a very good liar."

He laughed at that. "Not at all," he replied. "Your children are quite charming, Mrs. Harper."

"Oh. Thank you."

His mouth curved. "You needn't sound so surprised. I like children. Though I will confess, I haven't a clue what to do with babies."

I laughed a little at that. "Yes, that is usually the case unless one has experience. But you will— " Then I stopped myself, as I had been on the verge of saying something terribly foolish. Something like "you will learn once you become a father."

Mr. Dorian stared at me for a moment before he seemed to intuit the reason for my sudden silence. Then he looked down at the tabletop and began drawing circles with his finger. "I rather think that ship has sailed for me," he said softly.

Though I knew nothing of why his marriage had ended, apart from the gossip, of course, my heart ached for him in that moment. For there was no mistaking the regret etched on his face.

"There's still plenty of time for all that. You . . . you could marry again," I ventured.

But he let out a huff. "I'm afraid I've lost my taste for holy matrimony, not that it was terribly strong to begin with."

It was a frankly scandalous admission, but I maintained my sympathetic expression. "Don't say that," I urged. "What if you meet someone else?"

"What if I do?" he said with a challenging look. "We're on the cusp of a new century, Mrs. Harper, though it's easy to forget that here." He gave a dismissive glance towards the window before meeting my gaze once more. "Not every woman is intent on becoming a wife these days."

Now he was just trying to shock me. "I am aware," I said tightly. It was true. I had met enough so-called New Women while at Girton. Why, if I hadn't married Oliver, I could very well be one of them: sharing a flat in Chelsea, wearing a pair of bloomers while riding my bicycle, smoking cigarettes in public, and whiling away the evenings at literary salons.

It sounded rather lovely, to be honest.

"I had no idea you were such a romantic," Mr. Dorian drawled. "Given that *you* haven't married anyone else."

His insouciant comment caught my full attention. "I'm not a romantic," I insisted. "But it's hardly the same—" I stopped as cold panic shot through me. I very much wished I could shove those words back into my mouth.

Mr. Dorian narrowed his eyes and cocked his head. "Why?" he said archly. "Because your spouse died and mine simply decided life with me was intolerable?"

"I shouldn't have said that," I murmured. But he was absolutely right. I did think it was different, as I would undoubtably still be married if Oliver was alive. "I'm sorry."

Mr. Dorian let out a mirthless laugh and looked away. "Don't be. Of course it's not the same. Insulting to suggest otherwise."

"It wasn't," I said, but Mr. Dorian didn't seem to hear.

"How long were you married?"

I hesitated at the sudden intensity in his gaze. "Eleven years."

He gave me a thin smile. "We didn't even make it to our first anniversary. She demanded an annulment within a month, in fact, but I refused. Still had a scrap of pride left."

Then he shook his head, as if trying to rid himself of whatever memories were plaguing him. But I sensed it would take far more than that, given that the man couldn't even bring himself to say his former wife's name. "I should go before it gets too dark," he said abruptly and stood to leave.

"All right."

I suppose I should have insisted that he stay then. I could have compelled him by mentioning Paxos or possible questions to ask Doctor Campbell tomorrow. But instead I remained firmly in my chair, held in place by some invisible band pressing against my chest. For once we had exhausted those topics, we might talk more about his failed marriage. And then I would feel obliged to speak about mine, all while that little wave of panic rippled in my chest.

"Good night, Mrs. Harper," he said with a nod. "Thank you for the fine meal and even finer company."

I had to clear my throat before I could speak. "Good night, Mr. Dorian."

But he had already disappeared into the night.

Later, after I'd tucked the children into their beds and changed into my nightgown, I sat at my dressing table. As I looked at my reflection, I let out a sigh. Somehow, I looked even more tired than I felt, a situation that was not improved by my furrowed brow. I forced my features to relax and began to remove my hairpins, dropping each one into the small enamel dish I kept just for this purpose.

You haven't married anyone else.

Mr. Dorian was hardly the first person to bring this up. Indeed, it was rather obscene how often people casually mentioned it the first few years after Oliver died.

Clink.

But back then it had been much too soon to even consider the idea. Now, though . . . now it was well past the time when a widow could remarry without raising eyebrows.

Clink.

Perhaps that was why I had such a visceral response to his careless remark.

Clink.

Because, much like Mr. Dorian, I had no desire to marry again, ever.

Clink.

I had found a man who loved me. Really, genuinely loved *me*. Who thought my faults paled in comparison to my better qualities. Who let me win even our pettiest fight. Who never hesitated to get up in the dead of night when one of the children began to cry so that I could rest a little longer.

Trying to find another man like that in a single lifetime seemed a futile quest. And not only because the men of my acquaintance were lacking, but because I had so much less to offer another person now. The bloom of my youth had faded long ago. I was older and so much more cynical. Life had dug its claws into me and left behind scars that would never fully heal.

And aside from my own limitations, I had two children whom I loved madly and who drove me mad every day. I couldn't imagine someone else wanting to take them on. But more importantly, I didn't trust anyone else to love them as fiercely as I required.

No. It seemed that I was destined to live the rest of my days in a similar manner. That is, until the children left me one by one. And then . . . well, I could not think on that now.

My morose thoughts had distracted me from my task, and half of the pins still remained. I made quick work of the rest and tugged a comb through my hair before tying it in a loose braid. Then I climbed into my empty bed and willed sleep to come before I could torment myself any longer.

The next morning, I arrived at Mr. Dorian's villa a little before nine. I had taken to letting myself in so as not to disturb Mrs. Nasso, though she usually came to the study with a pot of tea and some biscuits not long afterwards. As I walked down the hall to the study, I braced myself. Last night had ended on an awkward note, and the more I thought about the exchange with Mr. Dorian, the more my uncertainty grew. It seemed we both had revealed some things to the other. Things we weren't quite ready to share, perhaps ever.

I resolved to hide my apprehension behind a mask of cheerful vigor and stay focused on the work. Now I could only pray that Mr. Dorian had decided to do the same. I paused just outside the doorway, took a deep breath, and entered the study.

"Good— "

It was empty. I glanced at the clock on the mantle. It was only just nine now. I pushed aside the apprehension in my chest before it could turn into rejection and sat down behind the desk. A fresh stack of notebooks had been left beside the typewriter, and I raised an eyebrow. Mr. Dorian must have been very busy last night. My chest eased a little at the thought, for if he had been up late, that would certainly account for his absence now. Then I rolled my shoulders back. Enough dawdling. There was work to be done.

The rest of the morning passed quickly. I reached the climax of the story and was surprised by the twists Mr. Dorian had added to this draft. There was still another notebook left, but it would have to wait for tomorrow, as I needed to make the journey into town to speak with Doctor Campbell. I tidied the desk and collected my things, then hesitated in the doorway. Though this had been how our working relationship had begun, now it felt odd to leave without even speaking to Mr. Dorian.

I've rather gotten used to our work schedule, he'd said.

As it turned out, so had I. Then I gave my head a shake. I was being terribly silly. The man wasn't avoiding me. He had been up all hours and was only getting some much-needed rest. Tomorrow he would be here—if only to hear what I learned from the doctor. And yet the thought wasn't very comforting. I let out a sigh and shut the door softly behind me. I had an investigation to resume.

* * *

After serving the children their lunch and helping Tommy write a short essay describing Napoleon's defeat at Waterloo—which seemed a rather advanced assignment for an eight-year-old—I set out for Corfu Town in the donkey cart. Like most of the shops on the island, nay all of Greece, Doctor Campbell closed his surgery during *mesimeri*, or the hours of two to five in the afternoon, to avoid the hottest part of the day. I arrived just after one and entered the tiny office.

"Hello there!" I called out.

The waiting area was empty, as the doctor employed no secretary. Not even an assistant, though I wasn't sure if this was a choice on his part or because no one wanted to work for him.

An exasperated grunt came from the back room. "Give me a moment, will ye?"

I pressed my lips together. The doctor was in, all right. "Yes, of course," I called back and sat down on a hard wooden bench to wait.

Rumor had it Doctor Campbell was once a promising young physician in Glasgow, but he came to the island after being banned from practicing medicine in Scotland. While it was not exactly a great comfort, no one could agree on why he had been banned. Some claimed it was because he accidentally killed an important politician during a routine procedure, while others insisted he fled after romancing the wife of his mentor. Given that the doctor hadn't managed to kill any of us over the years, I was in favor of the latter—though it was hard to imagine that Doctor Campbell had ever been young or in love.

After a few minutes, the doctor appeared in the doorway of the examination room, drying his hands on a tea towel. He was a small, rotund Scotsman of advanced age with a shock of white hair and absolutely no bedside manner to speak of. He conducted himself in a brusque, business-like style, no matter the circumstance, which I generously attributed to the long-ago heartbreak that drove him from his home country. But regardless of the source, it was still rather off-putting.

For example, not a minute after he had declared my poor Oliver dead, he headed for the door and called over his shoulder that a cart would come along shortly to remove the body, as if he was speaking of sacks of grain and not my beloved husband. I had forgotten that particular memory—or, perhaps, forced myself to forget is a better way to frame it—until he stood before me.

"Mrs. Harper," he said, with a touch of surprise before frowning, "you don't have an appointment." Though he had lived here for decades now, his brogue remained remarkably strong.

"No, I was hoping to have a quick word. Only if you have the time," I added solicitously.

He gave a brief nod. "Come through, please."

I walked past him and entered the examination room. "Take a seat," he prompted and gestured to the chair by his desk. Then he moved to sit across from me.

"Now then," he began with his usual brusqueness, "what brings you here? I haven't seen you in some time." Then he raised a bushy eyebrow. "Are you having feminine troubles? Is it the change? That usually starts around your age. Why, you must be nearly *forty* by now."

"Thirty-three, actually," I said with a tight smile, while I fought the urge to slap him. "And I am in excellent health. No, I came to ask about the girl that was murdered. Daphne Costas."

He reeled back as if the slap had actually been delivered. "Whatever for?"

"Well, you see, I knew Daphne a little. And I was the one who found her."

"A terrible business." He clicked his tongue and shook his head. "I haven't dealt with a body in such a state since I was in medical school. I don't think there has been a murder in these parts for years. And certainly not one like that."

I tilted my head. "What do you mean?"

He shot me an arch look. "I shouldn't be talking to you about this."

"Please, Doctor." I placed a hand over my heart. "I am the picture of discretion. And I know how very insightful you are in such matters. Why, I never would have known what killed my poor husband if not for your expertise."

The man preened at this shallow flattery, and I only wished I had the stomach to do it more often.

"Well, I suppose it's all right," he began slowly, "seeing as you have a personal connection to the deceased."

"I know she was strangled," I prompted before he could change his mind. "I saw the bruises on her throat. I'm guessing that was how she died."

"Yes," he admitted reluctantly. "Although"—the doctor paused and tilted his head—"usually when someone is strangled to death, there are signs of a struggle. They fight back. Quite fiercely." A shutter tore through me at his words. I couldn't help but imagine the sensation of strong fingers tightening around my throat, pressing and pressing until there was no breath left.

It is not a crime of convenience, but of pain. Of anger.

The doctor, unaware of the direction of my thoughts, continued: "But I couldn't find any evidence."

I frowned. "What do you make of that?"

He shrugged. "The victim could have been unconscious, though I can't say how. She had no injury to the head. Nothing physical that would have rendered her so."

"The autopsy didn't show anything?"

"I didn't perform one," he said blithely. "The police didn't think it necessary, as the cause of death was straightforward enough to them. And the Belvederes wanted her buried as soon as possible."

I sat back in my chair. "That sounds suspicious."

Doctor Campbell shrugged again. "Not necessarily. Things run a bit differently here, as I'm sure you know. We simply don't have the resources to keep bodies intact for very long," he added with a pointed look.

My jaw tightened as a metallic taste filled my mouth. "Right." Oliver had died in August, and I remembered all too well how hastily we had to bury him. It felt like one moment he was here and the next he was in the English cemetery under a pile of dry, crumbling dirt.

"Can I get you anything, Mrs. Harper?" Doctor Campbell's sharp question cut through the memory. "You're lookin' a bit peaked."

"No. No, I'm fine. Thank you." I swallowed hard and cleared my throat. "Were . . . were you able to establish a time of death?"

"Between five and eight the night before you found her," he replied, staring at me with a mixture of contempt and concern.

I inhaled sharply, as it was much earlier than I had thought. And according to Florence, she was still alive between six and seven. That only left a couple precious hours at most for Daphne to leave the house and encounter her murderer. "Why did the police waste all that time on poor Gregor?"

"It is not for me to say, Mrs. Harper," he said diplomatically. "I only told them what I found. They did the rest. And I'm sure they had their reasons." I snorted at this, but he turned thoughtful. "May I give you some advice? Tread carefully. The culprit, whoever they may be, is still on the loose, and they have gone to a great deal of trouble to hide their tracks. That is not the kind of person you want to cross."

My breath caught a little, but I maintained a skeptical expression. "I think you've been reading too many novels, sir."

His face suddenly lit up in a way I had never seen. "Have you met that Mr. Dorian yet? I'm a great fan of his. I've heard he's come to Corfu to finish his latest book."

"Yes," I grumbled, "I heard the same."

I submitted to listening to the doctor wax on about Mr. Dorian's brilliance for a few more minutes before I made my excuses and left.

Between five and eight.

If that was true, then Daphne must have left the Belvederes' right after Florence went off to bed. I never did learn if Mr. Dorian had found out whether Christopher had seen her when he returned home that evening. That could help narrow the window of time even more. His office wasn't far from here, and I immediately turned around and headed in that direction while my mind continued to whirl.

Now it seemed reasonable to assume that Daphne hadn't had time to stray from the neighborhood. My throat tightened a little. For if she had gone to someone else's home, that left very few places. She wasn't at my house, nor with Mr. Papadopoulos and his sister, which left only one other residence, occupied by one man.

Like Doctor Campbell, Christopher closed his office each afternoon, so I had to knock several times, and at increasing degrees of strength, before he finally opened the door.

"Minnie! Why, this is a surprise." He looked a little bleary-eyed but genuinely happy to see me. "Come in, come in," Christopher beckoned me into his tiny office and pulled out the chair where prospective clients usually sat. Though he was nearly sixty, Christopher carried himself like a much younger man. Only the dusting of silver at his temples gave him away. Florence always complained that he worked too much, but I couldn't imagine him mindlessly puttering around the garden like other men his age. The work gave him a purpose, and that purpose kept him youthful.

"I hope I'm not interrupting anything."

"Absolutely not," he said as he took his seat. "Only a lease agreement. Terribly boring business, as you know." He rubbed a hand over his face and attempted to straighten the scatter of papers. Given that the hair on the right side of his head was noticeably flatter than the left, he must have nodded off and only woke when I knocked.

I glanced around. "You've added some plants since I was here last."

Christopher let out a puff of breath. "Yes, Florence keeps bringing more and more over. I live in fear that I'll kill the blasted things and then there will be hell to pay."

"Yes," I agreed. Florence was fiercely protective of her plants. "They do look nice, though. That one in particular is beautiful." I pointed to a lush plant with eye-catching purple flowers just behind him on the windowsill.

Christopher turned to look. "I haven't a clue what it is. You'll have to ask Florence, though I think half of them are poisonous."

"Many houseplants are," I murmured, still staring at the petals. Funny how the most innocuous-looking things were often the most deadly.

"Now, Minnie," Christopher began, and I was forced to meet his gaze, "I'm sure you didn't come all the way here to compliment my décor," he said with a fond look.

I blushed and looked down. "I happened to be in the area."

He was right, though. I had come here with a purpose. And now I was dithering.

"If you're looking for extra work, I'm sure I can find something for you to do . . ."

"Thank you, but I'm fine. Mr. Dorian pays me very well," I added.

Christopher looked relieved. "Glad to hear it. When he mentioned his troubles, I immediately thought of you."

"And I am forever in your debt," I said with a smile, but he just waved me off.

"Is it something to do with Oliver, then?" he asked gently. "Have you had any more trouble from his brother?"

"Oh, no," I said and shook my head fiercely. "Nothing at all like that."

After my husband died, his eldest brother Harold—the current viscount—claimed that Tommy should be educated in England and threw around every bit of power his title commanded. He even threatened to travel to Corfu himself if I didn't willingly give up my son. It had been a terrible business, especially since I had never even met the viscount. Luckily, Oliver had had the foresight to draw up a new will with Christopher not long after we first settled on Corfu that made his wishes quite plain.

The viscount had no legal recourse, so the matter was settled. Unfortunately, he had only daughters, while their younger brother, Archibald, was a known libertine, so Tommy was, for all intents and purposes, the heir. I still held out hope that Harold would manage to have a son and take some of the pressure off Tommy, but so far, my prayers had gone unheeded. The viscount was permitted to write to Tommy and had generously set up a trust for his university education, but that was all I allowed.

I let out a breath. "I'm sure Florence told you that Mr. Dorian and I are investigating Daphne's murder."

He gave me a diplomatic nod. "She did mention it, yes."

No doubt there was quite a lot more she had said on the subject, but Christopher was a loyal spouse. It was a quality I greatly admired in him, especially since Florence could be difficult.

"And I understand Mr. Dorian himself spoke with you yesterday?"

Again, he nodded. "I told him my whereabouts the night before she was"—he caught himself, and a pained look crossed his face—"until you found her," he amended.

"Right." I swallowed.

He is the kindest of men.

I recalled Daphne's look of genuine affection when she had spoken of Christopher, and I could personally attest to his gentle character as both an employer and a friend. It was not surprising then that he had difficulty speaking about what had happened to the poor girl.

"Did you see Daphne at all that evening?"

"No." He shook his head. "I got home at about seven, and Florence was already abed with a headache. I never saw her."

Seven. I leaned forward in my chair. "Did you know that Doctor Campbell established her time of death between five and eight p.m.?"

Christopher's eyebrows rose. "No, I didn't. But I'm not sure about the significance of that."

"Florence said she went to bed between six and seven, but if Daphne wasn't there when you got home, then we know she must have left not long before you returned. That only leaves about an hour at most from the time she left the house and the time she was killed."

"Minnie . . ."

I heard the wary note in his voice, but I couldn't stop. Not now. The pieces were coming together too quickly, and I didn't want anything to slip past me. "Which means she can't have gotten very far. So where was she going at that time? It would have been too far to come all the way here, unless she was intending to spend the night—" Christopher tsked, and I raised an eyebrow. "Well, you can't think she was going door to door selling her soaps at seven o'clock in the evening," I said boldly.

He slumped in his chair. "All right. You have a point," he relented, now looking every bit his age.

"I'm sorry," I said. "You were fond of her, I take it?"

He glanced at me, distracted. "What? Oh, yes. I was, rather. She reminded me a bit of Celeste, our youngest. Florence butted heads with her from time to time, but that was nothing unusual." Then Christopher paused as he considered something. "Though to be honest, I didn't think she would stay with us for very long."

I frowned. "Because of Florence?"

"No. She . . . she always seemed distracted. Like something else was taking up her time. Something bigger than soap anyway," he added with a knowing look.

"Something, or someone?"

Christopher exhaled. "I know what people have been saying about her. Thought it was a load of rubbish at first. But now, perhaps . . ."

"Perhaps all the details aren't correct," I suggested. "But the general sentiment is. And there aren't many places she could have been going to that night." I was growing more and more certain that Mr. Dorian's villa had been her destination. It was closest to the Belvederes and would have been easy for her to slip away from and return home—though it remained to be seen if she had ever made it there in the first place.

"I suppose that's true," Christopher murmured, before giving himself a shake. "Minnie, I understand your concerns about the police, really I do. But you must leave them to it." As I began to protest, he held up a hand. "Florence and I are dedicated to finding Daphne's killer. I believe she even wrote as much to the girl's poor aunt."

"But—"

"I will speak to the chief investigator as soon as I can and tell him your thoughts," he promised. "Will that help?"

I held his gaze for a moment before nodding reluctantly. "Yes."

"All I ask in return is that you promise not to interfere."

"I'm only asking questions, Christopher," I demurred. "I hardly think that counts as interfering."

"Perhaps you are only asking questions, but I'm not so sure about your companion," he said ominously. "I'm rather worried that Mr. Dorian may be using this incident as fodder for a future novel."

"What?" Though I suspected the man's interest in this case was more personal than he let on, that seemed a stretch—not to mention remarkably tasteless. "He's already written nearly a dozen novels. I hardly think he needs to use *this* murder for inspiration."

But Christopher only shrugged. "I don't know about that. Florence says his first book was practically autobiographical. Did you know his father was a detective chief inspector at one point? Until the poor fellow drank himself to death," he added before I even managed to respond. Though I knew better than to take Florence at her word, this was shocking. And so very sad. It also explained Mr. Dorian's reluctance to speak of his past. I certainly couldn't blame him for that.

"All I'm saying," Christopher continued, "is that it sounds like he's been spending an awful lot of time investigating instead of working on his book."

"He *is* working on it," I said, rather indignant on Mr. Dorian's behalf. "I've seen the pages myself."

But Christopher didn't look convinced. "Well, I heard that he lost a great deal of money in his divorce. If anyone needs a successful book, it is him. And you have to admit that this is just the kind of story audiences gobble up."

"I wouldn't know," I sniffed.

"It's certainly not *Clarissa* or *Pride and Prejudice*, I'll grant you that," Christopher said with a smile.

"For heaven's sake," I grumbled, "I do read other things."

"I know, I know," he said. "But I couldn't miss the chance to tease you a little. You are our resident bluestocking, after all."

I smiled and rolled my eyes, then gave him a considering look. "Do you know anything else about Mr. Dorian? Anything that isn't based on gossip, I mean."

Christopher shook his head. "He's as tight-lipped as a clam, that one. Though he did mention that he's a member of Bedivere's. It's a club," he added in response to my blank stare. I knew nothing of London's private gentlemen's clubs, other than the names of infamous establishments like White's and Boodle's. Then Christopher brightened. "Your brother Jack is also a member there, I believe."

"Is he now?" I responded in a flat tone. If that was the case, it must be very exclusive and even more expensive. For Jack valued nothing more than having a sense of superiority to wield over others—even if he had to pay dearly for it. I admit that it did not make me think any better of Mr. Dorian, though now I wondered if he knew my brother.

"He may not have been born a gentleman," Christopher said magnanimously, "but he has done well for himself."

"Even though he might be in terrible debt now," I replied with a wry look.

"Well, he certainly would not be the first man to find himself in such a position." Christopher nodded sagely. "And I am sure he has the wits to change his fortune. After all, he's done it once already."

"That is true."

"And they say the first million is the hardest," he added with a chuckle, but I didn't miss the despair that flashed in his eyes. Perhaps it wasn't only restlessness that kept Christopher at his desk.

I stayed a few minutes more before I took my leave. As I found my way back to Maurice, I thought over everything we had discussed. Though I still didn't think Mr. Dorian was participating in this investigation merely to find inspiration for his book, Christopher had presented an intriguing new angle of exploration—as well as a possible motive. For I couldn't deny that if Mr. Dorian really was in need of money, a pregnant paramour could be a complication he didn't need.

Chapter 14

The next day, I arrived at the villa promptly at nine a.m. and again found the study empty, aside from a new stack of notebooks. I bit back my disappointment and sat down to work. I had gotten through one pot of tea and half the stack when Mr. Dorian made an appearance, though I was so absorbed in my typing that he had to clear his throat before I took notice.

I tore my eyes from the page and found him standing on the other side of the desk. His hair was damp from a bath, and he wore a pair of loose grey trousers with his shirt undone at the throat and the sleeves rolled up. By this time, I had grown used to his informal state of dress—mostly.

"Good morning," I rasped, taking care not to let my gaze linger on his exposed forearms.

"It's nearly noon," he replied, before cocking one eyebrow. "I suppose I should be flattered?"

I sat back in the chair and blinked until I realized he was referring to his book. "Oh. Yes." That I could admit to. Easily. The morning had flown by thanks to the pages. "It's quite good."

The corner of his mouth curved up as he took the seat on the other side of the desk. "I'll take it. If we keep this pace, I'll be finished before my deadline. Well," he amended, "my extended deadline."

"You should be very proud. And I'm sure Mr. Howard will be pleased," I added, in the same gently encouraging tone I used with the children.

He huffed a laugh and leaned back in his chair. "After everything I've put him through the last year, he'll simply be glad it's done."

I very much wanted to know what he was alluding to, but then Mr. Dorian fixed me with a look, and for one ridiculous moment, I thought he would apologize for his absence yesterday.

"So then," he began. "did you learn anything of interest from the doctor?"

"Oh. Yes," I said, trying not to sound disappointed. "I did, rather." Then I repeated the two most important pieces of information: the time frame during which the murder had occurred and that there was no sign of a struggle, which Doctor Campbell found strange. However, I declined to mention my visit to Christopher, as while I had learned some things of interest, I couldn't possibly share them with Mr. Dorian.

"Hmm. When I spoke to Belvedere, he said he returned home at about seven o'clock and that he didn't see Daphne, though that wasn't unusual. But I think it is safe to assume that she had left the house by that point."

I already knew this, of course, but nodded as if I were considering new information.

"If she was then dead by eight, or earlier, she couldn't have gotten very far. And there aren't many places in the area she could have gone to," I added, watching him closely.

But Mr. Dorian only shrugged. "I suppose not. She could

have arranged to meet someone, though. Perhaps close to where you found her."

"Yes," I allowed. "However, don't you think it's more likely she went to someone's house?"

He looked directly at me then, and my breath caught. Had my question been too obvious? "Why does it have to be a house?"

"I . . . well," I began, blushing furiously, "where else would they—"

Mr. Dorian let out an impatient sigh. "If you're trying to suggest she went to meet a lover," he drawled, "do keep in mind that plenty of assignations take place outside."

Well, he had me there.

I glanced away. I was hardly some innocent virgin, but the very last thing I wanted to do was admit something personal merely to prove my experience to this man.

"Remember, Mrs. Harper," Mr. Dorian continued, as if he hadn't just been speaking of fornicating *en plein air*. "We cannot assume. Only theorize."

I raised an eyebrow, my embarrassment forgotten for the moment. "Are you . . . quoting yourself?"

"I am quoting Inspector Dumond," he corrected. "And it's good advice."

I let out a rather indelicate snort. "Very well. Florence estimated that she went to bed between six and seven, while Christopher stated that when he returned home around seven, Daphne wasn't there—"

"No," Mr. Dorian gently interrupted. "He said he didn't *see* her. She could still have been in the house."

I pursed my lips and tried again. "All right. Perhaps she was still in the house, but I am *theorizing* that she left the Belvederes' home around six-thirty or so and walked to someone else's home. And if that was indeed the case, there aren't many places she could have reached before she died."

"She could have been accosted en route," he interjected. "Or she arrived at her destination only to be killed immediately. Remember the crime scene. Her body was rolled down that hill."

A shiver crawled down my spine at the thought. "Yes."

Mr. Dorian pinched the bridge of his nose and let out a sigh. "This is impossible. There is still far too much we don't know about Daphne. About her motivations—and what the hell she was *doing* that night." I bit back the instinct to reprimand him for language while he shook his head. "If we are to have any hope of solving this case, we must visit Paxos."

I blinked, thrown by the subject change. "Excuse me?"

"To speak with Miss Costas's aunt," he said with a touch of impatience. "We *should* speak to her, don't you think?"

"Yes. I do, but we would need to hire a boat for that," I said dumbly, for we very well weren't going to take the donkey cart there.

"Only for the day. Perhaps we can talk with this mysterious former suitor as well. The fisherman." Then he slanted me a glance. "I'll pay for it, if that's what you're worried about."

"No. Well—yes, that is certainly part of it. But . . ." I hesitated as Doctor Campbell's warning and Christopher's assertions echoed in my head. Spending time with Mr. Dorian in his home with Mrs. Nasso near was one thing, but could we really go to Paxos together if I actually suspected him of murder?

Mr. Dorian's gaze suddenly sharpened as if he had heard my thoughts. "Not to worry. We will be the picture of discretion, so as not to offend the Florence Belvederes of the world. Yes, she gave me a good dressing-down," he added, misinterpreting my look of confusion. I hadn't even been thinking of Florence. "Said you were a respectable widow and I shouldn't lead you on."

At that my mouth dropped open. "She said that to you?"

"That woman has absolutely no qualms about sticking her nose where it doesn't belong, and I told her as much," he said, looking quite pleased with himself. "I also assured her you were far too intelligent to fall for my pathetic attempts at seduction."

I pointedly ignored that comment. "When . . . when did this happen?"

"Two nights ago. I met Mr. Belvedere on my way home from yours, and he invited me in for a drink. Mrs. Belvedere then pulled me aside when her husband stepped out of the room."

I began to massage my temples. "If you said all that to Florence, she will have told half the island by now."

And if anyone then saw us traveling to Paxos together, it would be hard to stop the rumor mill.

Mr. Dorian crossed his legs. "I think not, as I reminded her that it is your reputation that is most at risk from gossip. That seemed to shut her up." Then he let out a sigh. "I had no idea this island would be like living in a fishbowl, the way you all carry on. Honestly, it's worse than London."

"Yes, I can see that," I said with a grimace.

He looked at me intently. "No wonder you keep so much to yourself."

I made a noncommittal noise of agreement, but that wasn't really the truth. At least, not since the murder. For I had been listening to a great deal of gossip lately. And let it influence me far too much. But that wasn't fair to Mr. Dorian or to Daphne, for that matter. At the very least, I owed it to her to seek out the truth. Perhaps that did involve Mr. Dorian, but perhaps it did not. At the moment, I had no real evidence. And I wouldn't find out anything more if I stayed on Corfu.

He tilted his head. "I suppose I could always make the trip without you—"

"*No.*" The word seemed to vibrate off the walls and Mr. Dorian raised an eyebrow. "That is, I would like to go," I amended calmly.

"Good," he said with a self-satisfied little smile that was, admittedly, rather charming. "I will head down to the harbor today and make arrangements. Shall we say in two days' time?"

I gave a halting nod. "That should be fine."

"Excellent."

Mr. Dorian then stood, and as he moved towards the door, I recalled something that had occurred to me last night just as I drifted off to sleep. Something that had nothing to do with rumor but my own intuition.

"Wait a moment," I called out, and he looked back. "I've been meaning to ask: how did you know where Daphne's room was?"

"I didn't. I looked in three other rooms first." Then he narrowed his eyes. "Why?"

"What was it like?" I asked instead. "Her room, I mean."

He turned fully to me then and considered the question. "Plain. Small. Not much in it besides a bed, a wardrobe, and a washstand."

"Where was the letter?"

He kept his gaze on me as he stepped closer and I resisted the urge to move back. "The wardrobe. I found a small wooden box in there filled with a few other trinkets. Nothing worth noting," he added before I could ask. Then he placed his palms on the desk and leaned towards me. "Why, Mrs. Harper, are you growing suspicious of me?"

My heart skittered a beat. "I'm only asking questions," I said carefully.

Mr. Dorian stared at me for a moment before he straightened and let out a *hmm*, though he hardly looked convinced.

"I was just curious," I added, trying not to squirm under

his assessing gaze. "I find that a person's bedroom can offer a window into their private life."

That was, at least, the truth.

"It can," he said with a sage nod. "But I didn't notice anything else of interest. She was a servant in the house. And a poor one at that," he added softly. Something flickered in his gaze then, and I was gripped by a sudden remorse. For my questions *had* been driven by suspicion.

"I'm sorry," I said. "I didn't mean to suggest—"

"I know. Good afternoon, Mrs. Harper." Then he turned on his heel and strode out of the room.

But I couldn't shake the feeling that both of us were only trying to save face.

I did not see Mr. Dorian for the next two days, though we communicated through short notes, solely about the book, that he left on his desk. Though my first instinct was to assume once again that he was avoiding me, I pushed the thought aside. He was making extraordinary progress on the book, and it was far more likely that he simply needed seclusion.

But on the third day, the note on top of the usual pile of notebooks didn't contain any authorial directions:

Meet at the port tomorrow. 9 a.m.

I inhaled sharply. It wasn't that I had forgotten about the plan to go to Paxos, but I assumed—or, perhaps, hoped—that Mr. Dorian had become too consumed with the book to follow up. A ridiculous assumption, I know. But at that time, I still hadn't learned the extent to which this man could deftly juggle entire worlds in his head. Planning a little excursion while writing a novel and investigating a murder was nothing for him.

When I returned home that day, I asked Mrs. Kouris to stay over the following night, in case we were unexpectedly delayed on the island. Of course, she immediately asked why, and although I already had an answer prepared, I couldn't shake my sense of unease. For if I wasn't honest with her, then Mr. Dorian would be the only person who knew my true whereabouts. Should something happen, even something entirely innocent like a weather delay, I didn't like the idea of her not knowing the truth.

"I am traveling to Paxos with Mr. Dorian to speak with Miss Costas's aunt. We only intend to stay for the day," I insisted, as if our intensions somehow lessened the potential for scandal. "But there is always the chance we may be delayed. For weather and such."

Unfortunately, admitting the truth did nothing to quell my unease. If anything, stating my plans aloud only made it impossible to ignore what I was actually about to do: travel alone with a man who was not a relative and barely qualified as a friend. A man whom I suspected, just a little, of murder. It was the most outrageous thing I had ever done—though I supposed there were plenty others who would have found my decision to leave England for Athens merely the beginning in a series of outrageous choices . . .

Mrs. Kouris let out a grunt. "I *knew* he did not find that letter."

"Yes, well." I cleared my throat. "I'm sure you won't need to spend the night. But just out of an abundance of caution—"

"I understand. It is no trouble," Mrs. Kouris said, even while her tone and bearing radiated disapproval.

I braced myself for her usual screed against Mr. Dorian and my involvement with him, but she only turned her back to me and continued to roll out phyllo.

Later, when I informed the children at dinner that I would be away all day and possibly into the night, working on Mr. Dorian's book, they greeted this news with barely a blink. Well, first, Cleo asked if I would go to London when the book was published. When I told her that was ridiculous and of course not, she only shrugged and went back to her plate. Tommy then asked if he could start a grub collection, for what he vaguely referred to as "research purposes." But he bore his disappointment with a resigned shrug and, like his sister, returned his attention to his food. Meanwhile, feeling horribly guilty for both lying to my children and leaving them overnight, I let them each have two pieces of *milopita*, or apple cake, after dinner.

I then spent most of the night tossing and turning against the doubts filling my mind. It seemed that I had only just drifted off to sleep when it was time to wake up. I dragged myself from my bed, washed and dressed in my beige traveling ensemble, and then packed a small valise of necessities—again, only out of an abundance of caution. When I asked for a second cup of coffee, Mrs. Kouris wordlessly handed me one she had just finished preparing with a disapproving look. Apparently, the dark circles under my eyes gave me away.

The children didn't have school that day, but Cleo wished to visit Juliet, so I asked her to take me into town first, claiming I needed to pick up some stationery for Mr. Dorian. For once, I was grateful for her self-centeredness, as Cleo didn't bother to inquire why I needed to perform this task, how I would get to Mr. Dorian's villa afterwards, nor why I was carrying my smallest valise.

As we rode into town, I listened to her seemingly endless chatter about her classmates and, occasionally, their parents. We had just reached the outskirts when an unsettling thought occurred to me.

"Darling, do you ever hear anything about Mr. Dorian?" I asked the question as lightly as I could manage, but Cleo still stiffened.

"Not really, no," she said hastily and glanced away.

In matters like these, I found it was most effective to keep quiet and let the other party fill the silence. When she finally looked at me again, I tilted my head in question, and she let out a breath.

"Sometimes," she admitted and bit her lip.

Then I raised an eyebrow. "Juliet has newspaper clippings about his divorce," she said in a great rush. "Her cousin sent them to her. They even have pictures of his wife."

Hopefully, no one would ever have to depend on Cleo to keep a secret.

"Good lord," I murmured. Whatever I had been imagining, it most certainly wasn't that.

"She looked very beautiful. Glamorous, even," Cleo continued breathlessly, as if this were a confessional and she was relieving herself of a great moral burden. "And they printed all sorts of things about the two of them in the papers. That he was a drunkard who only married her for her money. And when she found out, she refused to have his child. But actually she was in love with another man the whole time, and they ran away to France to be together, and then—"

"Cleo, that is enough," I said sharply. "Mr. Dorian's divorce was sensationalized to sell papers."

But I didn't know that. Not really. And if the papers had been bold enough to print their full names, those details likely came from the court proceedings. Still, it was a horrible invasion of privacy. That was indisputable.

"He is my employer," I continued. "He has been a guest in our home. And I have certainly never seen anything to suggest that any of that is true."

But as I said the words, images of Mr. Dorian in his dressing gown, looking like he hadn't slept in weeks, flashed through my mind. Along with his bitter words after dinner the other evening.

Why? Because your spouse died and mine simply decided life with me was intolerable?

Possibly intolerable enough to abscond to France with

another man. I shifted in my seat, uncomfortably aware that this new information didn't exactly help quell my suspicions. Still, I was determined to remain impartial. And "intolerable" could simply be a matter of opinion. I let out a sigh and wished there was a way to ask the man about it all directly without feeling like a horrible gossip myself.

Beside me, Cleo hung her head. At least she had the decency to look embarrassed. "I know."

"Just . . . promise me you won't listen to any more rubbish about him. Or repeat it."

"I promise," she said dutifully. It had been a good while since she'd agreed to anything so readily. I only wished it had been under different circumstances. For the more people gossiped about Mr. Dorian, the more my own association with him would be questioned. And as much as I hated to admit it, perhaps Florence had a point.

Cleo dropped me by the stretch of shops near the stationer's store, but once she was off, I pulled down the gauzy veil attached to my traveling hat, ducked down another street, and headed for the port, all the while praying I wouldn't cross paths with anyone I knew. Luckily, it was still early for most of the British inhabitants, and I saw no familiar faces as I hurried towards the water.

I spotted Mr. Dorian immediately, as he stood out in his grey linen suit against the assortment of fishermen already returned from an early morning at sea and haggling with various merchants, and a rush of excitement swept through me. As I approached, he gave me a subtle nod and gestured for me to follow. He then turned and headed away from the crowd. I followed a few steps behind, but I'm sure it was clear to anyone who took notice that we were together. Still, I appreciated this effort at discretion.

A man with weather-beaten olive skin and a thick black beard waited for us on the dock by a small fishing boat, known as a caïque. The boat looked even more worse for wear than its owner, and my chest tightened with apprehension. Mr. Dorian shook his hand and then extended an arm towards me.

"Spiro, this is my companion," he explained in mangled Greek, hesitating before he said the last word.

I pursed my lips at this description. Not exactly subtle. "Thank you for taking us to the island today," I said to Spiro.

He nodded and gave me a broad, gap-toothed smile. "It is a fine day to sail."

"Yes, I do hope so." I smiled back before remembering that he could barely see my face through the veil.

The man nodded again and climbed onto the boat. Meanwhile, Mr. Dorian was frowning beside me, but said nothing as he helped me aboard.

I took a seat near the bow and stared out at the water. It was indeed a fine day. The sky was a clear, brilliant blue, and the sea was calm.

"Is everything all right?"

I glanced over as Mr. Dorian sat down beside me, and he gestured to my hands, which were tightly clasped on my lap. I hadn't even realized I was doing that and immediately released them, but he let out a huff and looked away.

"You never mentioned an aversion to sailing," he grumbled.

"I don't make a habit of it," I admitted. "But when I do, it's usually not on a boat that looks like it played a role in the siege of Troy."

Mr. Dorian rolled his eyes. "We'll be fine. Spiro is very well-respected by his peers, and his boat is supposed to be the fastest in the Ionian Sea."

"According to whom? Spiro himself?" I made the comment in jest, but when his jaw tightened in response, I let out a hum of disapproval. Then something else occurred to me. "Does he know the purpose of our journey?"

"Of course not," Mr. Dorian said, looking offended.

I narrowed my eyes. "Then why does he think we are going to the island?"

Mr. Dorian slanted his gaze away from mine. "I told him we have an interest in mythology . . . and wanted to see Poseidon's love nest."

"You did not!" I hissed.

According to legend, Poseidon had split Corfu with his trident to create the island of Paxos to enjoy with his wife, Amphitrite—as well as a number of lovers.

Mr. Dorian shrugged off my outrage. "Well, he had no trouble believing me and didn't ask any questions," he insisted. "Apparently, we are not the first English people to make the request."

"Do try to pick something less salacious next time," I said primly.

But Mr. Dorian didn't appear to pick up on my sarcasm. "Noted," he replied, looking far too pleased with himself.

I scoffed and faced the sea. As Spiro maneuvered the boat towards open waters, I was determined not to spend the next two hours looking at Mr. Dorian's grin.

Chapter 15

Despite my resolve, I spent most of the journey with my face over the side of the boat as my stomach did not care how fine a day it was for sailing. Mr. Dorian did not gloat, but instead gently patted my back while I groaned my thanks. By the time we arrived in Lakka, the small fishing village where Daphne grew up, the worst appeared to be over—though that was likely because there was nothing left inside me to cast up.

Once Spiro docked the boat, Mr. Dorian insisted that I have something to eat before we did anything else, and I was too weak to argue with him. Spiro directed us to a café not far away and said he would wait for us in the local tavern until it was time to depart. I was then forced to lean heavily against Mr. Dorian for support, which did little for my pride. I only hoped he would not lord this incident over me too much in the future.

Paxos was known for its outstanding natural beauty, which was perhaps why Poseidon had made it his love nest in the first place, but I confess I was not able to take in much of my surroundings, apart from what was directly in front of me. From what I could tell, Lakka looked like any other sleepy fishing village in this part of the world. There was a collection of buildings gathered all along the harbor, while a gentle hill covered in cypress and olive trees rose behind it.

Our destination stood at the end of this collection of buildings, a freestanding structure painted a faded yellow that glowed in the late-morning sun. The proprietor easily spotted us hobbling up the road and greeted us at the door. "Kalimera," he began in heavily accented English. "Welcome to Estiatório Tou Déntrou. I am Mr. Karahalios and am very happy for you to—"

"A table for me and my wife," Mr. Dorian interrupted. Then he shot me a glare as I elbowed him for being so rude and addressed the proprietor once again. "If you please."

Luckily, the man seemed unaffected by his behavior as he quickly ushered us inside and down a short hallway.

"The Restaurant of the Tree," I murmured, translating while we lagged behind. "Odd name."

Mr. Dorian let out an exasperated huff. "That's what you're thinking of right now? I'd have thought you'd be asking for a priest."

"Nonsense," I replied, though failing to mask the weakness in my voice. "No one ever died from a little seasickness."

Mr. Dorian merely grunted in response, and together we followed the man through a doorway and into a wide, open courtyard hidden from the street. It was filled with lush potted plants, while a giant purple bougainvillea wound its way around, yes, a large tree that grew right in the middle of the space. It was quite extraordinary, and I would have thoroughly enjoyed the sight if I hadn't been in such a state.

But my companion seemed entirely unmoved by our surroundings. "Give us bread and some of those little spinach pies." He uttered the swift command while helping me into a chair.

Mr. Karahalios gave us a blank look, and I let out a sigh before I wearily repeated the order in Greek, along with a pot of mountain tea. The man nodded and hurried off.

I tipped my head back to let the sun warm my face and slowly inhaled the fragrant air. Now that we were on solid ground, I was beginning to feel a bit better. After a few more breaths, I straightened and found Mr. Dorian watching me with another of his inscrutable looks.

"You really should learn more of the language," I said, suddenly feeling self-conscious. "Or at least speak more slowly."

He arched a brow. "I confess that, in the moment, I was more concerned with making sure you had some food."

"I do appreciate the effort," I said, not wanting him to think I was entirely ungrateful.

"You're right, though." Then he sighed and looked away. "I have never had much of an ear for languages, even under the best of circumstances."

I frowned. "What do you mean?"

"Well, I wasn't exactly planning to come to Corfu, Mrs. Harper," he said flatly before meeting my eyes. "It was more of a . . . a last resort, you might say."

I thought of the vicious stories Cleo had repeated. Things that had been printed in the newspapers, for goodness' sake. Of course the man had fled. I certainly would have in his place.

Now it was my turn to look away. "I am sorry it came to that."

Mr. Dorian rightly huffed a laugh at my stilted attempt at sympathy. "It's fine. This trip has proved to be quite surprising, actually."

I glanced over at him then, but before I could probe that statement, Mr. Karahalios returned with my tea, a plate of brown bread still warm from the oven, and an assortment of savory pastries.

"I brought you some mastiha as well," he added and set down a small glass filled with golden liquid. "Good for the . . ." He hesitated and gestured to his stomach.

"Thank you," I said, managing a smile. "That is very kind." Then I took a sip and winced. It was both tart and incredibly sweet.

Mr. Karahalios gave me an encouraging nod, so I finished the rest in one long swallow.

"Bravo," he said. "You will be recovered very soon."

As the man walked away, Mr. Dorian shot me a skeptical look. "What on earth did he give you?"

"Mastiha syrup," I explained. "It is made from the resin of the mastic tree."

Mr. Dorian's frown deepened. "You mean to tell me you just voluntarily ingested tree sap?"

I chuckled a little at his incredulousness. "It is considered something of a miracle cure here. People use it for all kinds of ailments."

My stomach then let out a loud growl, and I was gripped with a sudden, ravenous hunger.

"Well," Mr. Dorian murmured in surprise. "Two cheers for the tree sap. Go on, then. Eat."

I chose a square of phyllo dough stuffed with cheese and took a bite. It was just as good as the ones Mrs. Kouris made, though I knew better than to ever admit it. As soon as I finished the pastry, I took up another, followed by a slice of bread. While I feasted, Mr. Dorian seemed content to sit back and observe.

"Your color is better," he said after I had eaten nearly half the plate's contents.

"I feel better," I replied and poured a cup of tea.

"We should move along then." Mr. Dorian signaled for the owner, who hurried over. "I told Spiro to take us back to Corfu at three."

That left only a few hours to track down Daphne's aunt

and speak with her—if she was even willing—as well as this mysterious fisherman.

I quickly downed the rest of my tea while Mr. Dorian settled the bill. When the owner came back with the change, I gave him a grateful smile.

"Everything was delicious," I said in Greek.

Mr. Karahalios beamed with pride. "My wife makes it all," he replied, gesturing towards the back of the restaurant, which must have led to the kitchen.

"Please give her my compliments. But before you go, I was hoping you could help us."

He tilted his head. "Of course."

"We are looking for someone. I'm not sure of her name, but her niece Daphne Costas was working on Corfu," I added, but the man had stilled as soon as I mentioned Daphne.

"Ah, you mean Sophia," Mr. Karahalios said, and the sadness in his eyes indicated that Florence's letter had reached her after all.

At least we would be spared from breaking the news.

"She lives on the top of the hill." He pointed north. "She is a laundry woman. You will see," he added with a sage nod.

"Thank you very much," I replied.

He gave me a warm smile and bowed a little. "You must come again," he said in stilted English.

"We will," Mr. Dorian said hurriedly. He was already out of his seat and extended his arm to me.

We exited the restaurant and headed towards the hill, which took us away from the village center. At this hour, the streets were mostly empty as people were at home, either eating their midday meal or sleeping off the hottest part of the day. Indeed, the bright sun beat down on us, and I pulled down my veil for extra protection.

"Well done," Mr. Dorian said after a moment. "Butter the man up first before asking for information."

"How do you know I was buttering him up?"

"Because of the way you smiled at him and your tone of voice. It was far nicer than the way you speak to me."

I scoffed, but Mr. Dorian grinned. I was starting to think he liked getting my hackles up.

"I told Mr. Karahelios the food was delicious, which was true," I insisted. Then I shot him a look. "But I probably would have said that regardless."

He chuckled. "I rather like this devious side of you, Mrs. Harper. It makes me feel less villainous."

"*Villainous.* What on earth are you talking about?"

"You know," he began, lazily waving his hand as he spoke. "The scandal-plagued man corrupting the innocent, upstanding widow. That sort of thing."

I very much wanted to point out that widows by their definition were hardly innocent, but kept that thought to myself. "It sounds like something out of one of your books," I huffed instead.

He let out a surprised laugh. "It does, rather. I should make a note of it, actually. It's hard coming up with interesting villains." Then he began patting his pockets and pulled out the small notebook and pencil I had seen him carry. As we walked, he scribbled something down, then put it back in his breast pocket.

"Is that how you get your ideas?" I asked. "From things people say?"

"On occasion." Mr. Dorian shrugged. "I might hear something that sparks an idea, but it's a bit like building a fire. I have to feed it before it can grow big enough to give off heat."

"Hmm. An interesting analogy." I hesitated before asking what I really wanted to know. "Have you ever been inspired by a real case?"

He turned to me sharply, with that dark gaze that seemed to miss nothing. "You think I'll write about this?"

"I have wondered."

Mr. Dorian looked back to the road. He was quiet for so long that I didn't think he would answer. "I based my first book on a real murder case that had gone unsolved," he began. "I suppose . . . I suppose I wanted to give the victim a kind of justice."

"Oh."

According to Christopher, Florence insisted the book was autobiographical. And from what I could recall, in that book the inspector investigates the murder of his first love—a woman he had known in childhood, but lost touch with as an adult. The pain of this lost love is one of the defining features of the character and colors how he approaches his investigations. It also explains why he remains a bachelor despite the appeal of both the duchess and Miss Linley.

Mr. Dorian's jaw tightened. "It was a silly idea. I haven't done it again. So, to answer your question, no. I will not be writing about this, Mrs. Harper."

"I didn't mean to pry," I said softly. My chest ached at the thought of Mr. Dorian, or anyone really, suffering that kind of loss—though it would certainly explain some things about the man beside me.

He glanced at me and smiled a little. "It was a fair question, and you're hardly the first to ask. People are always suggesting crimes to me, some of them much too grisly to mention in mixed company," he said with a shudder. "The public's capacity for blood and violence never ceases to amaze me."

In Mr. Dorian's books, the violence usually did not appear on the page, which was part of what I liked about them, but he was right. One only needed to peruse a London newsstand to see the range of sordid behavior on offer.

"However," he continued, "I will admit to finding inspiration in my life for other things, like characters and settings. Motivations. But it usually comes at the oddest moments."

"Interesting."

He raised an eyebrow. "Is it?"

"I like learning about your process," I said honestly. "And I really had no idea the great deal of work that went into writing a book. That sounds silly, I know. But seeing it firsthand has been . . . illuminating."

He grinned and shoved his hands into his trouser pockets, looking quite satisfied. "I think that might be the best compliment you've given me yet, Mrs. Harper."

"Does that count as a compliment?" I asked while raising a teasing eyebrow.

"From anyone else? No. From you? Absolutely."

I laughed at that, but then quickly sobered. After all, I harbored suspicions about this man and his own motives. Suspicions I could not yet dismiss. But Mr. Dorian made it easy to forget. Or perhaps . . . perhaps that was his intention, and here I was playing right into it.

The poor lonely widow easily manipulated with just a little male attention.

The thought sank through me like a stone, and I squared my shoulders, determined to be more careful moving forward. I could feel his questioning gaze upon me, but I resisted the urge to explain myself. To put him at ease. No. Let the man wonder. There is power in silence, I knew. And it was time to reclaim some.

We met a few people as we walked, along with a surly goat that bleated loudly as we passed. But as we reached the top of the incline, the houses grew more scattered until there was only one up ahead. The restauranteur had been right. The tiny stone house was surrounded by clotheslines filled with laundry hung out to dry under the warm, midday sun.

"This must be the place," Mr. Dorian murmured.

It was eerily quiet as we approached the house. The only sounds were the flapping of linens in the light breeze and the soft bleating of the goat down the hill.

"Do you think she's in?" Mr. Dorian asked.

"I certainly hope so," I said and moved faster. The front door was open, and I let out a sigh of relief. She couldn't be far, then. And there was still hope that this trip wouldn't be a waste.

"Yassou!" I called out as I carefully stepped through the maze of hanging linens.

A muffled reply came from inside, and an older woman appeared in the doorway. She was about Daphne's height and shared her dark hair color, aside from a streak of pure white at her temple. But it was her brown eyes that struck at my heart, for she had the same kind of listless gaze I recognized from those early months of widowhood.

Blackmail or not, this woman was clearly grieving her niece.

"Yassou," I repeated and continued in Greek. "Are you Daphne Costas's aunt?"

"Yes." Sophia narrowed her eyes. "Who is asking?" she said pointedly in English. I then recalled Daphne's words: *My mother and aunt worked on Corfu when they were young and made sure to teach me.*

How long ago that exchange felt.

I hesitated and glanced at Mr. Dorian. We hadn't discussed whether to keep up our pretense as a married couple, but since we expected, nay, *needed* some honest answers from this woman about her niece, it didn't feel right to lie. He gave me a subtle nod, and I turned back to her.

"I am Mrs. Harper, and this is Mr. Dorian," I replied in English, following her lead. "We knew Daphne on Corfu," I explained. "May we speak with you about her?"

Her expression began to soften, but then she caught herself. "I am very busy," she said and gestured to the laundry-filled yard.

"Of course. We only want a few minutes of your time."

She continued to frown at us for a moment, but then relented. "Fine." Then she cast a look around the still-empty yard and waved us inside. I had no doubt that plenty of eyes had seen us walking towards her house and that our presence would be a topic of conversation between her neighbors.

The house was blessedly cool and a comforting respite from the sun. As we entered, I cast a quick look around. It was quite small, but clean and well-kept. The entire house seemed to be made up of only three rooms: one main living space that contained the cooking area, along with a table and chairs and two doorways that I assumed led into bedrooms or storage. Sophia gestured for us to sit at the table, but Mr. Dorian opted to stand, since there were only two chairs. She put a kettle to boil over the hearth and produced some light brown biscuits.

"Thank you," I said and took one before offering the plate to Mr. Dorian.

He dutifully took one as well, and we ate while she prepared the tea.

"Your English is very good," I said in a bid to fill the silence. "Daphne said you and your sister learned it while working on Corfu?"

"No. My father was a schoolteacher in Gaios, and he taught us. If you know English, you find more work. That is the way on Corfu."

Sophia then went to fetch the kettle. I glanced at Mr. Dorian and tilted my head. It was his turn to coax more than a sentence from her.

"I don't believe I know your surname," he began.

She gave him a sharp look and held his gaze while she poured the water into the teapot. "I am also a Costas."

"I see," Mr. Dorian murmured.

Daphne had been illegitimate then. Possibly another reason why she had left Paxos.

"Yes," Sophia said wryly, as she placed the tea pot and cups on the table. "We did our best for her, her mother and I, but it is hard in a place like this. Everyone knows your business. And they never forget," she added as she met my eyes.

"I'm very sorry for your loss," I said. "I didn't know your niece well, but she seemed like a determined young woman."

Sophia's lips trembled, as if she were holding back some great emotion, but she mastered it and sat down. "Thank you. It has been a difficult time."

Behind me, Mr. Dorian cleared his throat, but I ignored him. We needed to gain this woman's trust before we accused her of blackmailing her niece. Besides, her pain seemed genuine to me. Something wasn't right here, and I needed to tread carefully.

"She once told me that her parents died when she was very young," I said.

Perhaps her father died before he and her mother had the chance to marry. It would hardly be the first time a woman found herself in such a precarious position.

Sophia's mouth tightened. "My sister died when Daphne was a child. Six or so."

"And the father?" Mr. Dorian prompted.

I shot him a glare over my shoulder, but when I turned back, Sophia had moved to stand. "I'm sorry you came all this way just to pay your respects to an old woman, but now you must be going."

"Miss Costas, we did not come here only for that," I said gently as a suspicion took hold. "Do you know how Daphne died?"

"Of course I do," she snapped. "Mrs. Belvedere said it was a fever. But it was quick and she had medicine, so at least she died without pain."

I wasn't terribly surprised Florence hadn't been truthful

about the grisly nature of Daphne's death, especially since the perpetrator was still at large. Sophia spoke with such urgency that it was clear she needed to believe this lie. And who was I to deprive her of a source of solace?

But Mr. Dorian had no such qualms. "No," he said calmly. "I'm afraid she was murdered. It was Mrs. Harper who found her. I am sorry to say that the police have been useless, so now we are trying to find her killer."

I winced at his matter-of-fact tone as Sophia brought a trembling hand to her brow. "Excuse me," she said and hurried from the room.

I shot a glare at Mr. Dorian. "What is the matter with you?"

But he didn't seem to hear me as he stared at the doorway Sophia had gone through. "She didn't look very surprised." Then he turned to me. "Did you notice that?"

I let out a huff and rose from my chair. "Wait here."

I approached the room and gently knocked on the door, which Sophia hadn't bothered to close. She was sitting on a small bed against the wall and looked up. Perhaps she wasn't surprised, but she did look incredibly sad.

"May I come in?"

She gave a weak nod. "This was Daphne's room."

Like the rest of the house, it was small but well-kept. Curtains embroidered with brightly colored flowers hung from the lone window, while a matching quilt covered the bed. My heart clenched as I noticed the worn doll in Sophia's hands.

Regardless of whatever had happened between them, Sophia had kept her niece's room ready for her return. And now that day would never come.

Sophia moved over and patted the space beside her.

"I'm very sorry," I said once more as I sat down, though it sounded even less adequate now.

"I suppose I knew it could not have been as simple as

that," Sophia said thickly, "but I had hoped she hadn't suffered . . ." As her voice broke, I handed her a handkerchief, which she used to dab her eyes.

"What do you mean?" I asked, recalling Daphne's words about her aunt.

She did not want me to come here.

"Did . . . did you think Daphne was in danger?"

Sophia looked at me carefully, and I could tell she was deciding whether or not to be truthful with me. "She did not tell you about her father?" she finally asked.

"Only that he died," I said, and she sighed a little. Mr. Dorian had appeared in the doorway by then, but Sophia didn't seem to mind his presence.

"After my mother died, my sister and I both went to Corfu to find work. Our father did not take our mother's death well, and it was better to be away from him. He drank, you see," she added, giving me a significant look before continuing on. "We were about Daphne's age then. Younger, even. We were both hired by different English households. But Maria was the pretty one, so she was an upstairs maid, while I was in the kitchen of another."

As she spoke, her mouth curved in another small smile. I sensed that there hadn't been a competition between the sisters, but rather a genuine friendship, and my heart ached for what she had lost—along with a twinge of envy for what I lacked. If I were to pass on, my own sister would not speak of me with such fondness. We had been frequent adversaries as children and were little more than strangers now.

"Maria and I always made sure to meet up on our half days. Then, one day, things suddenly changed. I wouldn't see her for weeks at a time, and she never explained her absences. I could tell she was hiding something. Then one day she told me she was with child. By the master of the house."

"Oh goodness," I breathed, and Mr. Dorian muttered a curse.

Sophia shook her head. "As soon as she told me the truth, I knew what would happen to her—to us—but poor Maria had somehow convinced herself that he would divorce his wife and marry her." She let out a dark laugh. "So I took on all the extra work I could find until . . ."

Mr. Dorian leaned forward. "Until what? What happened?"

Sophia shrugged. "What else? She was dismissed by the housekeeper as soon as she began to show."

"But what of the man?" Mr. Dorian barked. "The father?"

Sophia met his genuine outrage with a sanguine look. "She appealed to him, but he would admit nothing and even questioned whether the child could truly be his." I sucked in a breath at this appalling behavior, but Sophia was not done. "In the end, he gave her some money and jewelry and sent her on her way. Our father had died by then, but Maria would not return to Gaios, so instead she came here to Lakka, where no one knew her. She told people she was a widow, but they suspected the truth anyway. It is a common-enough story," she said with a shrug. "I came back to help with Daphne's birth, and then we started the laundry together. I haven't left since." Sophia then paused for a moment, as if she were gathering strength to relay the rest. "Maria was never the same afterwards. She never truly recovered from her heartache. And poor Daphne was a constant reminder of the man she had lost. With each year, she grew more frail until finally, she . . . gave up."

Sophia blinked as unshed tears shimmered in her brown eyes, and my nose began to sting.

"That must have been such a difficult time for you and Daphne," I said hoarsely, appalled by how much loss they had both endured, only for Daphne to then lose her own life in such a violent manner. It only strengthened my resolve to find the culprit and see that they paid for their crime.

"What was the man's name?"

Sophia balked a little at Mr. Dorian's sharp question.

"What does it matter? He has been dead for many years now. Maria never spoke of him, and she promised me never to tell Daphne the truth."

"But you broke that promise," I said with sudden understanding. "Or at least, partly."

She turned to me then, and guilt flashed in her eyes.

"You told Daphne about her father," I continued. "That was the secret. That was why you disapproved of her going to Corfu. You knew she would look for him."

Sophia gaped at both of us. "I— "

"The name," Mr. Dorian urged. "Or are you hiding something else as well?"

"No, I am not," she insisted and shot him a glare. "It was something like Granville or Granthem. Your English names all sound the same to me." Sophia threw up her hands in frustration, then softened. "Though it is true I did not want her to go to Corfu because I knew she would look for her past. We argued about that often. I told her to focus on the future, but it is easy for me to say that, isn't it? I always knew who I was and where I came from. It was never the same for her, though, especially as she grew older. I thought if I told her a little, that would help. But she only wanted to know more and more, until there was nothing left for me to tell. So she went to find answers."

"Even though her father was likely dead?" I asked.

"He had children from his wife, though they were much older than Daphne. She thought that if they knew the truth, there was a possibility they might . . ." She tilted her head side to side.

"Welcome her into the fold," I supplied.

Sophia nodded. "I told her that was very unlikely. And that she was probably not his only illegitimate child."

I winced at this uncomfortable truth. "Do you know if she ever found him?"

"No. But, as I said, her story is hardly unusual, and not many people would remember a maid who worked on Corfu for a few months twenty years ago. Maria did not confide in anyone aside from me."

"You are certain of that?" Mr. Dorian asked.

"As certain as I can be," she answered crossly before addressing me. "I had hoped Daphne had given up the search once she found her position with Mrs. Belvedere. I understand she is a very respectable woman. And Daphne would have learned much from working in such a household."

"Yes," I answered diplomatically, even as I recalled Florence's litany of complaints against the girl. "And Daphne seemed quite industrious herself." That was, at least, the truth.

Sophia smiled a little. "Her soaps, yes. She was very proud of them. She wanted to open a shop of her own."

I returned her smile. "A fine idea."

"You hoped," Mr. Dorian interrupted. "Or you knew she had given up the search?"

Sophia shifted in her seat. "In her last letter, she admitted to asking questions of the older workers she met, but no one remembered her mother. So I suppose I *hoped* she had given up, though I knew how stubborn she could be."

He then leaned forward with a strange gleam in his eye. "What else were you hiding from your niece, Miss Costas?"

"Mr. Dorian!" I cried out, horrified by his behavior, but he continued lobbing accusations at the poor woman.

"Is that why you resorted to blackmailing her? To stop her from poking into the past?"

Sophia looked genuinely affronted. "I did no such thing."

He whipped the letter out from his breast pocket. "Then explain this." I rolled my eyes at his dramatics. The man appeared to be acting out a scene from one of his novels.

"It's a letter from you to Daphne that Mr. Dorian found

after her death. In it, you mention disapproving of something and allude to a secret—though we know what that is now," I added tightly as I shot Mr. Dorian a scolding look.

But he merely lifted his chin in defiance. "You also demanded money in exchange for keeping said secret."

"No," Sophia said, with far more grace than I would have under the circumstances. She snatched the letter from him and quickly scanned it before she jabbed her finger at a line of text. "I *warned* her against continuing to ask about her mother because we did not know what the family would do if she confronted them with the truth. That they *might* assume she would want money to keep quiet. You need to work on your Greek," she added with a narrow look.

Mr. Dorian stared at her for a long moment. "Oh," he said mildly before raising an eyebrow at me. "Then it appears our translator erred."

I held up my hands. "You're the one who didn't want to ask Mr. Papadopoulos."

Mr. Dorian muttered something under his breath that I couldn't make out. "Please accept my deepest apologies, Miss Costas."

"Thank you," she said, though continued to eye him suspiciously. "I am grateful for your concern."

"Is there anyone you can think of who would have wanted to harm Daphne?" I asked after a moment, hoping to steer the subject away from any more unsavory accusations.

"Not here on Paxos," Sophia said firmly. "Her killer is on Corfu. I am certain."

"Does she have any friends in the village?" I asked. "Someone else she may have confided in?"

This seemed like a better approach than directly inquiring about a suitor.

Sophia hesitated and bit her lip. "Well, there is Milo. But I don't think they spoke after she left."

"Is that the former fiancé?"

I closed my eyes at Mr. Dorian's utter lack of tact. We really should have discussed our questions beforehand.

"They were *friends*," Sophia protested with more force than necessary. "Never more than that."

Mr. Dorian shot me a skeptical look that I ignored. "Where can we find this friend, then?"

"The harbor. He is a fisherman, of course."

"And you think he will speak with us?" I asked.

Her countenance darkened. "If Daphne was murdered, Milo will want justice for her as much as I do."

I shivered a little at the quiet fury in her eyes, though it was entirely understandable.

Before I could reassure her, Mr. Dorian gave a short bow. "We will do whatever we can, Miss Costas," he said with real feeling.

Their earlier contention appeared entirely forgotten as she gave him a genuine smile. "Thank you."

Mr. Dorian held out his arm for me, and I stood.

"I will write to you as soon as I have any new information," I promised. But as we headed for the door, I turned back. "One last thing. Did Daphne have a gold necklace?"

Sophia laughed and shook her head. "No. My sister eventually sold everything she had been given. We could not afford to keep such luxuries."

I blushed a little and flexed my left hand, uncomfortably aware of the simple gold band on my ring finger. "Of course. Thank you again, Miss Costas."

Mr. Dorian said his good-byes as well, and together we stepped back out into the yard.

I donned my hat and pulled down the veil to shield my face against the hot mid-afternoon sun, while Mr. Dorian pulled down the brim of his hat. We walked a little way back down the hill, each of us lost in thought, before Mr. Dorian broke the silence.

"So, then, do you think she's lying?"

I turned to him, aghast. "About what?"

He shrugged. "All of it."

I shook my head. "Are you really that cynical?"

"Skeptical. The word is skeptical, Mrs. Harper," he said with that maddening smirk. "And, yes, I am."

"I believed everything she said," I admitted, then blew out a breath. I felt hopelessly naïve once again.

"There, there," he replied, though his tone was more chiding than comforting. "In time, you will learn to question everything and everyone, which is not to say that Miss Costas was lying. But rather that— "

"We need to make sure," I finished.

He nodded in approval. "Exactly. And I think this Milo person is just the chap to help us with that. Come now," he said as he moved faster down the hill. "We don't want to keep Spiro waiting."

Chapter 16

When we arrived at the harbor a short time later, I was nearly out of breath from trying to keep up with Mr. Dorian. But if he noticed my agitated state, he refrained from making a comment—and certainly didn't bother to slow down. The first group of fishermen we asked knew of Milo and pointed towards the other side of the harbor.

I sighed inwardly as Mr. Dorian charged ahead and then scurried after him. A young man was tying up a small fishing boat that made Spiro's look like a yacht in comparison, while a much older man shouted criticisms at him from the boat's deck.

The younger man, who I assumed was Milo, said nothing as a litany of complaints was lobbed at his back. Everything from his work ethic to the manner in which he held the rope was critiqued until the older man caught sight of us approaching and abruptly stopped. But I could see that the words still had an effect. Milo's face was twisted in the kind of surly glare I was quite familiar with, as Cleo had mastered it over the last year, though all his focus was directed on knotting the heavy rope in his hands.

"Kalispera," I said to the older man before explaining who we were looking for.

"There he is," he answered in Greek as he pointed at Milo. "My worthless grandson."

Milo let out a heavy sigh and rose. As he pulled off his cap, I bit back a gasp. Milo was, well, beautiful. No other word could adequately describe him. He looked very much like an Ancient Greek statue brought to life, with broad shoulders, slender hips, and a thick head of tousled black curls.

Beside me, Mr. Dorian loudly cleared his throat, and I snapped to attention.

"Kalispera!" I said again, but with far too much enthusiasm this time.

Milo smiled shyly. "Kalispera."

"I am Mrs. Harper, and this is my associate, Mr. Dorian," I explained in Greek. "We are from Corfu and came to speak to Miss Costas about her niece. I understand you knew Daphne?"

Milo's shoulders hunched when I spoke her name, and he nodded, albeit reluctantly. "I did." He was surprisingly soft-spoken, especially when compared to his grandfather.

"What are you talking about?" The older man shouted at us from the boat. "What do you want with my useless grandson?"

Before I could answer the man, Milo stepped towards the boat and sharply told his grandfather to be quiet and that he would be back in a moment. To my surprise, the old man actually listened and shuffled off to a different part of the boat.

Milo let out another sigh before he turned back to us. "Follow me," he said, then walked towards the town. Mr. Dorian and I exchanged a look before we did as instructed.

"Will you be able to be objective," Mr. Dorian murmured. "Or shall I take the lead here?"

"What on earth do you mean?"

Mr. Dorian glanced at Milo's eye-catching form up ahead. "You seem rather taken with the boy," he explained, adding too much emphasis on the last word. "Remember, in an investigation, one cannot allow their personal feelings to cloud their judgement."

I scowled at his high-handedness. "Firstly, I don't have any feelings to speak of. Though I will admit he is handsome," I added primly.

Mr. Dorian snorted. "Well, at least you're honest," he grumbled.

"And, secondly, you don't speak Greek. So you'll just have to trust me."

Before Mr. Dorian could respond, Milo stopped and turned around. He had taken us to a shaded area by the harbor. I was grateful to be out of the direct sun for a little bit. Milo looked past us in the direction we had come from and seemed satisfied.

"Thank you for coming here," he said. "My grandfather can be difficult. If he knew we were speaking about Daph—Miss Costas, I would never hear the end of it. He . . . he did not approve of her."

Though he did not explain why, I surmised it was on account of her illegitimacy, and once again, I was struck by the number of difficulties Daphne had experienced during her short life.

I gave him a sympathetic smile. "It's good of you to help him with his boat."

But Milo let out a barking laugh. "It is not his boat. Well, not anymore," he amended. The young man looked out at the sea as he gathered his words. "His mind is not what it once was. I take him with me on the boat only because my mother cannot have him at home with her all day, criticizing every step she takes."

"Ah," I replied. "That must be difficult. For all of you."

Milo shrugged and glanced down at the ground. "Some days are harder than others."

Mr. Dorian gently nudged my side. Our time was growing short.

"I won't keep you from your work, so I'll get right to the point," I said briskly. "Daphne did not die of a fever, as you may have heard. She was murdered, and we are trying to find her killer."

Milo muttered a curse, but otherwise did not look as surprised as I expected. "It sounded very suspicious to me," he admitted, noting my own surprise. "Daphne was strong. And never sick. Ever. I told her aunt as much, but she didn't want to hear it," he said in a bitter voice.

"I'm sure that was simply too much for her to consider at the time," I said gently. "But she has accepted it now."

He met my gaze and nodded. "That is good. I've been meaning to go to Corfu myself and make inquires, but it is hard to get away."

"That is understandable," I said, thinking of his grandfather.

Mr. Dorian nudged me again. "Ask him about Daphne," he said impatiently.

"Yes, I'm getting to that," I hissed. Then turned to Milo. "Miss Costas told us about your friendship with Daphne."

He raised an eyebrow. "Friendship?"

"Unless it was more than that," I said hesitantly.

Milo let out another sharp laugh. "We were in love. For all our lives." He said the words so plainly that I was a little dumbfounded for a moment.

"Then why did she leave?" It wasn't the most tactful question, but he had surprised me yet again.

His face darkened. "To get away from her aunt."

My mouth dropped open just as Mr. Dorian whispered in my ear. "What is he saying?"

"That Daphne left to get away from her aunt."

He frowned, but didn't pester me with any more questions.

"What do you mean?" I asked Milo. "Miss Costas seemed quite upset over her niece's death."

"Of course she was. Daphne was her whole life," he explained. "We played every day as children, but once we grew older, her aunt did not approve. She was terrified that Daphne would make the same mistakes her mother had, so she kept her close. Too close much of the time. Not that it mattered. We found ways to be together," he said with a sly smile that would have sent my heart aflutter if I had been a young woman.

"Ask him why she went to Corfu," Mr. Dorian cut in.

I repeated the question, and Milo's smile faded. "She wanted to find out who her father was. She believed there were people on the island who would know."

"But that wasn't what her aunt thought," I pointed out.

Milo gave me an arch look. "She lied to keep Daphne here because she was angry and bitter over having lost her sister. She couldn't understand why Daphne was so curious about her father. But Daphne was six when her mother died," he explained. "So she remembered her stories of life on Corfu very well, and what her mother told her was much different from her aunt's version."

I was skeptical of this, given that Maria had found herself alone with a child. Then I thought about what Sophia had said about Maria. How she had been heartbroken for the rest of her life over her failed romance and was struck by how they each seemed to occupy a role: the serious, responsible sister and the beautiful, reckless one. The former forever cleaning up the latter's messes. Admittedly, it was a dynamic I was quite familiar with from my youth, and I could easily imagine myself in such a situation with my own sister.

Milo and Daphne both may have chafed against the boundaries Sophia set, but it was clear to me that her intentions had been good. She had given Daphne a stable home life after her mother let her romantic disappointment consume her. Even though I had experienced my own devastating loss, I couldn't imagine giving myself up to grief completely. If anything, my children had given me a reason to go on. But then perhaps I was being too harsh on Maria. Not everyone possessed the kind of resiliency needed to recover from life's slings and arrows.

"In what way did they differ?" I asked, though I could very well guess the answer.

"Daphne's father really did love her mother," Milo insisted. "He wanted to marry her, but it was impossible. His wife would not give him up."

Then he should not have taken her to bed, I thought.

"But they remained in contact until he died. Daphne even had a small box filled with things from him."

My heart began to race. *The necklace*. But I tried not to get ahead of myself. "Do you know what kinds of things?"

He frowned, remembering. "Some jewelry, I think. Maybe a letter or two? She only showed it to me once," Milo said. "She was so fearful her aunt would discover it. That woman destroyed or sold off everything she could get her hands on."

"I see." If Daphne had brought a necklace with her to Corfu, then perhaps she had brought a letter as well. And if it was signed, then we would be able to identify her father and perhaps at least solve one mystery. I could only hope that Florence hadn't gotten rid of the rest of Daphne's things. "Thank you. This is all very helpful. I just have one more question," I said. "Did you ever visit Daphne after she left?"

He shook his head sadly. "I wanted to, but as I said, it is hard for me to get away for very long because of my family. And . . . I am not sure she would have welcomed it."

I tilted my head. "What do you mean?"

"When she first left, she wrote to me every week. Such

beautiful letters," he said on a sigh. "I am not as learned as Daphne, so I had my cousin help me write her back. He is the village priest, you see. And I thought if I could woo her, she would miss me and return," he added sheepishly. "But after a few months, her letters grew shorter and more infrequent. I began to think she found someone else. When we learned she had died, I hadn't heard from her in weeks," he admitted and hung his head.

Perhaps I *was* naïve because Milo looked so utterly heartbroken that I couldn't possibly see how he could have killed her.

"Do you have any idea who?" I asked gently. "It might help us find her killer."

He shook his head. "The only man she ever mentioned was her employer, Mr. Belvedere." Then his eyes flickered, and he looked at me with a sudden sharpness. "No. That isn't true. She also mentioned someone else in her last letter. An Englishman who took the house next door."

My throat suddenly went dry. "Oh?" I croaked.

"He was a writer, I think. Yes"—he nodded with new enthusiasm—"she said he was a famous writer and she was excited to meet him."

I inhaled sharply. "Did she ever mention him again?"

"No. But do you know him? Do you think he could have killed her?" The anxious hope in his face was nearly as wrenching as his words.

Mr. Dorian chose that moment to butt in: "What's he saying?"

"I'll tell you in a moment," I snapped. I truly didn't know what to make of this information. Was it simply a coincidence, or was there something more sinister at play here? My stomach began to turn. For what better way to cover up your crime than encourage a silly little widow to pursue the case and then lead her in exactly the wrong direction?

"I'm not sure," I told Milo. In that moment, I'm ashamed to say it was the truth. "But I will look into it."

He nodded in resignation, but then clenched his hands into fists by his side. "I could not provide for her as I wished to when she was alive, but her killer will be found. Even if it takes the rest of my life," he vowed as a steely determination came into his eyes.

I found myself momentarily captivated until I felt a hand on my elbow.

"Mrs. Harper," Mr. Dorian said gently, "I'm afraid it is time for us to leave."

"All right."

Though I wanted nothing more than to get off this island, the journey home grew less appealing by the second. How on earth could I spend the next few hours in Mr. Dorian's company trying to act as though everything was normal? What I needed was to be alone so I could reason through everything.

I managed to say a stiff good-bye to Milo and promised to write him within the week. He didn't seem to notice that anything was amiss and thanked me profusely.

"You are very good to come all this way for her," he said with great feeling as he took my hands and squeezed them tightly.

"I hope to do more," I answered honestly.

"Come now," Mr. Dorian cut in as he took my arm. "Kalimera," he said to Milo as he steered me towards the tavern where Spiro waited for us.

"You just wished him 'good morning,'" I said dryly and stepped out of his grip.

Mr. Dorian huffed. "Well, at least I'm trying. What else did he say?"

I translated everything Milo had shared except for the bit about him. A mixture of guilt and apprehension began to build inside me until I found myself hoping my seasickness would return so I would at least be spared from any further discussion.

"You feel sorry for him."

"Of course I do," I snapped. "He lost his love."

"Right," Mr. Dorian said after a moment, and my cheeks heated.

Couldn't I make a simple observation without inspiring his pity? "I wasn't thinking of—" I paused and shook my head. I would not speak of Oliver now. "He seemed genuinely upset to me," I finally managed. "Do you not agree?"

"I suppose." He let out a sigh. "But grief can also look a lot like guilt."

My lips pursed, though he had a point. "I would think someone capable of murder could hide their guilt behind any kind of façade."

Even him, for example.

Mr. Dorian hummed for a moment in consideration. "What of the aunt? Do you still think she seemed genuinely upset?"

"Yes," I said, ignoring the skepticism in his voice.

"Then one of them has to be lying about the nature of their relationship with Daphne."

"Not necessarily," I began. "Two people can have very different impressions of the same event, no? It could be true that Daphne's aunt was overbearing and also true that Daphne told her she only saw Milo as a friend to quell her suspicions. And Miss Costas didn't know they were still in contact," I pointed out.

"Yes, all right," Mr. Dorian acknowledged. "But if Daphne did reject him—and for another man at that—that is a motive. And the clearest one we have so far."

"Fine," I admitted. "But I still don't think he did it. And before you say anything, no, I don't have a reason beyond a . . . a feeling."

Mr. Dorian laughed. "Very well. Then you have another reason to find the culprit."

I let out a little groan and pressed a hand to my forehead.

"There now, Mrs. Harper. You're doing a fine job on your first investigation."

I gave him a curious look. "Is this not also your first investigation? Not including your books?"

Surprise flashed in his face. "Ah, well, no. Not exactly," he admitted, but when he didn't continue, I tilted my head, encouraging him to explain. "My father was a detective. Scotland Yard."

I already knew this, of course, but played along. "He was?"

"Yes. He often brought his work home with him," he added.

Now that truly was surprising. "And he let you help him?"

Mr. Dorian shrugged off my incredulous response. "Sometimes. I intended to follow in his footsteps back then, so I suppose he thought of it as training."

But clearly he'd changed his mind. "What happened?"

Mr. Dorian swallowed and looked out to sea. "I saw how often the people my father was certain were guilty walked free, either from lack of evidence or plain old corruption. And the toll it took on him."

My heart clenched as I recalled Christopher's assertion that the man had drunk himself to death.

"So you write books to make sure justice is served," I said softly.

He turned to me with a grim smile. "Something like that."

"Then the case in your first book . . ."

"Was one of his," he finished. "Miss Maggie Murphy. My father's first love."

"I had thought—"

"That I wrote about my own?" He chuckled rather bitterly. "No, Mrs. Harper. I have never been in love."

Given that the man had been married, I very much wanted him to expand on this, but we had reached the tavern by then, and raucous laughter drifted from the open door, capturing our attention. I instinctively hung back, as women weren't welcome in such establishments—not that I had any desire to go inside. But Mr. Dorian took notice of my apprehension and pointed towards a large pear tree nearby.

"Why don't you wait in the shade?" he suggested. "I'll be just a moment."

As I retreated to the spot, my mind whirled.

Careful now. Don't let him manipulate you.

Was Mr. Dorian putting on a grand performance meant to inspire my sympathy and distract from his guilt, or was he simply telling the truth? I truly wasn't sure. And the more I thought over everything, the more confused I became.

I wanted to believe him, but then it seemed I wanted to believe everyone we met. I had yet to encounter a single person I believed to be guilty of the crime. Instead, I found reasons to support their innocence. Perhaps it was time I adopted a little of Mr. Dorian's cynicism—if only to protect myself.

Just then, he stormed out of the tavern with a thunderous look on his face. "I don't believe it," he growled once he reached me.

"What's happened?"

He placed his hands on his hips and cast a dark look back at the tavern. "Spiro is inebriated and cannot sail. He ran into an old friend, and they proceeded to get filthy drunk. Though he does send his apologies," Mr. Dorian added with a touch of sarcasm.

"There must be *someone* who can take us back?" I asked as panic began to rise in my chest.

Mr. Dorian heaved a sigh. "I asked every able-bodied man there, and they all said no."

"But . . . why?" I shook my head in bewilderment. It wasn't dark yet, and surely someone needed the money.

"They're a superstitious lot," he began. "They won't take a woman."

I let out a mirthless laugh and turned away.

"The earliest we can leave is first light," he continued. "Spiro will have sobered up by then."

I whirled back around to face him. Then we would have to spend the night here.

"Oh, God."

"Try not to sound so enthusiastic, Mrs. Harper," he said dryly.

I fixed him with a glare. This was not the time for one of our sparring matches. "But where are we going to stay?"

He glanced away, and my stomach clenched. I could already tell I would not like his answer. "The tavern owner says he has a room available upstairs."

A room. Meaning we would have to share.

I let out a groan, and he pointed an accusatory finger at me. "You knew this was a possibility."

"Because of an act of God," I shot back. "Not a thoughtless man!"

But he was right. For I had anticipated this. Had even prepared for it. And when Mr. Dorian offered to come here alone, I insisted on accompanying him. I had no one to blame for my predicament but myself—and the feckless Spiro.

Mr. Dorian stepped closer then, with an anxious look in his eyes. "The children are being cared for?"

"Yes. Mrs. Kouris is staying with them tonight—though I'm sure she will have quite a lot to say when I return."

"Well, that's a relief at least." Then his concerned look returned. "I'd offer to sleep on the boat, but I don't like the thought of you being alone up there."

"No," I said, as I cast a wary glance at the tavern. "I don't think I'd like that either."

"I really am sorry about this," he began with genuine remorse. "But the time will pass quickly. We can have dinner and then go straight to bed. All we have to do is make it to first light. Then we'll be gone."

Though I appreciated his attempt to minimize the situation, it was much less effective, given my suspicion that he might be involved in Daphne's murder. Sharing a room with Mr. Dorian was one thing. Sharing a room with a potential killer was another. But I couldn't say that, of course. So instead I simply nodded and gave him a weak smile.

"To first light, then."

Mr. Dorian returned to the tavern and told the proprietor that we would take the room. When he emerged a short while later, he was trailed by a chastened Spiro.

"I will go fetch our things from the boat," he explained, then nodded to Spiro. "Go on, then."

The man shuffled towards me, and I caught Mr. Dorian's eye just before he turned around and stalked off to the harbor.

"I am very sorry for the trouble I caused," Spiro said quite pitifully. "One of my oldest friends is here, and I could not say no to his hospitality." He swayed a little as he spoke, and it was clear he was still feeling the effects of this "hospitality."

"Understandable," I muttered tightly, just to get him to stop talking. It would be pointless to harangue this man, though I took some satisfaction in the knowledge that a nasty headache awaited him.

He gave me a grateful smile that turned into a knowing smirk. "Though it is not all bad, no? To be stuck on Poseidon's love nest with your companion?" His dark eyes gleamed as he lingered on the word.

My jaw tightened in response, and I said nothing until Spiro's smirk faded into uncertainty.

"I expect you will have our boat ready to sail at first light. And no later," I snapped, then walked off in the direction of the harbor to keep myself from saying anything more.

"I will, madame!" he called after me. "I won't let you down again!"

"Yes, thank you," I shouted over my shoulder and continued walking until I reached the edge of the pier. I stared out at the calm sea until I felt a presence beside me.

"I could have done without his apology," I muttered, then turned to Mr. Dorian.

"Spiro was very insistent," he explained. "Said he hated to disappoint a lady." I let out an indelicate snort, and he tilted his head. "It will still be very early when we return, and I'll keep my distance," he continued in a gentler tone. "No one will see us together, Spiro doesn't know who you really are, and I'll pay him handsomely to keep his mouth shut about the rest."

I let out a short sigh, but the relief was a cold comfort. "If I had only myself to think of, I wouldn't necessarily care. But the children are at such an impressionable age. Cleo and her friends in particular."

Just thinking of the horrible gossip that could spread made me cringe. Cleo would never forgive me, and I wouldn't blame her. Why had I ever taken such a risk?

"It's all right, Mrs. Harper," he soothed. "Despite what you may have heard, I'm not in the habit of ruining ladies' reputations." His mouth curved in a teasing smile. "No one will learn about this. I promise. Not even a group of gossiping schoolgirls."

At that, I reluctantly returned his smile. "Well, if you promise."

"I do. Now, if you're amenable to it, I think we should see our old friend at the Restaurant of the Tree or whatever it's called and eat something."

"Yes," I said with a nod. "I think so too.

Chapter 17

After dropping my bag off with the tavern owner's wife, we proceeded to the restaurant, where Mr. Karahalios greeted us with a surprised smile. When I explained our predicament, he was full of sympathy.

"Come sit. Nothing lifts the spirits like a good meal," he said, as he ushered us over to the same courtyard table we had occupied hours earlier. Though it was still on the early side for dinner, a few people sat sipping wine from short glasses and nibbling from small dishes of nuts. I noticed more than a few curious looks directed our way as the owner pulled out a chair and I took my seat. When we had been here earlier, we were the only patrons, but now, with the company, it struck me that I hadn't dined in public alone with a man since Oliver.

"Quite right," Mr. Dorian said. "Bring us whatever you recommend. And a bottle of wine." Then he looked to me. "Do you prefer red or white?"

I hesitated. This entire situation was scandalous enough without the addition of spirits.

Mr. Dorian raised an eyebrow. "I seem to recall you enjoying the wine I brought to the Belvederes. Make it a white," he said to Mr. Karahalios. "Something decent."

"Yes, sir," he replied with a bow before he hurried back into the kitchen. The man seemed to understand that well enough.

"Is something the matter?" Mr. Dorian asked once we were alone.

"Aside from the fact that I'm stranded on this island and we're no closer to solving the murder? No. In fact, I've never been better."

Mr. Dorian's mouth curved. "All the more reason for the wine."

I narrowed my eyes. "In my experience, wine rarely makes anything better."

He leaned back in his chair until he was in great danger of slouching. "Ah, well, on that point I'm afraid we must disagree, as I've found that it improves most things—and most people."

"Do you really think that?"

His smile faltered, just a little, but then our host returned with the wine, two glasses, a dish of olives, and some bread that looked like it had just been pulled from the oven. He made a great show of displaying the label to us—not that it made any difference to me—and Mr. Dorian waved a hand. "Pour it, my good man."

Mr. Karahalios then opened it with a flourish and poured us each a glass.

Mr. Dorian raised his glass. "To Daphne."

I lifted mine as well. "To Daphne."

The wine was crisp and cool on my tongue, though not as smooth as the wine I'd had at the Belvederes'. Still, it would do. While I sipped, Mr. Dorian dished a few dark olives bathed in oil onto a plate along with a piece of warm bread.

"Here," he said, passing it to me.

Surprised, I set down my glass to take the plate. "Thank you."

It became second nature over the years for me to serve everyone else before myself.

Mr. Dorian cast me a quick glance as he spooned some olives for himself and shrugged. "Ladies first."

"Right."

But I couldn't even remember my husband doing such a thing—or perhaps . . . perhaps I hadn't ever let him. I had been so happy to be his wife—so grateful, really. For he had taken me away from London, so I never had to move back home after Girton and suffer through a season or three before retiring into quiet spinsterhood. Many women spoke of marriage as a kind of cage, and I genuinely believed that if I hadn't married Oliver, I wouldn't have married at all. But thankfully our marriage had been different. In fact, I found a degree of freedom I had never experienced before because Oliver understood me in a way my parents weren't interested in attempting. So I expressed my gratitude in every way possible and never complained. Not even when he worked very late or accepted assignments that took him away from home, sometimes for days at a time. Nor did I object when he first told me about Corfu and his plan for all of us, despite my reservations. No, I was always the dutiful, devoted wife. Up until the morning he died in my arms.

It struck me now that perhaps I had been operating under a kind of misunderstanding all those years. For Oliver certainly hadn't married me out of a sense of obligation. He wasn't doing me a favor by making me his wife, was he? And yet I had always seen it that way. Had never once considered that he had simply wanted it. Wanted me.

"Mrs. Harper?" I looked up and found Mr. Dorian staring at me curiously. I got the sense that it wasn't the first time he had said my name. "Building castles in Spain, were you?"

I took a long sip of wine before I responded. "Something like that."

His brow furrowed. "You aren't still worried about the children."

"No." I shook my head. "They are in good hands with Mrs. Kouris." Of that I was certain.

"She does seem dedicated to all of you. That's good," he added with a nod.

"Yes. I'm very lucky. I . . . I don't know what I would have done without her these last few years."

In the immediate weeks after Oliver died, there were days I could barely open my eyes, let alone get out of bed. So it had been Mrs. Kouris who kept the children fed and happy. And when I had gone too long without eating or washing, she made sure I was fed as well. I would never be able to fully repay her for what she had done for me—for all three of us. But Mr. Dorian's money was a start.

He gave a thoughtful nod. "We had a housekeeper when I was a boy who was like a member of the family. Mrs. Russell. Good woman. Took care of us after my mother died."

I swallowed hard. He so rarely mentioned anything personal that it felt like I was encountering a wounded wild animal and didn't want to scare him off with any sudden movements. "How old were you?"

He stared at me for a moment before answering. "Ten. My brother was a few years younger."

A brother.

I nodded and had to turn away from the echo of devastation in his face. Even after all this time, the loss had still left its mark upon him. "It is a hard age to lose a parent."

"Especially your mother," he murmured. "Your children are also lucky to have *you*."

I looked up, and his dark eyes were serious and intent as he held my gaze. "Thank you."

Just as the air seemed to thicken around us, Mr. Karahalios returned, bearing plates of food, and the moment was broken. As he placed them on the table, each one looked better than the last: a heap of steaming rice, grilled chicken seasoned with fragrant spices and wedges of lemon, potatoes sprinkled with fresh herbs, and a dish of plump wedges of ruby tomatoes covered with creamy feta cheese.

"Perfect," Mr. Dorian pronounced, and Mr. Karahalios beamed with well-deserved pride. Then he smoothly refilled our glasses and left once more.

We feasted for several minutes, only breaking our companionable silence to encourage each other to try a bite of this or some of that, until Mr. Dorian cleared his throat.

"May I ask you a question?"

I glanced up warily. Based on his tone, this would not be about the food. "You may."

He was giving me that thoughtful look again. "Why haven't you married again?"

I coughed a little in surprise. Of all the things I thought he might have possibly asked me, that was not among them. "I've never considered it," I finally said.

Mr. Dorian's eyes narrowed. "And you didn't want to return to England after your husband died?"

"Oliver and I agreed to raise our children on Corfu. And I saw no reason to change course."

You must promise me, Min. Promise you won't go back there.

I took a large sip of wine and shoved the unsettling memory aside. This was hardly the time to explore the meaning behind Oliver's strange demand. "Besides, they are very happy here," I added. That, at least, was the truth.

My answer didn't appear to satisfy Mr. Dorian. "But what about your family? Wouldn't it have been easier to be closer to them?"

I let out a dismissive snort. "Easier? No. My family can be . . . trying." It was the most diplomatic way to put it. "Do you know my eldest brother? Jack Everly?"

I refrained from mentioning the Bedivere Club, as I was loath to admit that I had asked Christopher about him.

Mr. Dorian furrowed his brow in thought. "The MP for Kensington?"

I nodded. "That's him."

"Hmm." He paused to take a sip of wine. "Bit of a twat, isn't he?"

I let out a sharp laugh and quickly covered my mouth, but Mr. Dorian gave me an encouraging look. "Well, yes. He is," I admitted. "Takes after my father, I'm afraid. The only one who stands up to them is my aunt."

"The meddling one?" he said with a teasing smile I returned.

"Yes. And I am quite fond of my other brother, Samuel, but he lives in Bombay now. As for the rest of them, though, we aren't close."

He nodded in understanding and took another sip of wine. "My brother and I aren't very close either," he said after setting the glass down.

I was beginning to suspect it was the grapes that had loosened his tongue. "Does he live in London?"

"Yes. He's with Scotland Yard, in fact."

I raised my eyebrows. "So he followed in your father's footsteps?"

"He did. Made detective inspector not two years after joining the force, too," Mr. Dorian said with a brittle smile.

"Hmm. What does he think of your books?" Though I had a feeling I knew the answer.

Mr. Dorian's smile grew, but there was a sardonic quality to it. "Not much. He thinks I'm making a mockery of our father's work—and his."

"He sounds like a bit of a twat as well."

Mr. Dorian let out a startled laugh, then turned pensive. "He is, actually. I'm not sure how that happened. We probably indulged him too much, Mrs. Russell and I. After our mother died, Father became wedded to his work. I suppose we tried to make up for their absence in other ways."

"I'm sorry he didn't appreciate it more," I said.

Mr. Dorian shrugged his shoulders with a self-deprecating smile and finished the rest of his wine, while I had yet to even touch my second glass. "He was a child. Surely you have experienced that yourself with your own?"

I let out a sigh. "Yes, though I certainly hope they won't resent me when they're older." But as I spoke the words, Cleo came to mind.

Somehow, Mr. Dorian was able to intuit my thoughts. "Have you come to a decision about your daughter's schooling?"

"No," I said pointedly and stabbed a tomato with my fork.

"But you will return to London," he continued, "if she does go to that school."

"I haven't given it much thought," I lied as I set down my fork. This was not something I was willing to discuss at the moment. "Now, may I ask *you* a question?"

Mr. Dorian settled back in his chair and spread his hands. "I'm an open book, Mrs. Harper. Ask me whatever you'd like."

Though I very much wanted to take issue with that, I managed to stay focused. "Will you ever marry again?"

He let out a loud snort. "No. I'm afraid I've lost my taste for the institution. I am sure you are well aware why," he said in challenge.

"I have heard some things," I admitted. "But nothing that should make you swear off marriage forever." He snorted again, and I pressed on. Though I had begun this line of inquiry hoping to discover if he really had been romancing Daphne, now I was suddenly determined to change his mind.

"You chose to marry once before. Can't you remember why?" Everything I felt the moment Oliver proposed to me suddenly came rushing back in a wave of aching tenderness that nearly took my breath away. "Surely—surely it must have been important to you—meant something at some point," I continued.

"You give me far too much credit," he said with a callow look. "It wasn't terribly complicated, Mrs. Harper. She was beautiful, wealthy, and well-connected. And I am a selfish, shallow man. As well as an idiot. I knew almost immediately that it was a mistake," he added bitterly.

I shook my head. "Then why—"

He raised an eyebrow. "Why did I not simply grant her an annulment and avoid a public spectacle? Because I am also prideful—or I used to be, anyway. And she hurt me, so I wanted to hurt her in return." He shook his head. "What a waste it all was."

Despite the fact that I still harbored very real suspicions about this man, I couldn't help feeling sympathy for him.

"I'm sorry."

He let out a scoff. "Don't be. I deserve everything that has happened to me. And can think of no better punishment than to live out the rest of my life alone. But you . . . you are too young to give up."

I bristled. "I haven't given up. And I am not so much younger than you."

Mr. Dorian eyed me for a moment. "True. I suppose it's because you haven't lost your spirit yet. You shouldn't," he added softly.

This conversation left me feeling even more out of sorts. Though Mr. Dorian admitted to being cruel and callous towards his former wife, he clearly wasn't without feeling, despite his insistence that he had never been in love. And I knew very well what it was like to be lonely on the island. It wasn't like being lonely or heartsick in other places. There were far fewer distractions here, especially compared to London.

Perhaps Daphne had stopped by to see Mrs. Nasso and ran into Mr. Dorian on her way out. Perhaps she asked him about the soaps she had left and his eyes had lit with recognition. How easy it would be to invite her to return later, when no one else was about. If that was the case, I couldn't blame him. She was a beautiful young woman and he a handsome man. They complemented one another in that way. But had he then gone and killed her? Despite what Christopher claimed about Mr. Dorian's expensive divorce, he certainly didn't behave like a man hurting for money. And even if Daphne really was pregnant with his child, it seemed quite a stretch to kill her simply to avoid a potential scandal after what he had already endured. An affair? Possibly. But murder?

It is not a crime of convenience, but of pain. Of anger.

Though Mr. Dorian could certainly be snide, dismissive, and arrogant, not once during all the time I had spent with him, often alone, had I ever felt unsafe.

No. I couldn't see it.

Mr. Karahalios returned then to clear our plates. When he mentioned dessert, I immediately groaned and shook my head, but was overruled by Mr. Dorian.

"He'll take offense if we say no," he murmured when our host disappeared once more.

It was a fair point.

"Very well," I said, then shot him a suspicious look. "But why should you care? It's not as though you'll be returning."

Mr. Dorian lifted a shoulder. "One never knows. This place has started to grow on me."

"It does have a way of doing that," I said.

A smile played on his lips as his gaze turned thoughtful. "When Howard suggested I come here to finish my book, I was set against it. Too far and too hot. But then he threatened me with breach of contract, in the nicest way possible," he said with a laugh that I returned. "He was right, though. I needed that distance. That perspective. I came here determined to kill off the inspector," Mr. Dorian added after a moment.

I couldn't hide my shock. "Truly?" I knew he had been struggling with this book, but hadn't imagined he'd considered taking such a drastic step.

He nodded as he toyed with the stem of his glass. "I was tired of it all. The writing, the thinking, the letters from insatiable readers demanding the next book or criticizing every word. Tired of everything, really. But now . . . now I can see a path forward."

"Well, I am very glad to hear that."

He lifted his gaze to meet mine. "Are you?"

"Of course," I said. "You are a good writer, Mr. Dorian, and people love your books. They are very entertaining. It would be a great shame if you stopped."

I suppose the wine had loosened my tongue as well, for I spoke with more feeling than usual.

The corner of his mouth lifted in an impish smile. "Turning you into a mystery reader might be my greatest accomplishment to date. Even more so than finishing this book."

A fierce blush began to warm my cheeks, but before I managed an equally pithy response, Mr. Karahalios returned with a glistening slice of orange cake and immediately launched into a lengthy description of its merits, and the moment was lost. The cake was, admittedly, quite worthy of its praise, and after taking a bite, Mr. Dorian demanded another as he knew one slice would not be enough. This was followed by a plate laden with fruit and then, finally, we headed back to the tavern. To my surprise, several hours had passed during our leisurely meal, and the sky was streaked with a brilliant shade of orange against dark blue.

"The sunsets here are incredible," Mr. Dorian said as he looked upward. "I've never seen anything like it."

I hummed in agreement. "All these years, and I still haven't grown tired of them."

His steps slowed a little, and he turned to me. "Shall we watch some of it from the harbor?"

I couldn't imagine *he* was nervous about sharing a room, and yet I had the distinct impression he was trying to forestall our return. "An excellent idea."

"So then," he began, once we were settled on a bench that looked out onto the water, "if you're certain Milo isn't our suspect, who should we look at now?"

I frowned in thought. "He said Daphne was trying to uncover her father's identity. Perhaps we should find out if she spoke with anyone. Any of these older workers Sophia mentioned."

We had already spoken to Mrs. Nasso and Mrs. Georgiou, but I wanted to speak with them again armed with this new information.

Mr. Dorian nodded. "Good idea. We should also look into this phantom suitor."

I paused, uncertain if this was more misdirection. But it was hardly the time to make such an accusation. For if I was wrong and Mr. Dorian took offense, it would make things very awkward between us.

"Milo wasn't even certain about that, though," I said weakly. "He assumed that was why she stopped writing as frequently, but it could have been anything."

"Yes, but it aligns with the rumors about her," Mr. Dorian pointed out. "We must determine once and for all if Daphne had a lover—or even more than one."

"I'm sure that was just gossip," I insisted. I was so tired of defending this woman's memory from those determined to paint her as a harlot, as if that somehow excused her murder.

"Perhaps," Mr. Dorian allowed. "But sometimes gossip contains a grain of truth. Believe me."

Though a part of me absolutely burned with curiosity to know which ugly rumor about him was based on the truth, I was dissuaded by the resignation in his eyes. "Very well," I said hoarsely.

Mr. Dorian looked away. "We should be going."

The sun had gotten much lower during our conversation and had begun to resemble a golden egg yolk simmering above the horizon.

We rose and walked towards the tavern, which now glowed like a beacon. The sounds of music, laughter, and boisterous conversation filtered out into the night. I instinctively moved towards Mr. Dorian, and he responded by taking my arm and drawing me close by his side.

"I told the tavern owner and his wife we're married. It seemed best," he added, slanting me a glance.

"Of course," I said with a nod. "I would have done the same." As if I had ever found myself in such a situation.

Together, we crossed the threshold into the tavern, where about a dozen men were scattered about the room. Some sat at small tables, while others stood by the lit hearth. The room fell dead silent as we entered. I don't think I had ever experienced having the attention of so many people all at once. I shrank back a little and could feel Mr. Dorian's fingers tighten over my arm.

He flashed a smile and addressed the room. "Kalispera"

Good evening.

Every man continued to stare back at him in challenging silence. I held my breath and was just about to suggest we leave when the tension was broken as a stout woman wearing an apron bustled into the room from the back.

"Ah, there you are," she called to us in Greek and motioned for us to follow her. She must be the tavern owner's wife. "I've just made the bed. It's all ready for you."

"Thank you," I said.

She then looked around the room and clapped her hands once. "What is the matter with all of you? Go back to your drinking. And if your glass isn't full when I return, I will throw you out myself."

The men grumbled and shifted in their seats, while a few gestured to the barman to refill their glasses.

Mr. Dorian quickly ushered me through to the room where the tavern owner's wife waited. She gave us a nod of acknowledgement and then led us up a narrow staircase at the back of the tavern.

"Thank you for accommodating us on such short notice," I said to her in Greek once we reached the landing.

"The room was empty, and I never say no to extra coin," she replied with a dismissive shrug. "Your husband says you must go before dawn, so I will leave a basket of food for you to take."

"Thank you. That is very kind."

The woman shrugged again. "He paid for it." Then she opened the door and led us inside the cramped room. A small bed with a trunk at the foot was pushed against one wall and a battered washstand against another. There was barely enough space left for the chair and table, atop which sat an old-fashioned oil lamp.

"There is water for washing in the pitcher and some extra blankets in the trunk, though I doubt you'll need them," the woman explained. "This room is always too hot." She fanned herself for emphasis, and I agreed that it was rather stuffy in here, even with the one lone window open.

"We'll be fine for a night," I said and gave her a coin.

She pocketed it in the folds of her simple brown dress and gave me a firm nod. "Sleep well." Then without another word, she turned and left, pulling the door shut behind her.

It closed with a soft thud, and Mr. Dorian and I looked at one another.

He cleared his throat and took off his hat. "Would you care to wash up first? I can step out into the hall . . ."

"I don't think that will be necessary," I rasped. Then I took off my own hat and hung it on the wall hook next to his.

The tavern owner's wife had set my valise and Mr. Dorian's even smaller bag on top of the trunk earlier.

"I didn't think to bring my nightgown," I said as I opened my bag and removed my toothbrush, flannel, and toothpowder. "Just another shirt." Why on earth hadn't I bothered to pack more?

Because you weren't truly expecting to spend the night here.

Hoping was more like it. But now here we were.

Mr. Dorian sighed at my back. "I didn't even bring that much. Only my toothbrush, my comb, and my pomade."

I smiled and looked at him over my shoulder. "Your pomade?"

"I admit to being a bit fastidious about my hair," he muttered, not meeting my eyes.

"We all have our vanities," I said, amused. "You can borrow my toothpowder."

"Many thanks. And I'll sleep on the chair. It's no trouble," he added. "I barely sleep as it is."

I cleared my throat. "All right."

The bed wouldn't be big enough for both of us unless we slept very close.

I went over to the washstand and quickly performed my nightly routine, while Mr. Dorian rummaged through the trunk. When I finished, he had folded an extra blanket on top of the table to use as a makeshift pillow.

I shot him a skeptical look. "Will that be comfortable?"

"Don't worry, Mrs. Harper," he said. "I've made do with much less in my time."

I lifted my chin at the gleam in his eye. The man seemed

forever trying to bait me. "I don't doubt it," I parried back and walked over to the bed.

Though the room may have been small and stuffy, it was undeniably clean. The tavern owner's wife had put fresh sheets on the bed, and the faint scent of lemon peel tickled my nose as I pulled back the coverlet. Only then did the full weight of the day hit me, and I was dearly tempted to collapse facedown onto the bed. Instead, I removed my shoes and my jacket. Then I looked back and found Mr. Dorian discreetly turned away as he occupied himself at the washstand.

For a moment, I considered remaining fully clothed in an attempt to maintain some degree of decorum, but it was simply too hot. I compromised by taking off my stockings, unbuttoning the top of my blouse, and rolling up my sleeves. Then I climbed into the bed and pulled the blanket over me. As I stared at the ceiling while listening to the sounds of Mr. Dorian washing up, my wedding night suddenly came to mind. In a small inn by the Cambridge train station, I had undressed in a mad dash and then hid under the covers, all while Oliver washed up. Only that room had been much nicer, the bed far bigger, and I nearly vibrated from nerves. He had been gentle though, my new husband, and so distressed when I shed a few maidenly tears.

I'm sorry, my darling, he said as he wiped my wet cheeks. *I hate to hurt you.*

If only we both knew then how much pain lay in store for me.

"Are you decent?" Mr. Dorian's wry question cut through the memory, and I turned towards him with a frown. He seemed to find this entire scenario extremely amusing.

"Yes," I said testily. "And already abed."

"Excellent," he said as he turned around. "Then I will bid you good night."

I let out a soft huff and turned onto my side, facing the wall. I could hear him pull out the chair and sit down. Then, after a moment, the oil lamp was put out and the room fell into darkness, apart from the faint glow of the crescent moon. I expected it would be difficult to fall asleep in a room occupied by another man. But as the soft murmurs from the tavern drifted through the floor and mixed with the drone of insects outside, along with the ever-shifting sea, it all faded into a dull buzz, and in less than a minute, I fell into a deep, dreamless sleep.

Chapter 18

"Mrs. Harper."

A hand gently shook my shoulder, pulling me from the firm grasp of sleep. I blinked in confusion, and it took a moment for me to remember where I was—and who I was with.

"I'm awake," I said, as I bolted upward.

The oil lamp glowed on the table, and Mr. Dorian stood over me with his face cast in shadow. "Good," he said. "It's time to leave. Meet me downstairs."

I nodded and rubbed my eyes. He left the room without another word, and I wondered if he had even slept. I quickly dressed and washed up before packing the rest of my things. Then I shuffled downstairs, still bleary-eyed and ready to sell my soul for one of Mrs. Kouris's cups of coffee to find Mr. Dorian standing in the deserted tavern holding a large basket nearly overflowing with food. It looked like he was ready for a picnic, and the oddness of the scene struck me. I stifled a laugh, and he raised an eyebrow while his sharp gaze skimmed over me in a quick assessment.

"You have everything?"

My hand tightened on the handle of my valise. "Yes. I think so."

"Then off we go."

Though it was just before dawn, the harbor was teeming with fishermen readying their boats. I looked at every man we passed, but did not see Milo among them.

Spiro waited by his boat, still downcast. "Did you sleep well?" he asked me.

"Well enough," I replied, then accepted Mr. Dorian's hand as he helped me into the boat. We took our seats, and he began rummaging through the basket.

"I'm not very hungry yet," I said, but he shook his head.

"Here." He handed me a vial from the basket. "I told the tavern owner's wife that you get seasick, and she packed some of that dreadful tree sap you like so much."

"How did you ever manage that?" As far as I could tell, the woman spoke no English.

Mr. Dorian arched a brow. "With a very poor pantomime and by repeating 'mastiha' over and over." He shrugged. "Eventually it worked."

"Well, thank you. That was very thoughtful."

"You needn't sound so surprised," he grumbled.

I ducked my head. It was true. I *was* surprised. But perhaps that wasn't very fair. Aside from that first disastrous evening at the Belvederes' and our argument the morning I found Daphne, Mr. Dorian had been mostly courteous—even gallant on a few occasions. As I opened my mouth to reassure him, Spiro called out that he was raising the sail. The boat then quickly caught the wind, and we were pulled out to sea. Mr. Dorian seemed fully occupied by the water, so I took a preventative sip from the vial and kept my eyes on the horizon, determined not to vomit in front of this man ever again.

A quarter of an hour later, my stomach growled. The mastiha had done its work. I nudged the basket with my foot. "What do you think is in there?"

Mr. Dorian finally looked away from the water and glanced down at the basket. "Judging by how heavy it was, enough food for thrice as many people." Then he met my eyes. "You're feeling well?"

"Yes. Enough to eat, anyway."

Mr. Dorian smiled a little and retrieved the basket, setting it between us on the bench. I drew back the cloth napkin and began inspecting the contents. Indeed, the tavern owner's wife had packed far too much food for us: small triangles of papery phyllo stuffed with spinach and feta, a loaf of butter-soft bread, an assortment of ripe fruits, a large hunk of hard cheese, and a wedge of something wrapped in paper.

"It's sykomaida," I said once I unwrapped it. "This is quite good. It's a fig pie."

Mr. Dorian eyed it with suspicion. "I'll take your word for it."

I smiled. "It is an acquired taste, I suppose."

We each picked out what we wanted and ate happily while dawn steadily approached. I had watched the Grecian sun rise countless times over the years, but never from the water. It was a marvel.

"Stunning," Mr. Dorian murmured, his gaze fixed on the horizon.

I hummed in agreement and chewed on a grape. Once we had eaten our fill, Mr. Dorian took the basket over to Spiro. They spoke for a few minutes before he returned.

"Spiro says we don't have to dock in Corfu Town. He knows a spot not far from the villa. An old pier some rich Englishman built ages ago that's fallen out of use."

"That is convenient." And, most importantly, discreet.

"So then," he said, stretching out his long legs beside me.

"Back to our case. What is the next step? Shall we speak with Mrs. Nasso once more?"

"Yes. And Mrs. Georgiou too, if Florence allows it, that is," I added.

Mr. Dorian considered this and nodded. "I don't think either of them purposely withheld anything from us, of course, but it won't hurt to follow up, considering this new information."

I had thought much the same and was about to say so when Mr. Dorian gave me such an open, expectant look that the grape turned sour in my mouth.

For while they hadn't been withholding anything, I certainly had been, and I couldn't in good conscience carry on this investigation while continuing to keep information from him—especially information that possibly involved him. Better to clear the air and make him aware of what was being said about him. Most of it, anyway.

"There are some things you should know," I began haltingly. "Milo said Daphne mentioned you in her last letter."

"She did?"

He looked so genuinely surprised that guilt began to coil in my chest, but I could hardly stop now. "And . . . I know she visited your house."

"To see Mrs. Nasso, yes."

I paused as he looked at me, but there was no trace of guilt in his dark eyes, no veiled malice. Only curiosity. Or was I just hopelessly naïve?

I took a breath. There was only one way to find out. "Mrs. Georgiou also thought Daphne might have been with child when she died," I said in a rush.

It took Mr. Dorian a moment to fully absorb my words, then he blinked. "What?"

I repeated myself, but he only furrowed his brow and shook his head. "When—when did she tell you this?"

Now came the worst bit. I looked down, unable to meet his eye. "That day at the Belvederes'," I admitted.

When I found the courage to look up again, my stomach tightened. His brow was still furrowed. His confusion was entirely genuine, of that I was now certain. Which could only mean one thing.

"And you didn't bother to tell me this?" But before I could answer, his face fell as understanding dawned. "You mean, you actually thought . . ."

My cheeks heated, and I had to look away once again while the blood pounded in my ears. "You said I shouldn't trust anyone. That I shouldn't be so naïve." But my reasons sounded petulant and juvenile to my ears. Perhaps I wasn't naïve so much as immature. I certainly felt like a child in that moment. Only yesterday morning, I had scolded my daughter over her penchant for the sensational, but how had I behaved any better?

Not only had I clearly offended Mr. Dorian, I had lied by omission. We were supposed to be partners in this, and I had willingly shut him out. If *he* had done such a thing, I would have been full of righteous indignation. And deservedly so.

"Yes, I did say that," he said in a flat tone that pierced my chest. "I am not a good man, Mrs. Harper. I will readily admit to that. But I am not a murderer." Then he shook his head. "I thought you . . ."

"I didn't think you killed her," I said quickly, desperate to reassure him. "Well, maybe a little at first. But only because I was trying to suspect everyone."

He looked far from reassured. "Then why hide anything from me?" he asked with a narrowed gaze.

I opened my mouth and closed it once or twice before I got the nerve to continue. "Because. I thought you might have . . . that you and Daphne were . . ."

Despite my awkward explanation, Mr. Dorian caught on.

His eyes widened. "You thought I got her pregnant? That—that *girl*?" He swore under his breath. "I knew you disapproved of me, but, my God, I had no idea you thought me such a bastard." Then he turned away.

My nose began to sting, and to my utter horror, my eyes had filled with tears. But what right did I have to cry? I wasn't the wronged party here. I blinked, desperate to hold them back, but one escaped, and I hurriedly wiped it away with the back of my hand. "I'm sorry."

But he didn't seem to hear as he whirled back to face me. "I treated you as an equal in this. No other man in this entire blasted *country* would do that. Not even that sainted husband of yours." He spoke the words with such surprising viciousness that I choked back a gasp. "And all this time while we were working together you thought—no, *suspected*—that I was capable of such a thing? How?" he demanded. I opened my mouth, but he shot to his feet before I could respond. "Never mind. Don't answer that. I don't want to know." Then he quickly walked away.

I rose as well. "Wait!" I called to his retreating form, but he waved me off without looking back.

Of course, there wasn't anywhere for him to go, really, but he didn't stop until he reached Spiro's side. Our captain was watching us with undisguised interest, and I could only imagine what he was thinking of this little drama. I turned to the water and braced my hands on the salt-burned wood.

You've made a mess of this, Minnie.

Then I muttered a curse of my own that would have lost the children their pudding and glanced over my shoulder. Now Mr. Dorian was talking with Spiro by the helm, and our gazes tangled for an aching moment before he pointedly turned away. It felt like receiving the cut direct, and with my shoulders slumped, I looked back at the sea. This time I kept my eyes on the horizon.

* * *

Mr. Dorian did not approach me again for the remainder of our journey. As promised, Spiro took us to an abandoned pier not far from my home. I recognized it, for Tommy and Mr. Papadopoulos liked to fish off of it sometimes, but thankfully it was still far too early for anyone to be about.

"You should go on ahead," Mr. Dorian said, once we docked. I turned to him, but he was staring at the shore with his eyes narrowed. "There are some things I need to take care of here."

"Oh," I said dumbly as my cheeks heated. "Of course." I highly doubted that was the case, but given the man couldn't bear the sight of me, it was understandable he wouldn't want to walk together.

I moved towards Spiro, who had already disembarked and was waiting by the pier to assist me onto solid ground. But as I gathered my skirts in one hand, Mr. Dorian was at my side. I hesitated a moment and stared at his outstretched hand. I certainly didn't need him to act like a gentleman merely out of some misplaced adherence to the rules of etiquette—Lord knew he hadn't bothered with them before—but if this was some kind of peace offering, I would gladly take it. I slid my palm against his, and his strong fingers grasped mine as he gracefully helped me off the boat.

I whispered my thanks, to which he merely nodded, just once. Spiro gave me a sympathetic smile as he took my other hand and helped me down. It took a moment for my body to adjust to being on solid land once again. Then I headed towards the dirt road that would lead me back home. I had only taken a few steps when Mr. Dorian called out to me.

My heart lifted in my chest, and I whipped around. "Yes?" I asked, unable to hide the eagerness in my voice.

"It has already been quite a day for both of us, I think," he said, still not meeting my eyes. "So no need for you to come tomorrow."

"I don't mind," I said as I took a step towards the boat. "And your deadline—"

His gaze snapped to mine then, and I shrank back at the coolness there. It was so much like the way he had first looked at me that early morning all those weeks ago.

"It will be met," he said with a finality even I would not argue with.

I turned away again, feeling like a naughty schoolchild dismissed from class. As I walked towards the tree line, I thought I felt his eyes on me, but when I finally got the nerve to look back, he was nowhere in sight.

I followed the path that led to my house in a daze, my thoughts so consumed with Mr. Dorian that I barely noticed my surroundings until I was nearly home. From the front window, I could see a faint light flickering in the kitchen. I let out a weary sigh. I was very happy to be home, with my children waiting for me. At this moment, I wanted nothing more than to pull them into my arms and listen to their stories—even the ones about Tommy's disgusting creatures and Cleo's schoolroom gossip.

As I pushed open the front door, the smell of something warm and delicious greeted me. I called out a loud hello as I dropped my valise and removed my hat and gloves. No one responded, which wasn't exactly the welcoming I had hoped for, but not entirely out of normal, either. I entered the kitchen just as my housekeeper was setting down an oval of warm bread.

"Good morning, Mrs. Kouris. How was last night? I hope the children weren't too much trouble."

"The same as always," she said with a shrug. "They are both still asleep. They stayed up much too late telling ghost stories."

Given that she then hid a yawn behind the back of her hand, I had a feeling she had stayed up with them too.

Mrs. Kouris was well-known for her storytelling prowess, and I had no doubt the children urged her to tell them the more macabre tales.

Then she finally looked at me with her eyebrow raised. "How was your trip?"

I cleared my throat. "Very informative. I can't thank you enough for spending the night. We fully intended to come back yesterday, but our ship captain fell ill."

Goodness. It really did sound like a lie.

Mrs. Kouris hummed in response, but the skepticism in her eyes did not fade. "When you told me your plans, I assumed I would need to stay here."

Then she turned away and began to gather her things, but I lifted my chin. I knew I spoke the truth and refused to feel ashamed for my choices. More importantly, there was still a case to solve. Heartened by an idea, I approached the worktable.

"Before you go, I have a question. Have you ever heard any talk about an Englishman who fathered a child with his maid? This would have been about twenty years ago."

Perhaps if I could uncover Daphne's father's identity, I could present the information to Mr. Dorian as a kind of peace offering and salvage our burgeoning friendship.

"There was always talk of such things, but I cannot think of anyone in particular," she replied.

My shoulders sank in disappointment. "I see."

"You should ask Mrs. Georgiou, though," she added with a sage nod. "She knew what those English were up to back then."

"Thank you. That is helpful," I said with a determined nod.

Then I would go back to the Belvederes' to speak with her. Though it might mean enduring more of Florence's disapproval, I couldn't avoid her forever.

Mrs. Kouris narrowed her eyes. It was much the same

look she gave Tommy when he tried to bring one of his lizards to the dinner table. "Is this about something you learned on Paxos?"

"Yes. It appears that poor Daphne came here in search of her father, who was a married Englishman."

Mrs. Kouris's mouth dropped open. "Then you really did go there for her," she marveled.

I blinked. I had never seen her surprised before, and it took a moment for the words to penetrate my brain. "Of course. Mr. Dorian and I have been trying to find the culprit." Then I frowned and shook my head. "Why on earth did you think we went there?"

In response, my housekeeper merely tilted her head and gave me a look.

Now it was my turn to be shocked. "Mrs. Kouris! My relationship with Mr. Dorian is strictly professional."

But she only shrugged, unconvinced. "If you say so."

I bristled. "I very much do."

"Then it is good of you both to do this for Daphne," she said. "Her killer should face justice."

"Yes, I certainly hope they do." I gave her a weary smile. My restless night was catching up with me. "Take tomorrow off as well, if you'd like."

Since I wasn't needed at Mr. Dorian's, the extra housework would be a useful distraction.

"Thank you. I will." Mrs. Kouris then headed for the door. "Good day, Mrs. Harper. It would not be so bad, you know," she added, looking at me over her shoulder, "if you and Mr. Dorian were not only professional."

But she hurried outside before I could object. The kitchen fell into an unnatural silence with her gone, and I became aware of a tightness in my chest. But as I stood there, other sounds slowly came to me: the gentle creaking of our restless house settling, the faint lapping of the waves in the distance, and the bleating and chirping of our various animals as they woke, along with the low buzz of the insects. With each new sound, the tightness slowly eased.

Indeed, this would be my future if I raised my children right. For then they would go off and have lives and loves of their own. And I wanted that for them, of course. Even if it meant leaving me. Even if it meant being alone.

Mr. Dorian's question from last night then came to me:

Why haven't you married again?

I had answered him honestly. Perhaps, though . . . perhaps it was time I at least considered the possibility if I did not want this to be my future. For as pleasant at this little domestic scene was, I knew it was far better to have someone to share it with. Question after question began to crop up until I shook my head. I did not need to have all the answers now—or any, in fact. I only needed to get through today. And then tomorrow I would start anew.

Chapter 19

I managed to capture a few blessed hours of sleep before the children woke me. They both ran into my room, jumped on my bed, and launched into a barrage of questions before I had even opened my eyes. Eventually, I regained my senses and was able to determine that Cleo had been invited to spend the night at the Taylors', while Tommy wanted to camp out with Mr. Papadopoulos to watch a shooting star that was supposed to be visible. Still groggy, I nodded my assent and begged the children to give me a moment alone. With my permission secured, they raced out of the room just as quickly as they'd entered.

I let out a breath and stared up at the ceiling. Then cursed myself. The crack still needed to be repaired, and Nico was still off the island. At least I actually had the money to pay him now, thanks to Mr. Dorian. I should have felt some sense of relief, yet my stomach tightened at the thought of my erstwhile employer. All I could see was his stern expression as he insisted my services were not needed tomorrow. But what about the day after that? If this was a way of dismissing me, I could hardly blame him. I let out a sigh and forced myself to get up. I would not waste any more time wondering. If I hadn't heard from Mr. Dorian by tomorrow, I would go to his house. Let the man sack me in person. I deserved it.

The rest of the morning passed quickly, as the children were each occupied with preparations for their evening. Preparations that, naturally, required my assistance. After I had found Oliver's old sleeping bag for Tommy and argued with Cleo over an appropriate amount of clothing to take for a single night away, Mr. Papadopoulos came by after lunch, and we enjoyed tea and a chat out on the terrace, while the children finished packing.

"It is very good of you to do this," I said.

"Nonsense. It is my pleasure," he insisted. "What will you do with your evening, then?"

It dawned on me that I would be entirely alone in the house. For the first time ever. I paused to take a sip of tea, as my throat had grown quite dry at the thought. "Perhaps I'll read. There's a book I've been meaning to get to." It was, in fact, the next Inspector Dumond novel, but I kept that detail to myself. "Maybe have a bath."

"An excellent plan," he said with a smile. "And how is your *work* with Mr. Dorian progressing?"

Given his emphasis on the word, I gathered he wasn't asking about the manuscript. "Slowly. It seems that Daphne had been searching for her father, an Englishman who lived here." I then gave him a much-abbreviated version of our trip to Lakka, leaving out the fact that we had been forced to spend the night. "But I don't know how any of it is connected to her murder," I said, shaking my head.

Mr. Papadopoulos looked thoughtful. "I take it Daphne was illegitimate?"

"Yes. And her aunt seemed to suggest that the man's surviving family would not welcome her with open arms."

He clicked his tongue. "A poor maid from Paxos? No, I'm sure they would not. I don't mean to speak badly of your countrymen, but the English have always seemed to me very preoccupied with one another's bloodlines. More than most, anyway."

I waved a hand. "No, it's true. But I don't know if she even found her family. And if she did, why kill her? They could have just as easily called her a liar and slammed the door in her face."

"That is true," he acknowledged.

"No. I still think the violent nature of her death suggests that it was personal. Whoever did it knew Daphne and her movements. This wasn't a crime of opportunity. They wanted her dead for a reason."

He hummed in consideration. "I imagine there are not many people who meet those requirements."

"No."

A part of me longed to tell him about my suspicions of Mr. Dorian, if only to gain another person's perspective on the matter, that I had been right to suspect him in the first place—and perhaps ease my guilty conscience. But if word of it ever spread, that would end any chance we had of making amends. And I could not take that risk merely to satisfy my wounded ego.

Mr. Papadopoulos worried his lip. "Please take care, Mrs. Harper. If the killer catches wind of your little investigation, they may feel compelled to put a stop to it," he said with a grave look.

Despite his vague words, the meaning was clear: murder.

"I will," I murmured, even as I wondered what I could possibly do to protect myself. But I didn't get very far before Tommy came bounding over to us with a rucksack slung over his shoulder. The bag was almost as big as he was, and Mr. Papadopoulos let out a laugh.

"I believe I told you to pack light, Thomas."

"I did!" Tommy insisted even while he struggled to set the bag down. "You should have seen it an hour ago."

Mr. Papadopoulos and I exchanged a look, each of us trying not to laugh. "Let me inspect it before we leave," he said kindly.

As I left them to it, I decided that Cleo's bag needed an inspection as well.

After some shouting, a few tears, and a rehoming of a frightening spider Tommy had tried to take with him in a jar, both children had repacked their bags. Cleo and I set out in the donkey cart while Mr. Papadopoulos and Tommy headed for the woods.

When we arrived at the Taylors', Virginia insisted I join her for some refreshments on the terrace while the girls got settled. It was a clear, balmy evening, and given that only an empty house was waiting for me, I immediately accepted.

"Wonderful!" she replied and led me outside to the spacious seating area.

"My husband is away on business for the week, thank heavens," she said blithely as we sat down. "That man is simply exhausting when he's here." Granted, I didn't know Mr. Taylor very well, but I found that hard to imagine. He had always struck me as a quiet, serious-minded man who often left his family to their own devices while he traveled to different Mediterranean ports. Between the two of them, Virginia seemed the far more exhausting one.

"Needless to say," she continued, unaware of my admittedly unkind thoughts, "I'm very glad Cleo is here to occupy Juliet tonight. We mothers so rarely have any time to ourselves, isn't that right?"

She gave me an expectant look just as a footman arrived carrying a silver tray with two glasses of sherry, and I was saved from having to come up with a response to this from a woman who lived in a massive villa with a full staff.

Virginia handed me the glass and then raised her own. We toasted and then each took a sip.

"Isn't this nice?" she said after a moment. "We should do this more often."

I made a noncommittal sound and took another sip.

"I paid a visit to Florence yesterday, you know," she began. "Poor dear still hasn't found anyone to replace that maid." She clicked her tongue. "I rather fear she is beginning to grow desperate, though she will never admit it. I'd send her one of my own maids, but you know how it is when you loan out help."

I didn't, but nodded anyway. "Perhaps she can't bring herself to hire anyone just yet. She did seem very upset by Daphne's death when I last saw her." Then I paused and took another sip. "I wonder if she'll even stay on Corfu," I mused.

Virginia let out a sharp laugh and then quickly sobered at my confusion. "You do know that Florence didn't return here out of a sense of nostalgia," she said carefully.

I cocked my head. "What do you mean?"

"I know she acts as though it was always her intention to come back here after her children were grown, and perhaps it was, but I also heard that Christopher made a bad investment—several, in fact—and eventually they had no choice but to sell up and leave England. I doubt they could afford to move back now, even if they wanted to."

"Goodness," I murmured and set down my glass.

I thought of Florence and her unshakeable pride in her roots on the island. How she never missed the chance to tell someone about her idyllic childhood or her parents' legendary parties.

It seemed unimaginable to me that such a formidable woman could end up anywhere she did not wish to be. But then, so many of us donned masks to hide our pain from the rest of the world. Perhaps that was just hers, and I would not tear it away from her merely to make conversation with Virginia Taylor.

"Well, even if that was the case at first," I said, "they seem to have found happiness here—apart from the murder, of course."

Virginia's eyes dimmed a little in disappointment, as I was not the gossiping partner she had hoped for. "Yes," she said quickly. "Quite right."

But our conversation grew stilted, and I left not long afterwards. Returning to my empty house no longer seemed so unappealing.

Despite what I had told Mr. Papadopoulos, a bath seemed like far too much trouble to go to at this hour without anyone to help heat the water, so I made a pot of tea instead. But when I reached Oliver's study, where all the books were kept, I found myself pulling down *Sonnets from the Portuguese* instead of Mr. Dorian's next book. I stared at the cover for a long while and let my fingers trail over the floral gilt border before I mustered the nerve to open it. Even still, seeing the faded inscription felt like a punch to the chest.

To Mrs. Harper.

Let us read these together on our journey eastward.

All my love,

Mr. Harper

It had been Oliver's wedding present to me. When I first unwrapped it, I came close to tears because it was so terribly romantic, while all I had given him was a gold stickpin. But that had always been the way between us. And it was his sense of romance and adventure that I loved so well.

Not even that sainted husband of yours.

Mr. Dorian's angry words came back to me just then, and I frowned. I had been so consumed by my own guilt at that moment that I hadn't given this accusation the proper consideration. But now, as I turned it over in my mind, I found I couldn't dismiss his claim outright—though I dearly wanted to. I knew that Oliver had loved and respected me. But treated me as an equal? In truth, it wasn't something I had ever expected from him. Hadn't even thought to expect. Then I shook my head. No. I would not listen to a man who had both gotten divorced and claimed to have never even been in love. Mr. Dorian may have some rather progressive ideas, but clearly he hadn't put them into practice himself. I snapped the book shut and put it back on the shelf. Now I felt much too tired to read.

I forced myself through my nightly routine, but as I was heading to bed, my gaze caught on the door. The front and back doors were both locked—of that I was certain, as I had checked them several times each before coming upstairs. Still, unease rippled through me, and I shoved a chair under the doorknob for good measure.

"There." I felt quite satisfied with my makeshift alarm. If there was an intruder, I would hear them, and this would keep them at bay. At least for a time.

But then what will you do? the irritating voice in my head demanded.

I didn't have an answer for that. For there were no weapons in the house, aside from our kitchen knives, but I very much doubted they were sharp enough to be of much use. Oliver had insisted on keeping a gun, which I never understood, but I sold the horrible thing soon after he died.

"The chair will keep them out," I reasoned.

What if he has an ax? What if he's very big? What if he has a ladder and comes through the window—

"Shut up," I said sharply to the empty room, and the voice fell silent.

Then I turned down the lamp and forced my eyes closed. Eventually, my mind relented and let me sleep.

Chapter 20

I woke with the dawn, still very much alive and fairly well-rested. The chair remained in its place, undisturbed, and now, in the dim light of morning, it seemed quite silly. Of course, no one was going to accost me in my own home. The voice in my head remained noticeably silent. I rose, donned my trusty wrapper, and quickly washed before padding downstairs. The ominous silence of the night had been softened by birdsong and the faint rustle of the trees. Now this wasn't so bad at all. In fact, I rather enjoyed the quiet. I did not even attempt to make a cup of bitter Greek coffee, as I could never replicate Mrs. Kouris's, no matter how hard I tried, and instead prepared a simple pot of tea, along with toast from yesterday's bread. Then I sat outside on the terrace and tried to enjoy the morning calm.

I needed to go to the Belvederes' soon, so as not to interrupt Mrs. Georgiou's workday too much. But the dull throb of guilt that I had managed to suppress last night was much sharper this morning. I should see Mr. Dorian first. I could even ask him to come along, if he was amendable. I was certain of his innocence now, and it would do no good for me to continue investigating without him, even if the man did intend to sack me. Besides, I owed him a better apology.

Fortified by tea and toast, I bathed and dressed for the day, taking more care with my hair and appearance than usual. Then I donned my sunhat and marched outside, deciding to cut through the olive grove. As I headed for Mr. Dorian's house, I gathered my thoughts.

"I'm sorry," I murmured aloud. "I should have told you about Daphne straightaway. I don't know why I even suspected you in the first place— "

But that wasn't right. I did know. My steps slowed, and I came to a halt. It was Florence who had first put the idea in my head the day we went to speak to her.

The man has a reputation, and a well-earned one at that. Who knows what he's been getting up to at that villa since he arrived—and with whom.

At the time, I had found her sudden change of heart regarding Mr. Dorian, as well as her strident insistence that I keep away from him, quite odd, but had chalked it up to little more than Florence being Florence. Now though . . . had she simply been swayed by gossip, or was something else afoot? After all, she had complained about Daphne an awful lot before her death. But that was hardly a motive for murder, especially since Florence complained about all her servants, excepting Mrs. Georgiou.

I had properly stuck my foot in it once already by entertaining such baseless suspicions, and that was about a man I had only just met, whereas I had known Florence for close to a decade. Guilt began to gather in my chest for even thinking such a thing about her. Then I cast a wary look in the direction of her house higher up on the hill, while a warm, soft breeze delicately rustled the trees. A shudder tore through me, as if she had heard my thoughts, and I felt that unnerving sensation of being watched, though there was no one about.

I resumed walking—faster this time—driven by a newfound sense of urgency. I couldn't sort through such knotty feelings on my own. I needed to speak with Mr. Dorian. Now. Within a few minutes, I arrived at the villa. I knocked loudly but didn't wait for Mrs. Nasso before I turned the knob and pushed the door open, only to walk right into it. I stepped back, startled. It was locked. The door was never locked during the day—and likely not at night either. I knocked again, even louder.

"Hello!" I called out.

But there was no answer.

The back of my neck tingled. This wasn't right. This wasn't right at all.

I hurried around to the front of the house and peered inside the first window I came across, but the shutters were drawn. Mrs. Nasso clearly wasn't inside. I slowly stepped back as the tingling sensation transformed into a full-blown sense of unease. It was entirely possible that Mr. Dorian had given her the day off as well and was still asleep. Perhaps he had stayed up all night working on the manuscript.

Or occupied by something else.

I couldn't help but recall the first time I ever saw him, when he appeared on the back terrace, a glass of brown liquid at his elbow and a haunted look on his face. I truly hoped my suspicions hadn't driven him to drink to excess. But as soon as the thought entered my mind, I quickly pushed it aside. It was ridiculous to think that I could have such an impact on that man. He had endured far worse, after all. And from people who knew him far better than I did.

Still, I couldn't shake this sense of unease. If he was simply asleep and I was merely overreacting, then so be it. I would face his ire head on. I walked around towards the back of the house, but the terrace doors that led to his bedroom were shut and the curtains were drawn. I rapped on the glass, but again there was no answer. Then I cupped my hands and called his name in a very unladylike manner.

"He isn't there, Minnie."

I let out a startled scream and whirled around. Florence stood on the path just below me, gazing up with her hand shielding her eyes against the sun.

"Florence, my goodness!" I braced my hand against my chest. "You scared me!"

"Sorry," she called out with an apologetic smile. "I saw you walking from my house and thought I'd meet you."

Then I hadn't imagined the feeling of being watched. Yet this only increased my unease, though it had only been Florence. "Where is Mr. Dorian?"

But she didn't respond to the question. "Come round to the front." Then before I could answer, she turned and walked away.

When I met her by the front door, she looked troubled, and my heart beat faster.

"Florence," I said, with as much gravitas as I could manage. "What is going on?"

She glanced away, and I realized then that Florence was nervous. My unease increased exponentially, as I had never seen her nervous before. Frankly, such a plebian emotion seemed rather beneath her. "Mr. Dorian was arrested this morning for Daphne's murder."

It felt as if my stomach had dropped to the dusty ground. I stared at her for what felt like hours but could only have been a few seconds. "What?" I finally managed to ask, though I certainly hadn't misheard her.

"Come back to the house with me," Florence said with her usual pretension. "I don't want to discuss such sordid business out here." There was no one about, but I was too stunned to protest and let her take my arm. "You poor thing. You must be in shock."

"No, I . . ." But I couldn't manage the words. Perhaps I *was* in shock. I was certainly confused. A jumble of questions raced through my mind as we made the short walk up the hill to Florence's home, but I voiced none of them. When we entered her house, she escorted me to the kitchen.

"Sit down, and I'll make you some tea."

"All right," I said dumbly, as she led me over to a chair.

"Christopher is with him now to represent him," she explained as she put the kettle to boil. "Good man. They've struck up such a friendship. But I can't think of what this will do to him when Mr. Dorian is found guilty."

I began to nod then caught myself. "Don't you mean if?"

Florence shot me a sympathetic look as she headed towards the large cabinet where she kept her teas. "Of course. *If.*" Then she hesitated. "But I believe they found some rather incriminating evidence."

My heart stopped. "What kind?"

"Well, they won't say, exactly," Florence began as she opened the cabinet and pulled out a few glass jars and set them on the worktable. "But whatever it is, it seems to indicate that Mr. Dorian was carrying on with the poor girl." She shook her head. "That knave. I'm so sorry I ever encouraged you to work for him."

I watched in a dull trance as Florence began to measure out ingredients for one of her tisanes as her words slowly penetrated my woolly mind.

"I can't believe it," I finally murmured.

She tilted her head and looked at me with pity. "My dear,

you know what kind of man he is. I did try to warn you," she said in her usual ever-so-slightly patronizing tone. Normally, it took no effort for me to brush it off, but not today.

My jaw tightened. "That he was a cad, not a murderer."

Florence let out a heavy sigh. "Be that as it may, I can't say it's much of a leap in his case. The man wasn't well at all, especially after that sordid business with his wife. That's why he came here to begin with, you know. To recover. And Daphne, well, she was dazzled by him, poor thing. We all were."

I slumped back in my chair. I couldn't argue with any of that. But still, how had he been so *convincing* yesterday? I needed to see this through now more than ever.

"Florence," I said as my mind sharpened, "where is Mrs. Georgiou?"

She raised an eyebrow. "In the garden gathering herbs. Why? Are you hungry?"

"No," I shook my head as my stomach revolted at the very idea. "I wanted to ask her about Daphne's parents."

Florence looked troubled. "What do you mean?"

"Her father was an Englishman from Corfu. She came here to find him or, rather, her relatives." Then the kettle began to sing, and when she poured the water, the room smelled like a spring meadow complemented by a faint scent of pepper. As we left my tisane to steep, I explained how Mr. Dorian and I had traveled to Lakka only yesterday to speak with her aunt, though I did leave out the bit about Milo and the fact that we were forced to spend the night, along with the unpleasant terms on which we parted. All the while, Florence listened quietly.

"My goodness," she said. "You two have certainly been busy."

"Yes, we have. But I truly don't think Mr. Dorian did it, Florence. Even if . . . even if they *were* having an affair, I don't see why he would have killed her and then have been so sloppy about it." Though it was difficult for me to say those words, my conviction only increased. "I just need to find out who Daphne's father is," I said and took another sip. "That could be the key."

Florence eyed me curiously. "How do you mean?"

I frowned in thought. "It was something Daphne's aunt said. Though it was unlikely that her father was still alive, his children or grandchildren very well might be. And they might not be thrilled to learn about their half sister. Especially if"—I had to swallow before I could continue—"if money or property was involved."

But as I spoke, I recalled something else. Something that had escaped my notice until now.

"You didn't tell Daphne's aunt the truth about how she died."

"I thought it for the best at the time," Florence replied, "since we had no idea who killed her."

"Yes," I said, as I had surmised as much. "But you didn't share that with Christopher. He told me you promised her aunt that you would find the killer."

Florence hummed in consideration as she finished preparing my tisane by adding another scoop of dried flowers along with a few drops from one of the small brown bottles she used for her tinctures. "Christopher must have misremembered. You know how he can be."

I frowned in confusion, as that was not at all my impression of him. And it seemed an odd thing to misremember. But what reason would she have to lie? Before I could press her on the matter, Florence handed me the teacup. "Here. Drink while it's still hot."

She gave me an expectant look, so I took a tentative sip, then another. The scent alone, delicate and fleeting, helped to calm my nerves. There was something familiar about it, though. Something I couldn't quite put my finger on. "What's in this one?"

"A little of this and a little of that. I follow my whims, you know," she said airily. "Drink up."

I obliged by taking another long sip and closed my eyes. It had felt surprisingly good to speak with someone else about what I had uncovered. And having laid out the facts, I was certain that the police had the wrong man. Now all that remained was to make them aware of that. As I continued to sip my tea, Florence put away her jars and wiped the work surface. It was surprisingly relaxing to watch her clean up and I found myself rather mesmerized by her quick, efficient movements.

"And where are the children today?"

I blinked, thrown by the sudden question. "Out. Both of them, actually. Cleo is at the Taylors', and Tommy is with Mr. Papadopoulos. I've had the house to myself since yesterday."

"Really?" Florence raised an eyebrow. "Not even Mrs. Kouris is there?"

"No," I said. "I gave her today off."

"And you were on your way to see Mr. Dorian."

I nodded, though my mind was beginning to feel a little foggy. Perhaps my broken sleep was finally catching up to me. "We quarreled. And I wanted to apologize. Then I was going to come here to talk with Mrs. Georgiou again." I hadn't meant to say all that, but the words just seemed to slip out of me. "And to see if Daphne had any more letters," I added.

"No," Florence said, "I don't think you'll be doing any of that."

I tried to focus on her, but it was rather difficult. "What do you mean?"

"So you won't stop, then," she demanded, "not until you solve your little mystery."

I couldn't make sense of the derision in her tone and shook my head. "Of course not."

"Well. I'm very sorry to hear that," she said with a strange finality and wiped her hands on her apron.

I looked up at her, though the movement took some effort. "What?"

"I truly thought you had more sense than this, Minnie," she pressed on, while my sluggish mind hurried to keep up. "First, I tried to warn you away, then I tried to distract you. But still you persisted. And all over that *girl.*" She shook her head fiercely. "What a waste."

"Florence," I said weakly, while understanding slowly dawned, "what did you do?"

Her gaze snapped to mine then with an ugly, twisted expression on her face I had never seen before. "What I had to do. Whatever it took."

"Oh God," I whispered, as a cold sweat broke out across my body.

"I always did like you, Minnie. But you have been acting like such a fool over that man. Have you given no thought to what Oliver would think? You are desecrating his memory, but that is nothing compared to what you are doing to your own children."

"Florence," I managed to say, "nothing has happened. We're only—"

"No," she snapped. "That's how it starts. How it always starts. Do you know how many women my mother had to suffer through right under her nose? For years. Her own friends. Her own *help*. It was an absolute disgrace. I left this place as soon as I could, and I swore never to return."

"Until you had to," I murmured.

She looked at me with such viciousness then that I shrank back in my chair. "Yes," she hissed. "After Christopher made some foolish investments, we were left with few alternatives.

I would never stoop to asking my children for support nor explain to my husband why I was loath to return here, so instead I made the best of it. Because that is what women like us are bred to do, are we not?" She gave me a pointed look but didn't wait for my response. "And with my father long dead, it wasn't so bad, really. Until she came."

"Did . . . did you truly not know? Who she was?"

Florence scoffed. "Of course not. Neither of us did, in fact. Then one day she was helping me get dressed. I asked her to find a brooch in my jewelry case, and instead she pulled out a pair of earrings my mother had given me. I had completely forgotten about them. I never wore them, hideous things. Daphne said she had a matching necklace on at that very moment. That it was given to her mother by her father, an Englishman who had lived on Corfu. Then I watched that idiot girl piece it all together right in front of me," she said, still outraged.

"Then you *did* know about the necklace."

"And I let her be buried with it, along with those hideous earrings I tucked in her dress pocket. The only blasted things that could tie us together," she said with marked pride. "Thank God the police here are so incompetent and easily swayed. Though you can thank Mr. Papadopoulos for ruining my initial plan. Once that vagrant was released, I was left with no other choice but to frame Mr. Dorian."

"But . . . why even kill her at all?"

"Because she actually thought we were equals," Florence hissed. "That because my father bedded her mother for a few months, that entitled her to my family. My *name*. The gossip that had been forgotten all those years ago would have come out, and my mother would have suffered all over again."

"Isn't she dead?"

"That's not the point!" Florence slammed her hands on the counter, and I jumped in my seat. "You know nothing of loyalty. Of filial duty. You left your whole family without a thought."

That stung, but it was hardly the time to chide her. I needed to get away from here. "I should go," I said, though I admit I was slurring a bit, and began to stand, but my legs felt weak. Heavy. Like I was trying to move through water. Then I really noticed just how sluggish and slow my mind felt. I was fairly certain that if I closed my eyes, I could have gone to sleep right then. I looked up to find Florence watching me with an impassive expression, and I noted she had made no move to stop me. My bleary gaze fell on my empty cup of tea, and Florence made a little noise of confirmation.

"I'm sure you can agree with me that people tend to overlook older women," she began. "I first noticed it when I was about your age. Men whose attention I had once easily garnered now looked past me to my daughters, while younger women dismissed my opinions as old-fashioned and outdated. They talked behind my back about how silly I was, as if I couldn't tell from the way they treated me to my face." She let out a huff of outrage and then her hands tightened into fists. "Even Christopher, who had once declared me the sharpest woman of his acquaintance, began treating me like little more than a child. Then he invested nearly all our money in that foolish investment scheme without one word to me about it. If he had, I know I would have stopped him. But here we are." She punctuated this with an odd, half-hearted laugh before narrowing her eyes on me once more. "Only Oliver treated me with genuine respect as a person of equal intellect, not just some silly old housewife," she spat. In that moment, I will admit that, despite the very real danger I was in, I felt a pang of regret. For I had judged Florence, just as she said, but then she continued to speak. "And yet you failed to properly appreciate him, so he kept things from you, Minnie."

A pit formed in my stomach. "What things," I managed to growl, as weak as I was.

"Things he didn't trust you to understand," she said ominously before moving on. "But I've found there is an upside to being grossly underestimated. You can get away with nearly anything—and all in plain sight."

"Not this, Florence," I said, with far more conviction than I truly felt. For it would all depend on whether or not Mr. Dorian could convince the police of his innocence.

However, Florence blithely continued on, as if I hadn't said a word. "I will admit that I was a bit worried the evidence against Mr. Dorian would be too weak, but not if we make it look like he killed you as well. Actually, it reminds me of the plot of one of his novels," she said with a strange laugh. "You know, the one about the dead woman who had been having an affair with the postman?"

When I didn't answer, she waved a dismissive hand. "Anyway, it doesn't matter. I am sorry for the children, though." She actually had the nerve to sound remorseful. "But it will be better for them to grow up in England. You should have moved back years ago," she added in that haughty tone I had begun to hate. "I can't imagine why you stayed."

"Because," I said hoarsely, as my mouth had gone dry, "Oliver wanted me to." She looked genuinely surprised at that, and I enjoyed besting her in this small way. Then my addled mind clung to something else. "Who is *we*?"

Florence ignored the question. "I promise it will be quick. Like going to sleep. You shouldn't feel a thing." She spoke as if she were doing me a great favor, and I was filled with such sudden, all-consuming indignation that I hurled myself to my feet, only to just as quickly fall to the floor. But I would not give up. If she was so determined to kill me, I would make it as difficult as possible. I tried to get up, and when that proved infeasible, I began to pull myself across the worn stone floor. Florence clicked her tongue. "Really, Minnie. Don't make a spectacle of yourself."

Behind me, someone entered the room and gasped. "Dia, what have you done now?"

It was Mrs. Georgiou. I forced my head to turn and saw her staring down at me in horror, a basket at her feet with bunches of herbs spilled across the floor.

"She found out," Florence explained, sounding bored. "I had no choice."

"Please. Get help," I begged the old woman. "I have children."

Her troubled gaze flicked to Florence. "How much did you give her?"

"More than Daphne." Florence then narrowed her eyes. "I learned from that."

Mrs. Georgiou frowned in worry, and I let out a groan as my head began to spin and my stomach cramped.

"You stupid girl," she hissed at Florence. "We will be caught this time, don't you see?"

But Florence appeared unmoved. "I have a plan."

They began to argue, but I couldn't keep my eyes open. They felt so heavy. I tried to drag myself a little farther, but instead I fell in and out of consciousness for a period of time, until I became vaguely aware of louder male voices entering the room. Then there was shouting and racing footsteps. I felt someone call my name as they pulled me into their arms and patted my cheek.

With the last bit of strength I could gather, I forced my eyes open to find Mr. Dorian staring down at me anxiously. "Oh," I breathed, "there you are."

He let out a startled laugh. "Yes, terribly sorry for the delay. We would have gotten here sooner, but I was briefly imprisoned."

"So I heard." My eyes then began to close on their own

once more. I tried to fight it, but I couldn't manage to keep them open.

"Dammit, Minnie. Stay awake," he cried out as he shook my shoulders.

But despite his order, I slipped into the waiting darkness.

The last thing I heard was a voice full of anguish.

No. Not yet.

Chapter 21

I can't say with any certainty how much time passed before I woke again. Only that when I did, I was no longer sprawled on Florence's kitchen floor. Instead I was in the white-walled infirmary of the local hospital—or so I assumed. It must have been the afternoon, as a stream of golden sunlight had fallen across my face and woken me in the first place.

I grumbled my annoyance and raised my hand to shield my eyes. Then I noticed Cleo fast asleep in a chair by my bedside. A mix of fierce joy and longing pierced my chest with such force that I nearly lost my breath. How close I had come to never seeing her dear face again. My eyes stung with tears, but I made no attempt to blink them away. Instead, I let them fall freely while my gaze traveled over my firstborn, taking in every feature like it was the day of her birth all over again.

Cleo's brow was furrowed, and her cheek rested against her fist, while one of Mr. Dorian's novels was splayed across her lap. In that moment, she looked so much like Oliver that my breath caught. I had found him in much the same position so many times, and my heart twisted anew from a different kind of ache. A different kind of loss.

While I was watching her, Cleo shifted in her seat, and her eyes fluttered open. Then she noticed me and bolted upright. "You're awake!"

"Yes," I began before she threw her arms around me. I pulled her closer and made a soothing sound as she started to cry. "It's all right, my dear," I murmured as I gently rocked us. "It's all over."

"Oh, Mama," she choked out. "I'm sorry."

I pulled back and pushed her hair away from her tear-stained face. "What on earth for?"

"I've been so awful to you lately. But don't worry. I'm going to change. Right away. I'll be nicer to Tommy and more helpful around the house. And I'm not going to England. I'll write to Aunt Agatha tomorrow and tell her—"

"Cleo, stop," I said firmly. "We don't need to talk about any of that now."

She hugged me even tighter. "I just don't want to lose you," she whispered. "I *can't*."

The pain in her voice sent a tremor of regret through me. For weeks, all I had thought of was solving Daphne's murder. I never really considered the danger I was courting, nor what it might do to my children, who had already suffered one devastating loss. I couldn't put them through another.

"You won't," I said with more certainty than I could guarantee. But that didn't matter at the moment.

After we embraced a little longer, I gently pried Cleo's arms away. On the bedside table was a tray with lukewarm broth and bit of bread that my ravenous stomach demanded. Cleo noticed and handed me the bowl and spoon, though she insisted on sitting beside me on the bed. She hadn't been like this in years, and I can't say I minded very much.

"Where is Tommy?" I managed to ask between spoonfuls of soup.

"With Mr. Papadopoulos and his sister," she said. "Don't worry. They're both making quite the fuss over him."

"I can imagine."

Then Cleo hesitated. "He knows you're ill, but that's all. I didn't think it appropriate to tell him that . . . well . . ."

I paused and gave her an arch look. "That the woman who used to give him lemon candies also served me poisoned tea?"

Cleo let out a startled laugh. "Yes. That." Then she quickly sobered. "How are you feeling?"

I handed her the now-empty bowl and settled back against the pillows. "Tired," I said and looked past her to the window. But it was not merely on account of my recent ordeal. No, this bone-deep weariness had been with me for some time.

A passing nurse noticed I was awake and did a quick check before leaving to fetch a doctor.

When she was gone, I turned back to Cleo. "How long have I been here?"

"Since yesterday," she said. "Mr. Dorian suspected you were poisoned by Mrs. Belvedere and forced you to vomit. Then you were brought in and given an antidote, along with something to help you sleep."

My cheeks heated. "Oh dear." Was I never to maintain a scrap of dignity before that man?

Cleo fixed me with a look. "Mother, he saved your life."

"No, of course, I'm grateful," I said quickly. "It's only . . ." But I didn't finish the thought before a painfully young man with a severe part in his dark hair arrived and introduced himself as Doctor Nikolaidis before subjecting me to a more thorough examination.

"The poison seems to have worked through your system, Mrs. Harper," he explained once he had finished. "But it would be best if you stayed here another night for observation."

Cleo immediately tensed, and her mouth flattened.

I gave him a kind smile as I took her hand and shook my head. "I need to be with my children."

He frowned in that disapproving way all doctors must be taught to do in medical school, but I merely smiled back until he relented. "Very well. But if you feel ill at all you must return at once."

"Understood," I said with a nod.

He then gave me a list of symptoms to look out for and left. Cleo pulled the privacy curtain closed and helped me out of bed.

"What's to happen with Florence, then?" I asked as I began to dress. "I don't expect she went quietly."

Cleo looked pained. "She's dead."

I stared at her in shock. "How?"

"Mr. Dorian said there was a great deal of confusion when they arrived at the house and found you. He couldn't say exactly, but she took a draught of something. Nightshade, maybe? I'm not sure."

"My goodness," I said softly. Florence had been so self-righteous during her confession, and so utterly convinced that she had acted accordingly, that I assumed she would fight tooth and nail for her freedom. Or at the very least, flee the country over taking her own life. But this . . . this was like something out of a penny dreadful. It felt sordid. And sad.

"She knew what awaited her," Cleo said with uncharacteristic bitterness. "So she took the coward's way out. Fitting for her, though."

"Cleo," I gently admonished, more out of motherly reflex than conviction.

"She tried to *kill* you, Mama," Cleo said. "I hope she rots for all eternity."

I relented with a sigh. "Fine. Just don't say such things around Tommy."

"I won't," she promised.

"I suppose that means Mr. Dorian is a free man once again?"

"Yes. When Mr. Belvedere went to see him in jail, they pieced everything together. But they had no idea you were in danger until they arrived with the police to speak to Florence."

My breath caught. It really had been a close call, then.

"He was still with you when I got here," she added shyly. "And only left because he needed to sleep."

My hands paused on the button I had been attempting to fasten. "Well, I'm sure he just wanted to give you all the pertinent details." It couldn't have been anything other than that.

Cleo gave me a skeptical look. "Mama—"

"Let's go," I interrupted and turned my focus to the remaining shirt buttons. "I've had quite enough of being in hospital."

My daughter would not argue with that.

The ride back to the Lemon Grove House proved to be more trying than I had expected, and by the time we arrived, I wanted nothing more than to crawl into my own bed. Mrs. Kouris met us in the yard and immediately began scolding me for almost getting myself killed. Some might have taken offense at such a greeting, but I knew Mrs. Kouris was acting out of fear and love.

"I am very sorry," I said with genuine remorse. "It won't happen again."

Her arm tightened around mine, which was the only hint of her true emotions I was to receive. Then she clicked her tongue in disapproval. "It had better not," she warned, then helped me into the house. Once inside, she and Cleo fussed over me terribly, forcing me to eat, fluffing my pillows, and nearly burying me under blankets until I had to banish them from my room so I could rest. I must have still been under the effect of the hospital's sedative because as soon as I was alone, I fell deeply asleep.

When I awoke, it was late in the morning the next day. At first, I was mortified to have slept for so long, but I felt undeniably better. After lazing in bed for a few minutes more, I rose and washed up. Then I put on one of my favorite caftans and headed downstairs without even bothering with my hair, as I was in great need of a bath anyway. Hopefully Mrs. Kouris and Cleo were still in a helpful mood. I wanted to bathe as soon as possible so I could then go to the Papadopoulos residence and see Tommy.

I was so preoccupied by these thoughts that I entered the kitchen before I realized Mrs. Kouris was seated at the table talking with someone—someone who just happened to be Mr. Dorian. I came to a halt while they both stared at me, stunned.

"Hello," I said awkwardly.

"Mrs. Harper. Good morning." Mr. Dorian then pushed his chair back and stood as if he were a guest in a Mayfair drawing room. He was staring at me rather intently, and I frowned at his odd manner, even while an undeniable rush of warmth blossomed in my chest.

No. Not yet.

It had been his voice, full of wrenching despair, that I heard just before the world went dark. But I could not think on that now, nor what it meant. Not with my housekeeper a mere foot away. I pushed the memory aside and glanced at Mrs. Kouris, who was staring at my hair in disapproval. My hand automatically pushed an errant curl back, but I doubt it made much of a difference.

He cleared his throat, but the tension on his face remained. "You are looking much improved."

Given that I had been unconscious when he saw me last, this wasn't exactly heartening.

"Goodness, I should hope so."

Mr. Dorian ignored my dry tone and pulled back a chair for me. "You should sit."

I wanted to make a comment about him being my guest, but decided against it as the man already seemed rather out of sorts. As soon as I sat down, Mrs. Kouris presented me with a plate nearly overflowing with food.

"Thank you," I said as my empty stomach groaned in approval. Then I glanced around. "Where is Cleo?"

"She went to fetch Tommy." Mrs. Kouris then shot Mr. Dorian a very unsubtle look. "They won't be back for a little while, though. She only just left." Before I could respond to this, Mrs. Kouris headed for the back door. "I will go feed the chickens," she proclaimed, and in another moment, she was gone. I blinked and turned to Mr. Dorian.

"Please," he said, gesturing to my plate, "go on."

"Would you like anything?"

"No, no," he said, leaning back in his chair. "Your housekeeper force-fed me earlier."

I huffed a laugh and tore off a piece of bread from the nearly half a loaf she had given me. "I'm sure she did. So then," I began lightly, "did you come over here this morning to receive my undying thanks for saving my life? Because you have it."

He stared at me in surprise for a moment before he chuckled. "No. When I returned to the hospital yesterday evening, Doctor Nikolaidis told me you insisted on going home. The young man was very put out over it," he added in his usual droll tone.

"I saw no reason to stay," I said with a shrug, relieved that the strange tension had broken and we were back to our old, familiar manner. "And I've been perfectly fine since I left."

Mr. Dorian raised an eyebrow. "Mrs. Kouris said you slept for fifteen hours."

I choked a little at the number. "Well," I began once I recovered, "that isn't surprising, when one considers what happened."

Mr. Dorian frowned. "What *happened* is you came very close to dying, Minnie."

My heart skittered in my chest as he uttered my name. I could not bear the earnest look in his eyes that accompanied it and had to turn away. It was all too much.

"Thank you," I said softly.

"There is no need. I only wish it could have all been avoided in the first place," he growled. "Why the hell were you even there?"

I bristled at the accusation, but when I turned back to him, he only looked pained, not angry. "I went to see you. Then Florence found me and said you had been arrested. That was why I . . ."

He let out a heavy sigh and closed his eyes. "I'm sorry. I was just so goddamn worried about you."

"Mr. Dorian—"

He gave me a quelling look. "It's Stephen."

I hesitated for a moment, then forced the name past my lips. "Stephen. You cannot blame yourself for what occurred." He opened his mouth to respond, but I pressed on. "Firstly, because it takes away from my own agency, which I very much enjoy having. And, secondly, because Florence is the culprit here."

Stephen shook his head. "But I should have warned you."

I blinked as I gathered his meaning. "Then you knew it was her?"

"No. Well, not the entire time, anyway." He shifted uncomfortably in his chair. "But I had my suspicions since the day we went to speak to her. That purple-flowered plant of hers looked very much like the petal I found."

"The tisane," I murmured, and he raised an eyebrow. "I

thought it smelled familiar. But I couldn't figure out from where."

"Monkshood," he said. "Beautiful, but highly poisonous. I thought it odd she kept it as a houseplant."

"It was in Christopher's office when I went to see him. She must have noticed your interest and moved it."

Stephen nodded. "When you mentioned that Doctor Campbell suspected Daphne was unconscious when she was killed, I started to think someone might have poisoned her first, then strangled her."

I stared at him in shock. "Why didn't you say anything?"

"I had no real proof. It was only a hunch," he said with a shrug. "And I didn't think you would believe me. Florence was your friend, after all."

I began to contradict this, but then shut my mouth. For I had never been honest with him about my complicated feelings where Florence was concerned. I had kept so much to myself, both for my own protection and out of a misguided sense of loyalty. He had every right to think that I would have dismissed his suspicions about Florence. And there was nothing I hated more than a hypocrite. Well, aside from a murderer.

"But when you told me that Daphne might have been pregnant, I confess I suspected Christopher. I . . . may have even accused him of as much when he came to the police station," he admitted rather bashfully.

"Oh dear."

Stephen raised an eyebrow. "Quite. Admittedly, it took a bit of time for us to sort through everything, and all the while, Christopher remained adamant that I had gotten it wrong, though even he acknowledged that Florence's father was a likely candidate for Maria Costas's married paramour—right down to the rampant philandering."

"What a horrible mess." Then something else occurred to

me. "But why were you even arrested in the first place? What evidence did they have?"

Stephen let out a harsh laugh. "I wasn't arrested, yet. Officially, they brought me in for questioning as someone had sent an anonymous note suggesting that I was Daphne's lover."

"Florence," I offered.

He nodded. "It wasn't signed, but Christopher admitted that it was likely composed on his stationery with his typewriter, as it has a habit of misprinting the letter 'o'."

I remembered that little quirk from my time working for him. "It was a manufacturing error," I explained.

"Quite so. After that, the police agreed to release me and question Florence. Christopher then asked me to accompany him, as I don't think he had the stomach to face her alone."

"And then you found me there," I said.

Stephen's expression turned grim. "Yes."

"How awful," I murmured. "It must have been a shock for all of you."

"It was," Stephen agreed. "Luckily, Mrs. Georgiou was there and decided she couldn't be a party to *two* murders, so she admitted to the poisoning. I knew what to do after that."

My lips pursed. "Right. Cleo mentioned as much."

"You have no memory of it?"

I shook my head. "None."

"It's just as well," he grumbled. "While we were attending to you, Florence drank a tincture laced with belladonna."

"Yes, Cleo mentioned that too," I said. "Was it quick, at least?" Even as I asked the question, I wasn't quite sure what answer I was seeking.

Stephen stared at me for a moment. "Not really, no. Though I suppose it was better than the gallows," he said darkly. "She lost consciousness after a while and never recovered."

I shuddered at the knowledge that while I had been recovering in a hospital bed, Florence had been taking her last breaths.

"Mrs. Georgiou stayed by her side the entire time," Stephen explained, his tone full of derision. "Loyal till the bitter end, even after everything."

"She had watched Florence grow up," I said, recalling how Mrs. Georgiou still treated her like the little girl she had once been. Her Dia.

"Yes, well, now that old woman will pay for it. She confirmed that after Daphne made the connection between them, Florence asked her to have tea on the terrace," Stephen continued. "Pretended as though she wanted to make amends, but then poisoned her instead." He paused and shook his head. "She didn't give her enough to kill her, though, so she had to strangle her."

I swallowed hard at the thought and recalled the vengeful look on Florence's face as she listed the many indignities her mother had endured. Daphne had no idea what she had unleashed when she made the connection. She must have been so overjoyed to finally find the answer she had been seeking that she didn't know she was walking right into the lion's mouth.

"Was Mrs. Georgiou there the whole time?"

"No. She really had left for the day, that bit was true. But then Florence went to her home in a panic after she killed Daphne and told her what happened. They waited until nightfall, then used a wheelbarrow to dump the body down the hill."

They must have been very determined, then. For it couldn't have been easy to trek through the forest in the dark, and neither woman was particularly spry.

"So she became an accomplice."

Stephen nodded. "Yes."

"And all the while Christopher had no idea this was going on."

"None."

"Poor fellow," I said sadly. "How is he?"

He leveled me a look. "As well as one might expect upon discovering his wife is a murderess."

I truly couldn't imagine what that must feel like—to realize that the woman you had been married to for decades, the mother of your children, had the capacity for such violence. It sounded like the worst sort of betrayal. "He must be rethinking everything."

Stephen tilted his head. "What do you mean?"

"Well, I'm sure he didn't marry her thinking she could *strangle* someone," I said briskly.

"No, but you would be surprised what people, even perfectly respectable ones, are capable of under the right set of circumstances."

I lifted my chin. Was he actually trying to defend Florence's behavior? "I cannot imagine any circumstances which would provoke such a reaction in myself, barring self-defense. And that was hardly the case here. No," I continued, now warming to the topic, "I think if one possesses an excellent character, then they will always find an alternative to acts of violence or betrayal."

Something flickered in his eyes then, an emotion I couldn't begin to identify. But it did bring to mind my own betrayal of sorts against him.

I glanced down at the worn kitchen table. "I went to your house yesterday morning to apologize for keeping so much from you. And for my unfounded suspicions."

"But you already apologized," he replied, his voice softer than I had ever heard it.

I met his gaze then. "I thought you deserved another."

Stephen stared at me for a long moment. "I'm sorry too. I

overreacted on the boat. Took it far too personally when you were only trying to remain neutral. And your suspicions weren't entirely unfounded," he added, raising an eyebrow.

I laughed a little at that. "I suppose. But, regardless, I think we both would have benefitted from trusting each other a bit more. We might have even solved this sooner, and I could have avoided a poisoning."

He gave me a small smile. "Yes, I suppose we would have." Then he cleared his throat. "I'm glad you said that, actually, because I didn't come here only to receive your undying gratitude." He straightened in his chair, and I tilted my head.

"What is it?"

He hesitated as his gaze traveled over me in assessment. "It can wait, if you aren't feeling well."

"You can't bait me like that," I said with a huff. "I'm perfectly fine. I did sleep for fifteen hours, after all."

That seemed to convince him, and he chuckled. "Good point." But then he quickly sobered. "In the interest of honesty, I must admit that, some weeks ago, I wrote to a friend who works in the Foreign Office." I wasn't sure why he was telling me this, but nodded in encouragement. "And asked him to look into your husband."

I drew back. "You what?"

"It sounded so odd to me," he continued, unaware of the effect of his words, "that a man in the prime of his career would willingly give it all up so suddenly to come *here*."

I shook my head, which seemed to be full of cotton wool. "I . . . I don't understand."

Stephen leaned towards me, his gaze growing intense once again. "But that's it, Minnie. Neither did I, nor did my friend. It didn't make sense. And to leave you in such a vulnerable position—"

"I told you," I said haltingly. "Oliver was tired of the constant jockeying, the paper-pushing, the favoritism. And he wanted the children to have space to roam."

My words came out faster and faster with each well-recited reason, but Stephen didn't respond to any of them. "I had a letter from him yesterday."

It felt as if a heavy weight was pressing against my chest, so much so that I struggled to take a deep breath. "What have you done?" I whispered.

But Stephen didn't appear to hear my accusation. He just stared at me for a moment that seemed to stretch for an eternity, and I came very close to asking him to stop before he could even begin, but I waited too long.

"Your husband was suspected of stealing Grecian artifacts and selling them to the highest bidder," he said plainly, as if he wasn't setting my entire life on fire. I grew very still while his words washed over me, but they were slippery, and I couldn't quite grasp the meaning. "However, he resigned before the investigation could be completed." Then Stephen's mouth pursed. "I suspect his brother the viscount intervened."

It was that small twist of his lips, his subtle disapproval, that wrenched me from my shock.

How dare this man judge Oliver. How dare he try to reduce an entire life to nothing more than one despicable act. Whatever Oliver had done—whatever he *may* have done—he was far more than that.

"I expect that little export business of his was a front for any contraband he may have retained," Stephen mused, and it was his casual judgement that finally caused the commitment to propriety at any cost, which had been drilled into me over the course of my life, to snap cleanly in half.

I let out a slow breath and attempted to gather my jumbled thoughts, but the only thing I could properly focus on was my mounting anger.

"You . . . you had no right," I said quietly, though by that point I was trembling with rage. "No cause to do that."

Stephen's eyebrows rose in surprise, which only made me want to laugh. Did the man think I would welcome this news? No. I'm sure he did not think at all. Did not even consider that he was maligning the memory of my beloved husband.

"I suppose not," he said dryly. "But you should know that he angered some rather unsavory characters when he retired. In fact"—he paused for a moment before continuing—"my associate questioned whether his death was natural."

Now that was far, far too much.

But, of course, he would see murder and violence at every turn. The man had built an entire fortune on such misery. A kind of hollowness opened up inside of me then. Something I have never felt before or since. I simply couldn't bear it. Couldn't bear any of the things he was saying. And so I attacked.

"Why should I believe you?" I began in an icy tone I barely recognized. "What proof do you have of any of this other than the word of your friend?"

"Minnie—"

"No," I said viciously, hating the sound of my name on his lips, "I cannot imagine why you would seek to ruin him like this."

"That was not my intention," he protested.

But I could only scoff at this. "Then what *was* your intention?" I demanded miserably, while my throat began to tighten.

He blinked, as if the question had taken him by surprise. "I—I don't know."

My breath caught. I believed him, and yet this answer only angered me further. Because he had been so bloody careless. "I think you hoped to discover something unsavory about him so that I could be as full of resentment and bitterness as you," I rasped.

Something flared in his eyes then, a deep hurt that would have silenced me if the circumstances had been even remotely different. But I would not stop. I couldn't.

"I *loved* my husband," I said, pressing my palm to my chest. "I didn't divorce him or drive him away. He *died*."

The word seemed to echo off the walls, and Stephen's gaze shuttered completely as he sat back in his chair. We stared at each other for a long moment, his expression distant and mine still daggered.

"I can see that I have upset you," he finally said. "As I explained, that was not my intention. I only thought you deserved to know the truth about your husband's activities. Furthermore, it seemed imperative that you understand the gravity of the situation should you or your children ever return to England."

"I—"

"But please accept my sincere apologies," he said as he rose stiffly to his feet. "Good day."

Then he turned on his heel and left without another word. Once I was alone, the hollow feeling gradually faded, and as I came back to myself, I choked back a sob. I inhaled deeply for a few minutes, which helped, but it was a long time before I regained any semblance of control over my emotions.

I sat in my empty kitchen now, turning over everything he had said, fuming with resentment. But as the minutes passed, something else hummed underneath. The doubts I had buried long ago so I could go on with my life. Because I hadn't wanted to know. Hadn't wanted to ask. For what would that have meant for myself, for my children, and the life I had been left with?

I buried my head in my hands and let out a sigh, but it did little to ease my worries. There was so much I still didn't know. So much I still had to solve. I had little time to ruminate, however, as the children arrived not long afterwards. I took great comfort in hugging Tommy as tightly as I could until he began to complain. He had no idea just how close to death I had come. And I had no intention of him ever learning otherwise.

Mr. Papadopoulos had come along as well, and once the children went off, I recounted my entire exchange with Stephen. He was quiet for a long moment as he mulled over my words. I didn't like repeating the accusation against Oliver, but I very much needed someone to confide in.

"Perhaps Mr. Dorian was trying to protect you in some way," he offered.

I balked at this explanation, as I don't think I had ever felt more exposed than when he coldly recited the charges against Oliver. "If he truly wanted to protect me, then he should have kept quiet," I grumbled.

Mr. Papadopoulos gave me a sympathetic look. "Even if you may be in danger?"

"I highly doubt that is the case," I huffed. "And besides, if Oliver was involved in that . . . that business, he has been dead for four years. What would anyone want with me or the children?"

"I don't know," Mr. Papadopoulos said with a shrug. "But we are speaking of criminals. They don't follow the same code of conduct as you or I. You think it would have been better not to know the truth at all?"

"If it is the truth," I said petulantly. "Just because someone at the Foreign Office repeated a rumor doesn't mean Oliver was guilty."

Mr. Papadopoulos tilted his head in acknowledgement. "Yes. And Mr. Dorian could have delivered the news in a better manner, certainly. But I don't think you would have liked him to have kept such information to himself. And if Oliver was, in fact, under investigation, don't you wish to have the chance to clear his name?"

I hadn't considered that, as at the moment, I was far too concerned with being angry with Stephen.

"What I wish is for him to have never sought it out in the first place," I insisted. "And, moreover, I can't understand what his interest was in Oliver to begin with."

Mr. Papadopoulos looked at me oddly, but then Tommy interrupted us with an alarming question about the mating habits of arachnids, and that was the last we ever spoke of it.

Chapter 22

I was still fiercely holding on to my anger the next morning when I trudged downstairs and entered the kitchen. My body seemed to have fully recovered from the ordeal with Florence, as I was now back to my usual broken sleep—and unfortunately, my argument with Stephen had occupied far too many late-night thoughts. I had just resolved to put him out of my mind for the rest of the day when my gaze caught on an envelope addressed to me on the kitchen table. I recognized his atrocious scrawl immediately, but resisted the urge to open it.

"What's this?" I asked Mrs. Kouris as casually as I could manage.

She was occupied with kneading a ball of dough, but glanced over at me, not the least bit fooled by my tone. "It was on the doorstep when I arrived."

"Hmm," I said, continuing to attempt nonchalance. The children were still abed, but likely not for much longer. If I wanted any privacy, I needed to get on with it. "I suppose I'll read it then."

My housekeeper arched a brow and turned back to her dough.

I picked up the letter and went outside onto the terrace. Then I sat down in a chair that faced the sea. I stared at the view while my mind whirled with possibilities. If it had been on the doorstep this morning when Mrs. Kouris arrived, then Stephen must have left it very early. But what could have possibly driven him to do such a thing? Surely there wasn't anything so urgent that needed to be said. I admit it brought to mind Mr. Darcy's letter to Elizabeth in which he explained his contentious relationship with George Wickham and defended his own behavior in dissuading his friend Mr. Bingley from pursing Jane. For a moment, I imagined that Stephen had stayed up all night composing a letter in which he explained his reasons for digging into Oliver's past. Reasons that somehow would be entirely understandable and make my anger vanish.

But I found the answer much different:

Mrs. Harper,

Enclosed is the remainder of your wages.

Your work was excellent.

I wish you well in your future endeavors.

Sincerely,

Stephen Dorian

I had to read the short note three times before the words fully penetrated my addled mind. And, despite the great deal of money I now possessed, I felt nothing but a sense of loss. As my heart sank in my chest, I realized just how badly I had wanted him to appeal to me. To mend this rift between us before it could grow into a chasm. But as with a great many things in this world, I could not wait for a man to come to his better senses. So I would have to do it myself. I rushed back upstairs, filled with a sudden determination to repair things between us, and threw on a clean dress, attempted to fix my hair, and quickly gave up in favor of a hat.

Then I bolted out the door, so I wouldn't be waylaid a moment longer.

With each step, I grew more and more certain of what I would say. I could do this. I could be brave. One of us had to be, and it may as well be me. By the time I reached the villa, I had managed to compose a short speech in my head. I knocked on the door and waited anxiously, as it no longer felt right to simply enter at will. Hours seemed to pass before Mrs. Nasso opened it and looked at me in surprise.

"Kalimera," I said, forcing a cheery note into my voice that barely masked my impatience. "Where is Mr. Dorian?"

The old woman frowned. "Gone."

"Oh." That was rather deflating, but I remained undaunted. "Well, not to worry. I will wait in the study until he returns." I stepped over the threshold, but Mrs. Nasso shook her head even as she let me enter.

"No, no. I mean, he left. For good. Back to England."

I paused mid-step and cocked my head, certain I had misheard her. "What?"

Mrs. Nasso repeated herself, then looked concerned. "Perhaps you should lie down, Mrs. Harper. I will get you some food."

"No, thank you," I said, still confused. "When? When did he leave?"

"Yesterday. He came home in a great rush, packed his bags, and left for town."

It must have been right after our disastrous encounter, then.

"But I had a letter from him just this morning," I stubbornly insisted, as if the woman was mistaken and Stephen was still asleep upstairs.

She bowed her head shyly. "He asked me to give it to you," she explained. "I didn't have time to deliver it yesterday, so I took it first thing. I hope that was all right. He didn't say it was urgent."

I held back the urge to curse her for this, as my panicked mind seized upon a possibility. "Then he might still be here," I said as my heart lifted. "He could be in town waiting for the next steamer."

And given that steamers in Greece rarely adhered to the printed schedule, there was still a good chance he was on the island.

But she shook her head again. "He intended to hire a boat to take him to Italy. That was why he went into town yesterday. I believe he meant to leave as soon as possible. He is gone, Mrs. Harper." Then she took my hand, her wrinkled face full of sympathy. "I am very sorry. Let me make you something to eat."

But food held absolutely no appeal as a sick, acidic feeling had come over me. Gone. And why shouldn't he have left, given what I had accused him of? My chest burned as I recalled the worst of it:

I think you hoped to discover something unsavory about him so that I could be as full of resentment and bitterness as you.

Strange how one could experience such a sense of loss over what they had never possessed. What an utter fool I had been.

"I . . . I'm fine." I gently pulled my hand away and lifted my chin, even while my nose began to sting. "I'm sorry to have bothered you."

Then I turned around and headed outside. Mrs. Nasso called out to me, but I didn't stop. I kept my eyes fixed firmly on the path ahead of me, for by then, the tears had begun to fall, and I would not show them to anyone.

Chapter 23

Five Months Later

"Really, Minnie," my aunt Agatha tsked, "what on earth were you thinking when you ordered this fabric?"

"That I needed a new dress," I answered mildly.

"But in *that* color? Brown?" My aunt screwed up her face in an almost comical display of distaste.

"It is fawn," I corrected her. "And I like it." I continued to admire my reflection in the shop's mirror. "The seamstress said it complements my eyes. Besides, I won't have to worry if it gets a little dirt on it."

I thought this was very practical reasoning on my part, but Aunt Agatha looked absolutely appalled. "You must let me assist with the rest of your wardrobe. At least while I'm here."

Cleo had kept her promise not to tell Tommy about my brush with death, but that hadn't stopped her from writing to my aunt. Agatha had arrived last month and still hadn't mentioned when she intended to leave. But it was no matter, as I was enjoying her company, apart from her criticisms about my clothing.

"I'm fine. I only needed the one dress."

She narrowed her eyes and muttered something under her breath that sounded awfully like "We'll see about that."

After I had changed back into my old dress and paid for the new one, we exited the shop. It was just after eleven, and the morning was growing warmer by the minute.

Aunt Agatha covered us with her parasol and looked around the busy street. "Where are we meeting Cleo and her friend?"

"By the water. Just up there," I said, pointing towards the Esplanade. She linked her arm through mine, and we strolled down the tree-lined street.

When Aunt Agatha had first arrived, I had been certain that she and Cleo would launch into a coordinated attack to convince me to send her to that school in England. But so far neither of them had said a word about it. Perhaps Cleo really did intend to stay on Corfu. The trouble was that now I was no longer sure I wanted to.

"And the roof will be done today?"

I nodded. My prodigal handyman had finally returned home last month, and I had been putting him to work ever since, thanks to Mr. Dorian's last payment.

Agatha knew I had been the man's typist for a time and that he had been on hand when Florence nearly killed me, but I told her nothing about his accusations against Oliver, nor the terms on which we parted. As for the riot of emotion that had driven me to his doorstep that fateful morning, they must have been brought on by the lingering effects of my poisoning. That was the only reasonable explanation for such impetuous behavior on my part. In fact, I was inordinately pleased that Mr. Dorian had already left by the time I arrived. Otherwise, I would have said some very silly things that I would have had to recant once I fully recovered my senses. By slipping away as he did, he saved us both a great deal of embarrassment. And for that, I was grateful.

"Good. I confess, I don't think I could take another day

of his hammering," Aunt Agatha admitted. "Did you still wish to visit Oliver, then?"

"Yes," I said. "Cleo offered to purchase the flowers after her errand with Juliet."

Since my perilous brush with death, I had begun to visit Oliver's grave regularly. Sometimes with the children, but usually on my own. I had been inspired to do so by Miss Costas and Milo, of all people. As promised, I wrote to Miss Costas about Florence's murder of her niece—though I left out some of the more distressing details of my confrontation, as I did not think it appropriate—and invited her to come stay with us for a few days. She responded and asked if Milo could come as well, which I readily agreed to, as it seemed far better that they not be at odds with one another. We even dined with Christopher one night, and it was unexpectedly touching as they exchanged memories of poor Daphne. Christopher then announced his intention to return to England as soon as he got his affairs in order—entirely understandable given the circumstances—and I was glad to learn that he would be staying with his daughter Celeste and her family. The one whom Daphne had so reminded him of.

But it was our visit to Daphne's grave in the little churchyard that made the greatest impact. For Miss Costas and Milo seemed to find a kind of peace there that I envied, even so many years after my husband's death.

Like many people, I had always thought of cemeteries as bleak, spooky places, but the English cemetery was nothing like that. It was almost bucolic, with plenty of flowers and trees among the timeworn gravestones and towering monuments to the dead. And in the early morning, it could be quite a peaceful place to reflect.

I didn't talk with Oliver during these visits, as some mourners are prone to do, but I did feel a glimmer of his presence each time I went to his plot, and my memories always seemed just a bit sharper. Or perhaps that was because it was the only time I really allowed myself to go over Mr. Dorian's accusations and tried to make sense of Oliver's reasoning. But I suspected it would take a great many more visits before I could accomplish that.

"There they are," Aunt Agatha trilled as she raised her arm. "Hello, girls!"

Cleo and Juliet spotted us and bounded over, each practically vibrating with excitement. Cleo was clutching something in her hands, and as they drew closer, I could see that it was not the expected flowers but a book.

"Mother! Look!" she cried out as she waved the tome before me. "Mrs. Taylor ordered Mr. Dorian's new book, and it came today!"

"We've just picked it up for her at the post office," Juliet cut in. "She had my father pay a fortune to have it shipped here as soon as it was published in London. It must be the only copy in all of Greece! Isn't it exciting?"

I managed a tight smile. "I didn't realize you were such a fan, Juliet. Nor you, Cleo."

My daughter rolled her eyes. "We aren't going to read it, Mother. But we know him! And you worked on it!"

I could see that she was determined to make a meal of this, but I would not take credit where it wasn't deserved and waved my hand dismissively. "I only did a little typing, my dear. I certainly didn't write any of it."

But Cleo wasn't the least bit put off. "Isn't it marvelous? A whole book!"

She then handed it to me, and I hesitated for a moment before taking it and staring at the cover.

A Murder in Middle Temple.

It was a good title, and despite everything that had happened between us, I was genuinely happy for him. After so much strife, he had finished it. I glanced up and realized all three of them were watching me, waiting for my reaction. Perhaps if I made a little fawning sound and complimented the typeface or something, then we could move on. I bit back a sigh and opened the book. But as I flipped through the first few pages, my gaze caught on the dedication.

For M.H. My undying thanks. I could not have done this without you.

My breath caught, and I made a strange kind of choking sound.

Cleo was at my side in a flash, craning her neck to see. "What is it?"

"Nothing," I said hoarsely and shut the book. For I must have misread.

Had to have.

But Cleo pried it from my hands and found the page. "Mother," she gasped. "M.H. He dedicated his book to you!"

I stepped back as Aunt Agatha and Juliet crowded around to see for themselves. Then I looked around for a place to sit, as I felt terribly lightheaded.

"Minnie?" my aunt asked, her sharp voice cutting through my tangled thoughts. "What is the meaning of this?"

"I haven't the faintest idea," I said. "Perhaps . . . perhaps it's someone else."

But neither Cleo nor Juliet would hear of it. And deep down, neither would I.

My undying thanks.

I had said those very same words to him with such flippancy, because even in that moment, I had been too much of a coward to be sincere. While they talked among themselves, I sat down on a bench and stared out at the endless sea before me as the blood roared in my ears. Eventually, Cleo sat down beside me.

"London must be very grand this time of year," she said after a moment.

"It is," I agreed as my mind filled with images of russet-colored leaves and crisp, smoke-scented mornings. Of long walks beside the fog-laced Serpentine, Mrs. Potter's apple pie, and warm mugs of mulled cider. A fierce longing swiftly followed, and for the first time in many years I wanted to go home.

"Mother," Cleo said gently, interrupting my little reverie. "I think it's time."

It was as if she had heard my every thought and I nodded in return. "I'll start making the arrangements this week."

"I'm sure Aunt Agatha will be more than willing to help."

I turned to her. "Yes. But first we need to see your father." For if we were to go to England, we would not return for a long while.

She squeezed my hand. "I'll go get the flowers. You wait here."

"Good girl." I squeezed back and then let her go.

Somehow, Cleo convinced Juliet and Aunt Agatha to come with her to the flower stand. Alone once more, I let my thoughts turn fully to him. Since that terrible morning all those weeks ago, I had been determined not to think of Stephen and done an excellent job. But now . . . now I allowed myself to wonder. *Really* wonder. Then hope soon followed. And I allowed that too.

Acknowledgments

Many thanks to my agent Amanda Jain for encouraging me to write this book after four historical romances—and for then reading my first draft and assuring me I didn't mess anything up. Thank you to John Scognamiglio for your enthusiasm and guidance. Thank you to Dawn Cooper and the team at Kensington Books for the gorgeous cover. Thank you to Nicole, Katie, and my mom for reading earlier versions of this book and offering valuable feedback. Thank you to my family and friends for their endless support. And last but never least, thank you to James for double-checking my Greek. Se latrevo.